My Summer on Haight Street

A NOVEL BY

♣ ROBERT RICE JR ♣

Fox Point Publishing
Santa Barbara, California

Fox Point Publishing

My Summer on Haight Street
Book website: www.mysummeronhaightstreet.com

First Published 2013 by:

Fox Point Publishing
P.O. Box 1362
Santa Barbara, CA 93102-1362
Website address: www.foxpointpublishing.com
Telephone number: 805.451.6669.

ISBN: 0615767583
ISBN-13: 9780615767581
Library of Congress Control Number: 2013932793
CreateSpace Independent Publishing Platform
North Charleston, South Carolina

Dedicated to all the Vietnam War Veterans and to those who served in the US military during the Vietnam era, and to all the 1966 and 1967 high school graduates across America.

Grateful acknowledgement is made to Terry Row, John Cronin, Nancy Fletcher, JoAnn Reck, Terry Tamminen, John Schliesleder, and Rosa Estarellas.

Some Deserving Praise for
My Summer on Haight Street

Robert Rice, Jr's novel, *My Summer on Haight Street,* follows in the footsteps of Jack Kerouac's *On the Road* and J.D. Salinger's *The Catcher in the Rye* as a story of youthful exuberance, the search for meaning and relevance, and the need for love, understanding, and companionship. Rice weaves a fascinating, but realistic tale about innocence, the desire for higher knowledge, lust, deceit, drugs, and experimentation in San Francisco during the Summer of Love 1967. His thoroughly entertaining novel underscores that people, places, and things are often not what they appear to be. *Terry Tamminen – author: Lives per Gallon; Cracking the Carbon Code; and Watercolors. Former Secretary-California EPA and internationally recognized environmentalist.*

Robert Rice, Jr's first novel is an impressive debut that juxtaposes the youthful pleasures of a promiscuous society in 1967 against the Vietnam War, casting a pall over a deeply divided nation. *My Summer on Haight Street* provides a unique window into a monumental time in America's history. We get to follow a young man's quest from Milwaukee to San Francisco where he ultimately has to decide between right and wrong when he finds himself in a life and death situation. The plot grows thicker with every chapter and the ending is deviously delicious. If you were in San Francisco in 1967, you will empathize. If you were not, you'll learn about what you missed. **Terry Row-author:** *Summer Capricorn; Untarnished Reputation-***winner, Best Western Fiction, Indie Excellence Awards;** *Phyllis Marie-***winner, Best Fiction, Pinnacle Book Achievement Awards.**

Although *My Summer on Haight Street* is a work of fiction, Robert Rice, Jr., has crafted a compelling story that is based on several real people and some real events. Robert captures the aspirations and fears of young men who elected not to go to college immediately out of high school in 1966 and 1967 and faced the prospect of being drafted and sent to Vietnam. *My Summer on Haight Street* validates what many have forgotten; it was a wonderful time for some, and an agonizing time for many others. ***John Schliesleder – Vietnam veteran, awarded the Purple Heart.***

Chapter 1

At dawn on June 8, 1967, the sun's brilliant rays danced off the placid green waters on Lake Michigan's eastern horizon. As the sunlight flooded my eyes, it looked like just another summer day in Milwaukee. My unenthusiastic observation was based on the WTMJ-TV's forecast that tomorrow would be "nothing out of the ordinary."

Perched on Lake Michigan's western shore, Milwaukee was a rusting and decaying Midwestern city, home to Harley-Davidson motorcycles, Schlitz beer, and Usinger sausage. The city's population of one million was declining steadily as white flight to the suburbs continued unabated, yet it was a relatively clean city known for its beer, good restaurants, and countless duplexes: a unique architectural style of placing one complete residence above another. On this sunny summer morning, thousands of elm trees that lined the city's streets were succumbing silently to Dutch elm disease. I was restless in Milwaukee and felt uninspired and captive.

Milwaukee was also known for its stability, and there were many examples of that. Henry Maier was Milwaukee's mayor for twenty-eight years, a record for the city. WTMJ-TV's weatherman, Bill

Carlson, was on the airwaves for decades. Milwaukee was considered a safe city and averaged fewer than thirty murders a year. And it was said that Milwaukee was a good place to raise kids.

By the summer of my eighteenth year, I was turned off by all this stability. I yearned for something that would break this cozy monotony. I longed for a meaningful purpose, something I was sure could not be found in Milwaukee.

Despite the blazing temperature and muggy humidity, this day was going to be a special day for 432 young men and women graduating from Riverside High School. I was one of them.

Riverside High School had the odd distinction of having two official names: Riverside and Milwaukee East. Boys received an E for letter sweaters, while girls received a R for theirs. When I questioned the dual lettering system, the vice principal quipped, "So you can tell the boys from the girls."

Riverside is one of Milwaukee's oldest high schools, located on the eastern shore of the highly polluted Milwaukee River. Despite the environmental degradation around it, changing demographics, and aging neighborhoods, it was still considered one of the city's best public high schools in 1967. The front entrance was even adorned with dark green ivy, during the warm months anyway. The high school district included some of the east side's more affluent neighborhoods, as well as parts of the city's poor black ghetto. In the 1966-1967 school year, Riverside's student population was thirty-six percent Negro and there were never any racial problems. Little did I know at the time that after graduation, I was never again to have as many black friends as I did at Riverside.

Several hours before our graduation ceremony and a couple thousand miles west in the obscure research community of Livermore, California, a bomb shattered the early morning calm. The blast blew out windows, partially collapsed a building, destroyed a laboratory, and killed four people. Too late to make the morning edition of the *Milwaukee Sentinel*, the story was later reported on page three of the afternoon edition of the *Milwaukee Journal*.

I had never heard of Livermore, California, but I read the story with curiosity. Despite being a self-centered, self-absorbed teenager, I was beginning to notice worldly events.

On graduation day, most of the students at Riverside knew me, or at least that's what I thought. I was six feet tall and a slim 155 pounds. My boyish looks resembled those of Timmy, the child actor on the television series *Lassie*. Due to my natural blond hair, people believed that I was of German descent. In Milwaukee that would not be unexpected, but I am of Irish Catholic decent. I must confess I know nothing about my family's Celtic ancestry. I knew that Irish people loved to drink at both weddings and funerals, both of which I had the displeasure of having to attend as a young child.

In my first three years of high school, I played on the varsity football and basketball teams. When school resumed on the traditional Tuesday after Labor Day in the fall of 1966, my name was conspicuously absent from the varsity football sign-up sheet. Both faculty members and students thought it was just a typographical error, but it wasn't.

A lot of introspection took place in the summer of 1966, and that changed my life forever. When Fall arrived, participating in organized sports was no longer one of my priorities.

On the Fourth of July, I watched a parade in Milwaukee with dozens of Vietnam veterans, many with limbs missing, carrying signs against the war. In August, just before school resumed, I accompanied my buddy, Jim Gaston, to the University of Wisconsin-Madison to see a French documentary on Vietnam. After watching the documentary, I couldn't help but feel that America's foreign policy was rooted in the longstanding "Domino Theory." The documentary stated that fear of the spread of Communism was nothing more than a cover for our blatant colonialism.

When Jim and I exited the theater we found ourselves in the midst of a large demonstration against the university's animal testing laboratories. While I stood there watching the demonstrators, I realized how little I knew about a lot of things. I was determined to use my senior year in high school to get informed about worldly events.

Chapter 2

Although it was just another party at the Billford farm, I knew the parties there were never ordinary. Freddy Billford's family had bought an old dairy farm thirty-five miles northeast of Milwaukee in the tiny town of Grafton and then remodeled the main house.

Actually, it would be inaccurate to call the place a farm, because no farming whatsoever took place there. The only crops were parties and the crops were strategically harvested year-round when Freddy's parents were not present.

The farm was blessed with a grove of majestic birch trees that bordered the deeply rutted dirt road that meandered lazily for more than a half a mile from the highway to the main house. Even when a strong northeast storm blew, only the slightest sound of rustling could be heard from the countless birch branches. Mister Robert Billford stored his collection of old Cadillacs in the wooden barn, and he and his wife, Betty, used the farm sparely as a weekend retreat. Billford's second son, Freddy, was tall, gregarious, and musically talented. He was the leader of a very popular high school band.

The farm was legendary for hosting rambunctious teenage parties, and its remoteness kept the din out of earshot of neighboring farms. I was a regular at these parties, sometimes drinking too much beer, but never getting too drunk or rowdy, except for the night Jimmy Gaston and I went down to a local cemetery, appropriated twenty-five gravestones and brought them back to the farm.

We had gravestones of all sizes and designs in the back of Gaston's tiny Peugeot station wagon. One was an angel heralding God with a trumpet; one was badly weathered from 1825; and one contained the names of all twelve family members. Why we decided to bring them back to the party I'm not sure. We weren't that drunk.

The gravestones were heavy and Gaston's French station wagon barely made it over the rutted road to the farmhouse. We made a grand entrance by flashing the headlights and beeping the horn, and then parked the car immediately adjacent to the swimming pool.

Systematically, Gaston and I carried each gravestone over to the pool and placed them, one at a time, on the diving board. Loudly proclaiming some reason for the impeding dunking, we began bouncing on the diving board until they toppled into the pool one by one.

"Far out, man," I slurred.

I asked the fifteen teenagers at poolside to judge the diving style of each gravestone and to give a thumbs up or thumbs down rating. After all the gravestones littered the bottom of the pool, the judging committee, Gaston, and I adjourned to the farmhouse. It never occurred to me the pain we caused individuals visiting the gravesites of their loved ones only to find that the gravestones had been stolen.

In early 1966, I knew nothing about marijuana, but it was making its debut in the Midwest, at both the collegiate and high school levels, and Billford's farm was a hot spot of pot activity.

Prior to the summer of 1966, beer and whiskey were the mainstays of getting high in Milwaukee. Along with numerous other high school students, I was using a fake identification card to gain access to local bars and taverns. An eight-ounce glass of draft beer and a shot of whiskey, commonly called a "boilermaker," cost $1.25. It didn't take much time or money to get high or drunk in Milwaukee, and taverns would sell liquor, beer, and wine over the bar to carry out.

Most attendees at Billford's parties liked rhythm and blues music. The Impressions, James Brown, Sam and Dave, and Otis Redding were big favorites prior to that memorable summer of 1966. Over a period of several months in early 1966, the music being played at the parties began to subtly change.

A new, sweet, and strange aroma in the air accompanied the music. More and more partygoers played psychedelic music on the 33-rpm record player. A Jefferson Airplane album was heard constantly. A guy named Bob Dylan, with his strange voice and unusual lyrics, was heard regularly.

Gaston warmed up to the musical change much quicker than I did. "Gracie Slick has a far out voice and Kantner is writing some heavy stuff," he said on a hazy Sunday afternoon at the farm.

"Who's Gracie Slick?"

Suddenly, someone thrust a joint in front of both of us. Gaston knew what to do. He grabbed it and inhaled deeply. I felt shocked to see my closest friend, someone I thought I knew well, smoking pot.

I thought smoking pot was scary and even dangerous. I knew it was illegal, nevertheless, it had a strong and mysterious appeal.

"It's OK, man. Don't be afraid to try it. It won't make you crazy or anything," squeaked Gaston, trying to hold in the smoke and talk simultaneously.

I hesitated before I took it from him.

"You been doing this stuff long?"

"For a while," he said, exhaling loudly. "Try it. It won't kill you, man."

Awkwardly, I tried to take the joint, but I burnt my fingers. "Shit!" I exclaimed.

Gaston, seeing my dilemma, reached into his jeans pocket and pulled out a roach clip made from a small electrical alligator clip. He attached it to the joint and handed it to me.

"You've been doing this for a while."

"A couple of months."

"How come you never told me?"

"Shut up and smoke it,"

I had smoked a few cigarettes so I was not totally unfamiliar with smoke entering my lungs. As I inhaled, I began to sputter loudly as the smoke blazed into my lungs. Gaston decided right then and there it was a good time for the pot apprenticeship of Bob Ralston.

Under his close tutelage, the two of us smoked every joint passed our way that afternoon. It was two o'clock on a bright and sunny Sunday afternoon, but soon it felt like midnight. I was in a dreamlike state and wandered to the living room where the party's main activities were taking place.

When the Jefferson Airplane's herky-jerky song "3/5 of a Mile in 10 Seconds" began to play, I was sure someone was purposely slowing down the record. My perplexed facial expression caught Gaston's attention.

"What's up, man?"

"I think someone is fucking around with the record."

"You're stoned, man," Gaston laughed.

"No shit," I giggled.

It was at that moment I knew what it felt like to be high on marijuana.

Directly across the living room, shrouded in cigarette and pot smoke, sat Donna Read. She was a full-figured girl with a glowing smile, green eyes, and summer blond hair and she was also a friend of Mary Beth Kingston, my ex-girlfriend. I had broken up with Mary Beth earlier in the year over my demands for more sex. I leaned over to Gaston and gurgled, "Read's got great knockers."

"I'll bet you she'd ball your brains out if you'd ask her," Gaston's proclaimed.

"And I'm the Pope," I replied.

"She's always had the hots for you."

I was trying to deal with all sorts of unfamiliar feelings, sights and sounds, and what Gaston had just said. Then I thought, maybe it's true girls really do like sex.

It must have been my Catholic guilt, because I always believed that I had to somehow trick girls into having sex with me. I got them drunk, or I used my popularity as a jock to win them over and get their clothes off.

It never occurred to me that a girl would like sex as much as I did. I always thought girls were incapable of feeling the way I did about it. That theory was reinforced by my recent break-up with Mary Beth Kingston, who had a considerably lower sex drive than I.

I found it difficult to rationalize that Donna Read liked sex, liked me, and was there for the taking. But it was equally difficult getting to my feet to walk over and speak to her without stumbling.

She was sitting in a large, red armchair and was slightly drunk on beer. She watched me walk toward her. As I stood next to her, I could see her deep cleavage, and I became sexually aroused.

"Did I see you smoking pot with Jimmy Gaston?" she asked.

"So what?" I said.

"Is that any way for a star athlete to behave?"

"I didn't know I had to behave."

Suddenly, three girls, followed closely by three boys, streaked through the living room naked and raced outside toward the pool.

In a flash, the whole party left the main house, and a crowd of revelers quickly gathered around the pool. By the time Donna and I followed the crowd outside, most of the partygoers had stripped-off their clothes and had jumped into the pool.

The pool was jammed with twenty nude teenagers frolicking and splashing. I looked at Donna and she was taking off her clothes. I felt obligated to do the same.

I found myself standing naked in front of a lot of my friends. Strangely, I felt no shame or embarrassment. I thought it was the pot, but maybe it was an unconscious yearning to free myself from the Catholic value system by which I had been raised. Donna and I jumped into the water together.

Although it was August, the unheated pool quickly jolted those unprepared for its briskness. While horseplay in the pool swirled around us, Donna and I stood face to face in waist deep water without speaking. I put my arms around her neck and drew her close; we kissed. We were soon oblivious to all the frolicking around us as she pressed another soft kiss against my lips.

I felt her supple breasts press against my chest and with each succeeding kiss our passion grew. The horseplay in the pool died down. Couples that were engaged in similar foreplay exited for bedrooms in the house. Only guys without dates continued the splashing.

Donna grabbed my hand as we climbed out of the pool to walk back to the house. As we neared the kitchen door, my mind flashed back upon all the times I had tried to impress girls with the ultimate goal of getting them into bed. Now, with a willing partner holding my hand, all those previous escapades seemed trivial and a complete waste of my time and energy.

We entered the house and went up a short flight of wooden stairs to one of four bedrooms on the second floor. The first bedroom door we tried was locked. You could hear the loud moans of a girl nearing her climax. The second bedroom was occupied by John Ball and Kate

Kozacka who were vigorously fornicating on the bed. We continued down the hallway until we reached the Billford's master bedroom.

Everyone knew that the master bedroom came with a well-established ground rule: it was strictly off-limits, but Donna opened the door, revealing a king size bed, neatly made up with a shiny, deep blue bedspread. She grabbed my arm, pulled me onto the bed, where we began to make love.

On that same Sunday afternoon, forty-three American Marines walked into a Vietcong ambush near Bien Hoa, Vietnam. Only twenty-one survived. Three minutes later, Tran Lua, a Vietnamese citizen, was standing on a railroad bridge over a small burbling stream. He was fishing with his six-year-old son when a US Air Force F-4 Phantom dropped a two-thousand-pound bomb. The bomb struck the bridge, destroying it instantly, and throwing Lua and his son into the stream. Tran Lua miraculously survived and spent the next six hours looking for his son. He never found a trace of him.

Chapter 3

Riverside's varsity football coach, Stan Burns, served as a marine drill sergeant during the Korean War. His military buzz cut hairstyle and forehead seemed to glisten perpetually from the perspiration of his previous gym class, and when I received his summons, written with his limited vocabulary, my heart ached at the thought of having to face him. As I entered his office on a particularly cloudy and dreary Tuesday, he pointed me to a chair in front of his immaculate desk. He sat down in his dinged up wooden swivel chair and wasted no time.

"What's this I hear you're not coming out for football this year?"

I started shifting in my seat and felt like I was on a witness stand.

"No more football for me, Coach."

"What do you mean, no more football for you?" he demanded, raising his voice."

Coach, I've lost interest in the game. I don't want to spend my last year in high school playing sports."

Burns drew a deep breath, got up from behind his desk and walked over to a team picture on the wall. It was a picture of my freshman team from three years earlier.

"When you walked on my football field three years ago, I knew you could play. I knew you could catch a football. And I spent a lot of time working with you, refining your talents and making you into one of the best wide receivers in the City League. Now you want to throw it all away, up and leave your teammates."

"My heart's not in it anymore."

I was not feeling the guilt I normally would in a situation like this.

"What the hell do you mean your heart isn't in it anymore?" he demanded in his forceful drill sergeant's tone.

"Coach, I've got new priorities and football isn't one of them."

"Son, I think you're making a big mistake. You're letting your school and your fellow teammates down," he said switching to a fatherly tone.

"I'm going to do my own thing."

After I said it, I regretted I couldn't think of something more intelligent.

"Nothing will change your mind?" he asked in a softer tone.

"Nothing," I replied with a knot forming in my throat, offering up my last line of defense.

"Get outta here," he said, resigning himself that no pep talk or laying guilt on me was going to change my mind.

As I got up and walked to the door, my feet felt like they were wearing cement shoes and the door looked like it was fifty miles away. I looked straight ahead, afraid to look back.

Chapter 4

While on a pumpkin buying expedition the day before Halloween, I fell in love with and purchased a used Golden Guernsey milk truck with money I had saved from years of summer jobs. It was a split axle, classic boxy-looking milk truck that for many years had delivered milk door-to-door in southern Wisconsin. It had the familiar goldenrod and black color scheme and the famous Bessie the Cow logo on both sides.

Wisconsin farmers, like most Midwest farmers, were experiencing the effects of corporate takeovers. Many small dairy farms were being consolidated while many others were just plain closing down. Most door-to-door milk delivery had been discontinued in Milwaukee, so hundreds of these milk trucks were for sale at giveaway prices.

On that same cool and windy Halloween eve, a bomb exploded on the campus of the University of San Francisco, killing a security guard and a student researcher. Hardly anyone in Wisconsin, including me, paid any attention to the story on the TV news that evening.

"What the hell is that?" exclaimed my dad, as I drove the former delivery truck into our driveway. Robert H. Ralston, Sr., was an executive with Wisconsin Bell, part of the country's biggest telecommunications monopoly. My dad's specialty was advanced technology with little-known equipment such as multi-routing computers. He used our den as a second office, and it was packed with experimental equipment not available to the general public.

My dad was two inches shorter than I with brown hair and brown eyes. When he wasn't preoccupied with his work, he was the proud father of five children: one boy and four girls, three older and one younger than I. Unfortunately, he relied on drinking as a crutch to deal with the enormous pressure of his job. He was not a warm or sensitive man. He never hugged me after the age of five, and he stopped kissing all of his children when they reached ten. He was a Marquette University graduate, and on occasion he would say that he wanted me to attend his alma mater in Milwaukee.

Even my dad, who was an extremely busy executive, noticed my changing interests. The arrival of a milk truck only heightened his concern.

"What do you think, dad? I'm going to convert it into a cool van," I announced.

He shook his head and said, "I don't know about you sometimes." He turned and walked away without articulating his displeasure.

Over the course of a couple of weeks, I transformed the milk truck into a customized van with a double bed on a wooden platform in the back and a heavy-duty stereo system with numerous speakers. Shortly after remodeling the interior, which included two royal blue captain's chairs for the driver and the front passenger seat, I paid for a shiny new Earl Scheib paint job. Instead of the familiar sounds of Otis Redding and James Brown, a new breed of music from The Jimmy Hendrix Experience and Cream blared from my truck's sound system.

During the Christmas holidays, my third oldest sister, Betsy, came home from Pennsylvania where she was attending college. Eager to show her my converted milk truck, I agreed to pick her up at the airport.

There was no mistaking Betsy Ralston and Bob Ralston for brother and sister. We looked like twins and she was as athletic as her younger brother. I quickly hustled her through the baggage claim area and into the waiting truck. A light snow fell and the bare trees over Lake Drive provided a stunning, white archway.

I kept a huge peace symbol flag in the back of the truck and used it as a bedspread. I adorned the interior with various posters of rock groups, including a band called Big Brother and the Holding Company with a singer named Janis Joplin.

"What do you think? Pretty out-of-sight machine, huh?" I asked.

Betsy surveyed the truck for a moment and then proclaimed, "You're a stoner!"

"What?" I stammered.

"You're smoking pot, aren't you?"

I was totally flabbergasted. Was it that easy to recognize, especially by a family member? I was busted by my own sister. Then to my astonishment, Betsy reached into her purse and pulled out a rolled up marijuana joint and stated, "Don't worry, I won't tell anyone."

She started laughing while she lit up the joint. After taking a hit, she offered it to me. I started laughing and took a deep draw on the joint.

"Holy shit, my sister is a stoner!" I exclaimed.

She quickly retorted, "Holy shit, my brother is a stoner!"

We laughed and joked all the way home and finished the joint before pulling into the driveway. My sister was no longer the straight-laced individual that I had gone to high school with for two years until she went off to college.

The holiday season at the Ralston household went well with only a few seasonal arguments. It seemed strange to my family not to attend any Riverside High basketball games. Since I was not on the team, no one was interested. My sister Betsy and I spent quite a bit of time together during the vacation. We would go off, smoke pot, and discuss world affairs. She also introduced me to hashish.

The Saturday morning after Christmas, Betsy and I drove to Terry Andre State Park along Lake Michigan. The park's coastline consists of a series of rolling sand dunes. Five months earlier, these dunes were covered with small tufts of grass and hordes of sunbathers.

The dull sun was low in the eastern sky and a heavy blanket of snow covered the dunes. They looked like an Eskimo village with numerous igloos. We decided to brave the twenty-degree temperature and go for a walk on the icy beach. The walk turned into a what-are-you-going-to-do-with-your-life discussion, that eighteen-year-olds often have. However, this conversation was delivered with love and great concern by my sister.

"So my little brother's eighteen now. Did you file with the Selective Service?" she asked as we walked briskly along the shore.

"Last week."

"Dad said you were considering taking some time off before you go to college. Is that true?" Her question failed to mask her concern.

The wind was pushing the waves up on the frozen shore and the few seagulls present seemed forlorn in this frigid environment.

"I don't want to go to college right now. After four years of high school, I want to take a break. I'm thinking about going out to California for the summer."

"If you don't get a student deferment, you are going to get drafted," she replied.

"I'm not going to worry about that now. You gotta be nineteen before they can draft you," I replied.

"You don't have any idea what's going on in Vietnam, do you?"

"A war."

"Damn straight a war! And let me tell you something, you don't want to end up in the infantry in Vietnam, and that's exactly where you will end up if you don't get a 2-S or 4-Y or 4-F deferment."

"What's all this 2-Y, 2-F stuff?" I asked, annoyed at her preaching.

"Bob, listen to me. I've been working with anti-war groups at school and I've seen how bad things are going over there. We are supporting a corrupt government, and they are shipping hundreds of dead American boys home every week and covering up the truth."

"How do you know all this?"

Before she could answer we came upon a group of dead seagulls frozen on the beach. She looked down at the seagulls and then looked at me.

"When I left Riverside High School two years ago, I had never heard of Vietnam. I recall it being named French Indochina in our geography books. But three months after graduation, my friend John Collins was shipped home in a body bag. When I stood next to his casket at his funeral, I decided I better find out what's going on. He was only nineteen. Why? What the hell did John Collins ever do to deserve to die at nineteen?"

Tears welled up in her eyes and she turned and gave me a big hug.

"Don't let that happen to you, Bobby. Don't let that happen to you," she said through her tears.

I was speechless. Could this Vietnam thing be that serious? So serious that it warranted a tearful warning from my sister? We didn't say a word as we trudged into a stiff northerly wind back to the truck. She wrapped her arm tightly around mine as we walked with our heads bowed against the wind. It was at that moment that I knew what it meant to love and be loved by a sibling.

The sun broke through and it turned into a brilliant winter day as we drove through the snowplowed but slippery county roads leading back to the highway. The truck's heater offered welcome relief from Lake Michigan's cold, damp air.

I couldn't suppress the great desire to know more about what was going on in Vietnam. As we pulled onto the clean black asphalt of the highway I said, "Everything you see on TV says we are winning the war. I'm hoping that it will be over before I'm nineteen."

"Our government is lying," she replied.

"Lying?"

"The Vietcong control most of South Vietnam. That doesn't sound like we're winning the war to me."

"On TV, I hear that their side has lost thousands of troops and we lost a few guys."

"Well, don't believe it. And if you are counting on this war being over before you're nineteen, think again. If I were you, I'd be thinking about getting my ass into college or some other way of getting out of the draft."

"I can't go to college now. I don't give a shit, and I'll just flunk out anyway. And I'm damn sure not going to run away to Canada and hide out the rest of my life."

"You better do something or they'll draft you right into the infantry and ship you over to the jungles of Vietnam. Do you know what the life expectancy for a new recruit in the infantry is? Six weeks. Six weeks!"

I just stared at the road, but she pressed on.

"Get your head out of the clouds, man. I don't want to see my little brother in a body bag."

Sensing that enough was enough and that she had made her point, she reached forward and turned on the radio. The Buffalo Springfield's lyrics "something is going on and it ain't exactly clear," filled the truck and added to my anxiety.

Weeks passed since my sister had returned to college and the smell of lilacs filled the air. Finally, the last of the dirty snow piles had melted away. The tiny, pink blooms in the apple orchards gave promise of an early spring in the Midwest. Although it was only April, some hearty souls were already putting their boats into the city's marinas.

My interest in Vietnam continued to grow. I read all the news accounts I could lay my hands on and regularly watched the nightly news. Meanwhile, I was drinking considerably more than usual at weekend parties. One weekend, students held a big demonstration at the University of Wisconsin-Milwaukee, a few blocks from my house. The students took over the chancellor's office and held it for forty-eight hours before the police and campus security dragged them out. I was oblivious to the event because I spent the weekend in bed having sex with Freddy Billford's girlfriend, Sharman Stromme, while he was out of town touring prospective colleges.

Chapter 5

Billford's parties were rarely devoid of girls, but a stag party was held in late April at the farm. Young men, acting far senior than their years, were drinking cognac out of Mr. Billford's crystal snifters and smoking cigars. At the circular breakfast table, a hot and heavy poker game was in progress. It was later reported that the big loser was out fifty bucks.

The main topic of discussion was who was going to take whom to Senior Prom. For those without steady girlfriends, strategic plans were being formulated to get as many of the guys dates as possible. After all, this was going to be the last chance before graduation for a guy to date a girl he'd been eyeing for years.

Moonlight flooded the adjacent cow pastures and the constellation of Orion was setting in the western sky with the great warrior's sword pointing to the horizon. This was a clear sign that summer was fast approaching.

Gaston, John Haus, and I reclined in three lounge chairs, drinking beer and smoking cigars. We gazed skyward, having a heart to heart talk about our respective futures. Gaston was normally a quiet and introspective individual, and he and Haus had graduated from Riverside a few months early in January as members of the 12-B class.

Riverside had two graduating classes every year, one in January and the other in June. Inexplicably, the June graduates were designated as the 12-A class and the January graduates were the 12-B class. Obviously, this odd class numbering system was created by the same administrator who devised the dual letter sweater system.

I felt deeply troubled as I lay there watching Sirius, the Dog Star, chase Orion to the west. With graduation about a month and a half away, I still hadn't decided what I was going to do about the draft.

Gaston drew on his cigar, exhaled, and told of his plan to outfox the Selective Service System.

"My physical is next week, and I haven't eaten a solid meal in three weeks. I've lost twenty-two pounds. If I get under one hundred and twenty-five pounds, I'm exempt for my height."

"That's all it takes?" I asked.

I looked at John Haus who was as close to an all-American boy as you could find at Riverside High School. He was a physical specimen. He was six foot two, two hundred and five pounds and his chest was broad, his forearms immense, and his facial features chiseled. He was the city's leading high school running back and owned a three-year undefeated record in wrestling. He often wrestled opponents that outweighed him by as much as fifty pounds. We nicknamed him "Hoss."

Hoss could have been anything he wanted to be. He was handsome, bright, with a commanding physical presence. What he lacked was charisma. He was basically a big, shy Midwestern kid, and he liked it that way. He could have won the title of Homecoming King anytime he wanted, but he never ran and declined all offers to do so. He often found himself having to fight a drunk in a bar who wanted a piece of him. He was not mean-spirited and always respected the rights of others. Hoss spoke softly as he revealed his future plans.

"I'm going to enlist in the army the day after the prom and get it over with. In two years I'll be back home."

"That's a dangerous plan, Hoss," Gaston chimed in.

"An infantry recruit has a life expectancy of six weeks in Vietnam," I stated, using information gleaned from my sister Betsy.

"Hey, I don't plan to end up in the infantry. My dad said that if I enlist I could request a particular job. I'm going to volunteer to be a cook. No one wants to be a cook so it should be easy to get it. And cooks are usually behind the lines-way behind the lines," he said.

"I'm not sure there are such things as lines in Vietnam," I said.

It was getting late and Gaston was the first to acknowledge the hour. "I'm not driving home. I'm going to sleep in my car," he said.

"I'm going home," Hoss said.

I was too troubled to sleep, get up, or leave. I quickly acknowledged their departure with a grunt. The party wound down and many of the attendees decided to sleep at the farm rather than to drive back to Milwaukee.

Once alone, I looked up at a continuous stream of shooting stars. I wondered if my life was going to be like a shooting star, just a brief moment in the universe. It was the first time since I was fourteen years old that I wasn't spending the majority of my time thinking about how to get sex. I took a swig of my warm beer and felt a psychological vise tightening around me. Summer was fast approaching, and I knew I wasn't going to college, at least not right away, but that meant that I had six months until I was going to have to take my US Army draft physical examination. If I passed the exam, which I most surely would, then on my nineteenth birthday in February, I would be inducted into the United States Army, most likely as an infantryman. If I got drafted, Vietnam couldn't be far off.

The peace movement that my sister Betsy spoke about sounded provocative and kept entering my thoughts. I stared at the stars and wondered how to join it. But alcohol and introspection didn't mix, and I soon nodded off to sleep. I dreamt vivid and perplexing scenes. One was a massive group of people marching as if they were part of an army unit. None of the marchers wore a uniform and some had long hair and beards. This long rag-tag column was made up of men and women and marched through city streets and down country roads. People lined the sides of the streets as they had done along railroad tracks for presidential cavalcades.

The column eventually arrived at a large field of tall grass. Then suddenly it stopped marching. Each marcher proceeded to lie down on the grass and once prone, became rigid and motionless. Around the perimeter of the field there were thousands of flags unfurled atop shiny stainless steel flagpoles. Some were American flags and some were unidentifiable. Drums pounded a marching beat, which seemed incongruent due to the prone and lifeless marchers.

I tossed and turned in the lounge chair. But just as the dream seemed to reach some sort of conclusion, somebody shook my shoulder. I struggled to my senses and when I opened my eyes, I was overwhelmed by the bright sunlight. It was nine o'clock.

Gaston said, "Get up, it's time to go home."

I looked up trying to see who it was, but the sun was shining directly into my eyes. I wasn't sure if I was awake or still dreaming. Gaston, seeing that his first effort at arousing me was not successful, shook me more violently.

"Get up, man!"

I was surprised and relieved when I recognized him. But when I began to describe my dream to him, he was already walking back to his car. Realizing he was my only way back to Milwaukee, I stumbled to my feet and followed him begrudgingly.

For the first several miles driving toward Milwaukee, neither of us had anything to say. We both suffered from a restless night, Gaston from his cramped station wagon, and me in an uncomfortable lounge chair. He offered me a joint and we both smoked it furiously, hoping it would make up for our lack of sleep.

Monday morning traffic on Highway 141, busy with semi-tractor trailers, zoomed past Gaston's underpowered station wagon, shaking us with violent blasts of air. Gaston opened his glove compartment and pulled out a psychedelic-looking flyer and handed it to me. Suddenly a bird flew into the windshield with a tremendous thud. It startled both of us, and Gaston struggled to stay in his lane as yet another semi-truck zoomed past us. After the jostling stopped, Gaston exclaimed, "Shit. I wonder if he knew what hit him?"

"I wonder how many birds are killed by cars every year in the US?" I asked.

Gaston looked at me with no intention of venturing a guess. Looking for the flyer he had dropped, he spotted it on the floor and picked it up and handed it to me. It was an advertisement to hear Doctor Timothy Leary speak at the Downer Room near the University of Wisconsin-Milwaukee.

On that same Monday, in California, someone stole one hundred pounds of dynamite from a highway construction site. The Fresno police chief stated in the local newspaper that they had no leads and no suspects.

Chapter 6

The Downer Room boasted a reputation as an avant-garde coffeehouse, part of the trendy Downer Avenue area near the university. Downer Avenue had been transformed recently into a beautifully landscaped shopping and entertainment district with progressive clothing stores, restaurants, bars, coffee shops, and a foreign film theater. I recognized the coffee shop's name, as I was a regular patron of the nearby theater.

Earlier in the year, Mary Beth Kingston and I had gone to see the classic Japanese film *Woman in the Dunes* at the Downer Theater. That was the last time I ever dated her.

My thoughts wavered back and forth between the flyer and my dreams.

Gaston finally broke the silence. "Do you know who he is?"

"Who, Leary?" I asked.

"Who do you thing I'm talking about, Lyndon Johnson?"

Embarrassed and annoyed, I replied, "Ahh, he's some sort of spiritualist."

"He's a Harvard professor who's into LSD."

I nodded in agreement even though I knew very little about Leary, and even less about LSD.

"It's this Friday night. Do you want to go?"

"Sure," I replied without really thinking about my answer. Nothing more was said during the remaining thirty-minute drive into the city.

It was supposed to be just another week of school, in which by now I had lost complete interest, but then I was summoned to a meeting by Christine McGovern, the student advisor and counselor.

Where my mind was, I didn't have a clue. I was having trouble concentrating on anything for more than fifteen minutes. Make that ten minutes.

As I walked to the student counseling office, I was reminded by Vice Principal Galding to tuck in my shirttails. And as usual, I was wearing penny loafers without socks. Before I reached the office, Gaston, who had already graduated and had no business being in the building, intercepted me. He pulled me aside and was bubbling over with good news.

"I did it. I'm exempt!" he blurted out.

At first I wasn't sure what he was talking about. Gaston grabbed my arm and did a little do-si-do with me in the hallway. It was then that I realized the reason for his great sense of joy and relief.

"I'm exempt! I am out! I spell that O-U-T of the draft," he shouted.

He hurriedly told me how his starvation diet plan had worked and that he had failed his military induction physical that very morning.

"All right, far out, man!" I exclaimed.

I was genuinely happy for him. Our impromptu celebration was ended abruptly when Counselor McGovern stepped out of her office into the hallway.

"You're late, Ralston, and I've got other appointments," she snapped.

Chapter 7

Posters of universities from all over the world adorned the walls in the student counseling office. The most striking poster was of the ivy-covered walls of Harvard.

"Well, Mr. Ralston, I have bad news for you," Miss McGovern said, getting right down to business.

It was hard for me, or any other male student, to concentrate on anything McGovern said. She was blessed, or cursed, with the finest set of perfectly round 36-DD breasts in Milwaukee. I was pretending to listen, but I was fantasizing about taking off her bra and kissing her breasts.

"If you fail any class this semester, you will not have enough credits to graduate," she continued.

"What?" I asked, finally paying attention.

"You need twelve credits to graduate and that means you cannot fail any class or you don't graduate with your class. Do you understand?"

The embarrassment of not graduating with my classmates was too much for me to bear. "But I'm not flunking anything," I protested.

"Well, according to your World History teacher, Mrs. Banks, you're a borderline failure. And if you like, I would be glad to relay what your English and Political Science teachers had to say."

"I admit I haven't been keeping up with the homework, but flunk me? Isn't that a little extreme for a senior who is graduating?"

"What I'm saying here, Mr. Ralston, is that if you don't get it together, you will not be graduating."

"That's a real bummer."

"If I were you, I'd get the homework done and buckle down and start studying for final exams. Then maybe you will graduate with your classmates."

All of a sudden the importance of the draft, Vietnam, the peace movement, and Senior Prom vanished. I got up out of the proud old armchair I was sitting in, probably still there from the time my mother attended Riverside, and walked out into the hallway. Fifth period had just ended, and the hallways were crowded with students. Sharman Stromme walked toward me in hopes of arranging another clandestine weekend rendezvous, but I never saw her. I walked off to my sixth period class with my head down and my thoughts in a thick fog. A fellow student intercepted me at the classroom door and reminded me that tonight was Timothy Leary's presentation.

Chapter 8

The Ralston household was truly surprised to find me home and studying, but it was short-lived as I got on the telephone and made arrangements to meet Gaston at the Downer Avenue coffeehouse.

I arrived first and I stood outside in my penny loafers, Levis, and button-down shirt. I felt out of place. Everyone entering the coffeehouse was older; most were university students or professors; many were dressed like hippies, and almost all of the men were sporting long hair and beards. I looked too clean-cut. I felt like I was entering a private club of which I was not a member.

Gaston arrived five minutes later with two attractive university freshmen coeds in tow. After brief introductions and the inquiring glares I shot at Gaston, we entered the coffeehouse. We sat near the back of the room with an unobstructed view of the stage.

When Doctor Leary walked out on stage, he received a long and cordial applause. He was dressed in a long, flowing white silk shirt and a pair of battered old jeans.

I leaned over to Gaston and whispered, "Is that how they dress at Harvard?"

Leary captivated and mesmerized the audience–and me–speaking with charm and wit for an hour and fifteen minutes. He expressed ideas on pursuing a higher meaning, having the courage to break the bonds of the mundane and materialistic world, and the essentiality of seeking spiritual enlightenment. Then he spoke about his experience with LSD. He stated that LSD had a profound effect on his ability to become a higher spiritual being. He recommended that everyone in the audience try LSD.

At the conclusion of his presentation, Leary asked for questions. The exchange between Leary, the professors, and the college students was electrifying. Questions on existentialism, life after death, and drug use in the pursuit of a higher awareness ricocheted off the coffeehouse's smoky walls and echoed deep into my mind. Someone handed me a joint, but I quickly passed it to Gaston. I didn't want to smoke pot in public, especially in a room full of strangers. Gaston didn't hesitate and neither did the two girls.

I was deeply engrossed in the conversation and the theories being bantered about. I was hearing words and terminology I had never heard before. I had no idea that LSD was originally used by the US Army for psychological testing. A majority of what was being discussed was way over my head. When Leary finally walked off stage, I wasn't sure if my karma was good or bad, or for that matter if I had any karma at all.

As we were leaving the coffeehouse Gaston announced, "My parents are out of town. Why don't we all go to my place?"

The two girls nodded their approval. I knew full well it was a school night, but I agreed to go.

Gaston lived in a three-story, eight-bedroom Colonial home with columns on the front porch and high stucco ceilings throughout the interior. Ornate fireplaces decorated every bedroom and art deco tile graced the bathrooms.

After a quick tour of the house, the four of us went outside on a large second-floor porch to take in the nocturnal view of the nearby University of Wisconsin-Milwaukee campus.

The girls were both nineteen years old. Connie Kelly struck me as the proverbial girl next door with a sweet face and flaming red hair. She joked that she was a good old Wisconsin girl and could drink beer with the best of them, and she admitted experimenting with hallucinogenic drugs. Anne Nitche was a foreign exchange student from Russia who spoke impeccable English. She entertained us with her knowledge of Greek mythology. I felt an immediate attraction to this striking blonde with dazzling green eyes.

Gaston began rolling a joint while Anne was explaining why the constellation Orion was next to the constellation Taurus and why Zeus disapproved of Orion's designs on the Seven Sisters of the Pleiades. I was completely enamored with this tall Russian beauty and was fascinated with her knowledge of the constellations. Gaston lit the joint and the four of us smoked it. The joint made several rounds before expiring. Getting stoned was a new experience for Anne and she became disoriented. I was stoned too. Standing next to this beautiful creature I could feel my heart pounding. Gaston suggested that we retire to the den where we could listen to Jimi Hendrix on his dad's new Kenwood stereo. Once in the den, Gaston turned up the stereo and turned down the lights. The room was swirling with Hendrix's guitar riffs, and I was sitting next to one of the most beautiful women I had ever seen. Although I was in awe of her beauty, the pot slowly put me at ease.

"That's some damn good pot," I remarked.

"It's from Thailand," Gaston shouted over the music. "It sure knocked my socks off."

Everyone giggled. Gaston built a fire in the fireplace despite the fact it was seventy-two degrees and one of the warmest days of May, so far. The reflections from the flames leapt about the room, caromed around the ceiling, danced on the pleats of the drapes and glistened on the marble mantle above the fireplace. Gaston and Connie were sitting on an oversized sofa and Anne and I were lying next to each other on large pillows on the floor. When Hendrix's record ended, it was followed by Cream, a group that featured a hot, lead guitar player named Eric Clapton.

Anne was on her back watching the flames reflect off the high ceiling. I watched her and wondered what it must be like to be a student living in a foreign land. Serious thoughts quickly gave way to carnal ones as I realized that she was braless. Gaston and Connie began kissing on the sofa but neither Anne nor I were aware of it. Connie's soft moaning caught our attention. I felt awkward watching another couple making out so close up. Connie opened her eyes and saw us looking at her. She got up off the sofa.

"I've got some window-pane acid. You guys want some?" she asked.

"I do," Gaston answered.

"What about you two?" Connie asked, standing over us.

Anne shrugged and said, "Sure."

I was more reluctant.

"Are you sure that shit is okay?" I asked.

"You don't have to take if you don't want to," Connie responded.

I was embarrassed. I didn't want to be the odd man out.

I nodded my head and said, "I'll give it a try."

Gaston went to the kitchen to get a pitcher of fruit juice and four glasses. The three of us followed him into the kitchen. Connie laid four tiny blue LSD tablets on the stark white kitchen counter tiles while Gaston filled four glasses with juice. With all of us holding both a glass and a hit of acid, Gaston proposed a toast.

"Here's to Timothy Leary. He takes you up and he brings you down on the very same day," he said, borrowing a lyric from a Moody Blues' song.

"I hope so," I said.

We raised our glasses and swallowed the pills. On the way back to the den, Connie said that she had heard Doctor Leary speak at the University of Illinois and that he was much better tonight.

Once we were back in the den, it didn't take long for the effects of the LSD to be felt. Connie and Gaston resumed their cuddling and kissing on the couch and it only seemed natural that I should lean over and kiss Anne. I didn't know what to expect but she didn't resist my advances. While I kissed her, she put her arm tightly around the back of my neck. Connie took a breather from her activities with Gaston to observe Anne's and my situation.

"Be good to her, she's never been high with a guy before."

Anne giggled and I felt compelled to respond, but I couldn't think of anything to say so I just nodded.

As the LSD came on, I looked around the den, awash with vibrant colors. Orange hues raced along the curtain valances and the green carpeting waved like a rolling pasture in a light breeze. Faint yellows from the fire shone on Anne's face like light from a faltering candle. Her face appeared as chiseled perfection. Rodin must have been summoned back to earth to create one more beautiful masterpiece. Her pupils were so dilated that she looked like a statue destined for immorality in the Metropolitan Museum of Art. The LSD raced through my body and I felt so warm and happy that I almost cried.

Anne smiled and pulled herself closer. She kissed my neck and then stuck her tongue into my ear. Lightening shot through my body and I felt my erection bulging in my pants. She felt my erection against her leg. Something magical was happening between us, but Connie interrupted us again.

"If you make love to her, you have to wear a rubber."

I was really coming on to the acid and I had difficulty understanding that having sexual intercourse with this beautiful girl was a foregone conclusion in everybody's mind. This added to my excitement. Before I could respond to Connie's command, Gaston and Connie took off their clothes. Anne and I watched them begin to make love. Anne appeared unaffected. I had never seen another couple make love and was frozen in my voyeurism.

The glow of the fire illuminated Connie's breasts as she mounted Gaston and began thrusting her hips down on him. I began to hallucinate as I watched Connie and Gaston copulate. Connie looked so beautiful. I thought she was a queen, a naked, free, regal woman. Anne touched my face and I saw that she had disrobed and was lying next to me naked. She looked up at me and whispered, "Make love to me."

I was all thumbs as I tried to take my pants off. But after what seemed like an eternity, I was naked too. There was no need for foreplay as the LSD had amplified our sexual desires to new plateaus. When I rolled on top of her she was warm with desire. We both shuddered. Making love to her was so natural it stirred my soul. Rather than immediately thrusting, we both lay very still and began to communicate as only a man and a woman can do when they are fornicating.

Across the den, Connie's and Gaston's sounds of passion grew louder as they neared their orgasms. Anne and I laid there listening to the sensuous sounds echoing about the den and the rhythm they pounded out on the sofa. Soon we began to create our own rhythm. As Anne neared her orgasm, she began emitting soft guttural sounds. My first orgasm felt like it lasted for an hour. Dawn broke before we reached the last in a series of mutual orgasms. We were so exhausted and overcome with a sense of joy that we both began to laugh uncontrollably.

Chapter 9

Detective William Swenarski, a twenty-year member of the San Jose Police Department, just happened to be driving by Power Systems Corporation's headquarters when he heard a call over his radio about a fire or an explosion. He was the first to respond to the emergency at the defense contractor's ordnance manufacturing facility, a mile north of San Jose, California.

Driving his 1966 Ford squad car at seventy miles per hour, Swenarski came to a screeching halt at Power Systems' front gate. The first person he saw was a pot-bellied security guard in a wrinkled blue security guard uniform pointing toward flames shooting out of a building three hundred yards away.

"What the hell happened?" yelled Swenarski out the window.

"I don't know. There was a huge explosion, and then another explosion, and now the fire."

"Anyone in there?"

"Yes, I think there are at least six people working in the storage building, and that's the one that's on fire."

"What's in the building?" Swenarski yelled.

"We produce munitions for the US Army. There are millions of M-16 bullets, grenades, and mortar rounds stored here for shipment to Vietnam."

Swenarski grabbed his radio microphone, "Swenarski, six seven six, code five emergency."

A clear and calm voice answered, "Headquarters command. What's up, Swen?"

"John, get all available fire units and a half a dozen ambulances out to Power Systems on Highway NN. They have–"

A deafening blast rocked Swenarski's car, throwing his head back against the seat. The security guard staggered backwards and fell to the ground. A three-foot section of a steel I-beam rose out of the brilliant flashes and came crashing down on the hood of the police car and impaled the engine. The car immediately burst into flames.

Fire trucks from every fire department within fifty miles of Power Systems raced to the inferno. Dozens of fire trucks clogged the highway with their bulging, sweating fire hoses crisscrossing the entrance road to the factory. The intensity of the blaze and the rogue rounds of ammunition exploding non-stop created such a dangerous environment that they forced the fire crews to pull back.

A specially trained fire rescue team of six men, dressed in inflammable suits with oxygen masks and flak jackets, trudged toward the flaming, exploding chaos in hopes of finding any survivors. But after two-dozen mortar rounds exploded, they quickly retreated to safety.

It took twenty hours to extinguish the blast and another four hours before ammunition and ordnance inside the storage building stopped exploding.

A smoky and foul haze hung over the scattered steel and aluminum debris when US Army and FBI agents arrived on the scene. An Army officer in a starched green uniform, with golden eagle insignias on his collars, spoke to San Jose Fire Chief John Cardinal, the local incident commander.

"Chief, I'm Lieutenant Colonel Peter Appleton, special anti-terrorist unit, Fifth Army Command, Washington, D.C. With me is FBI special Agent Richard Crens."

Crens stood next to the colonel in a neatly pressed blue suit with his FBI badge on a lanyard around his neck.

"What are the US Army and the FBI doing at a local fire?" Chief Cardinal asked.

"Chief, Power Systems is an army contractor supplying munitions for our war effort in Vietnam. The destruction of military supplies is a federal offense," the colonel said.

"Are you implying that this was arson?"

"At this point, we don't know. But Power Systems has been receiving terrorist threats for about a year."

The Fire Chief's face turned ashen and he slammed his helmet at the feet of the colonel and Crens.

"Are you telling me that this facility has been threatened, and no one told us? Why wasn't additional security provided?"

When the site was finally secured, six bodies were recovered from the carnage. The FBI's report cited sabotage as the cause. FBI forensic teams determined that the original explosion was caused by dynamite detonated in a mortar storage area. The evidence overwhelmingly indicated that it was a case of domestic terrorism.

Prior to the incident, Power Systems had never had a single workplace accident or fatality. They started making munitions for the army at the beginning of World War II.

Chapter 10

I tried valiantly to keep up with my studies, but my mind was filled with wonderful memories of the night with Anne. I was also dealing with another problem: I didn't have a date for Senior Prom, which was only three weeks away. I asked Anne, but she was going to be out of town. I felt the pressure, as it would be a big embarrassment if I showed up stag.

Even though Gaston graduated five months earlier, all January graduates were invited to Riverside's Senior Prom in May and he was taking Connie Kelly. They had become inseparable comrades and were experimenting with a variety of drugs; their favorites were hashish and magic mushrooms. He said he would ask Connie if any of her friends would be willing to go as my date.

It seemed an overly busy Monday at Riverside High School. For some strange reason there was always higher student attendance on Mondays. As the third period bell rang, the hallways were jammed with students moving between classes.

As I headed off to my next class, someone came up from behind me and slipped her hands over my eyes.

"Guess who?" came a soft and sexy voice.

Before I could answer, Sharman Stromme stood in front of me.

"Sharman, Sharman, Sharman, what am I going to do with you?"

"That's what I want to know?" she asked in an inviting voice.

"What about Freddy?"

"We're finished."

"What?"

"I caught him with Donna Read, and they didn't have their clothes on."

Before I could inquire into the details, the tardy bell rang and we both took off running to our respective classes before any plans could be discussed, much less finalized. I thought about asking Sharman to the prom as I entered the classroom, but a cold stare from my History teacher brought me back to the subject at hand.

Storms raged the week before prom, both meteorologically and at the Ralston household. My father grew increasingly impatient with my decision not to attend college. As the thunderheads rumbled overhead an argument ensued.

"I'm not going. I want to take a break and I mean it," I said.

"The odds of a student going to college decrease every year he doesn't attend after high school," my father answered.

"Dad, we've been through this a hundred times, and I'm not changing my mind. I have my own money saved up to do this and my truck is ready to go."

"What is this going to San Francisco shit anyway?" he asked.

"I just want to get a little change of scenery. I want to explore new places and new things."

"And plenty of drugs!" he interrupted.

"Dad, drugs have nothing to do it. If you want drugs, you can get anything you want right here in Milwaukee. Do you really think I want to be a druggie?"

"What the hell are you going to do out there?"

"I'm going out there for the summer, three months. Maybe I'll get a job or something," I said, trying to defuse his anger.

"San Francisco is a radical city. I don't think you are ready for it."

"I'm only going out to look around. I never said I was moving there."

The phone rang and thankfully my mom said it was for my dad. I seized the opportunity to escape to my room. I debated about going over to see Sharman, but the pile of homework on my bed put an end to my sexual fantasies. This was a night to stay home and do homework. An easterly gale gusted off Lake Michigan causing twenty-two foot waves and the rain hammered on the roof like a million pellets fired from a shotgun. Even WTMJ-TV's weatherman, Bill Carlson, warned people to stay home.

When the weekend arrived, I called Gaston and asked if he would come over and talk to me about my San Francisco trip. Gaston had been there the previous summer for a quick visit, and he had shared some pretty incredible stories. He said he would give me some tips on the do's and don'ts. Some of his stories seemed so outlandish that I was sure he was given to embellishment.

It was a classic May weekend: the sun shone brightly and the warm weather offered a tantalizing preview of the approaching summer. The interior of my truck was almost complete. I stopped at a local variety store to purchase several oversized pillows, which would come in handy for the drive out to San Francisco. I also stopped at the oil-stained and eternally greasy Wisco 99 station for gas. I often wondered what Wisco 99 sold more of, gasoline or cigarettes.

My truck's new paint job shone brightly in the sunlight, and I had just recently had all the bumpers re-chromed. I still hoped to paint a mural on the side of the truck, which reminded me to ask Gaston for suggestions on what to paint. I had paid the attendant standing next to the pump and was about to get back into the truck when a white MG-B screeched to a stop just inches from where I was standing. Up through the roofless car popped Sharman Stromme.

"You scared the shit out of me," I exclaimed.

"Next time, I might run your tight little ass over," she answered.

We both starting laughing.

"You got a date tonight?" she asked.

"No."

"Now you do."

"Ok, Miss Parnelli Jones, what do you have in mind?" I asked.

"I want to go see *What's New, Pussycat?* at the drive in."

"My car or yours?"

"You don't own a car. You own a truck."

"Ok, your car or my truck?"

"Sweet thing, what I want to do to you can't be done in this car."

She backed up her car and blew out of the gas station like a blustery wind.

As I drove to Gaston's house, I wondered if this impromptu date was actually planned by her.

As usual, Gaston's parents were out of town for the weekend. When I pulled into Gaston's driveway, Jim was washing his small station wagon.

"Guess who's going to the drive-in with me tonight?" I asked as I climbed out of the truck.

"Ursula Andress," he replied.

"I wish. Sharman Stromme," I proudly announced.

"What is Freddy Billford going to say about that?"

"Nothing. She broke up with him last week."

"Well, you sure don't waste time."

"I got a little secret for you. I screwed Sharman a couple of weeks ago."

If Gaston was surprised, he managed to not show it. He quickly finished his car washing duties and invited me in. Once inside, we retired to the all-too-familiar den to smoke a joint.

"I'm always going to have fond memories of the floor in front of this couch," I declared. "I call them rocking chair memories."

"If it wasn't for your old buddy Jimmy Gaston, you'd never get laid."

"What a babe. I wonder if all the girls in Russia are as beautiful and sexy as she is?"

"If they are, we should invite all their women to visit America, even if they are all spies."

Gaston lit up a joint.

I smoked pot but rarely ever bought any. The conversation quickly turned away from girls to contemporary politics.

In a somber voice barely audible I said, "I got a bad feeling about Hoss joining the army."

"We make our own decisions and then we gotta live with them."

"Yeah. Live with them. I only hope he does," I responded.

"I think he's crazy."

"He's going to be a cook. That's the job he wanted," I said.

"Do you think cooks don't get killed in Vietnam?"

My face tightened as the conversation began to rub a raw nerve.

"Vietnam, Vietnam, Vietnam! That's all I hear about! My History book still calls it French Indochina. What the fuck are we doing? What's going on?"

"I'm glad I'm not going over to some shit hole jungle and have someone blow my brains out," he answered.

"I don't understand. Vietnam isn't going to invade the United States."

"Nobody invades the United States," Gaston said through a blue smoke clouding the room. "Look, the US goes to war to make money. Have you ever heard of the military-industrial complex?" he asked.

"Don't give me some political jive."

"The military hires civilian companies to make its bombs, rifles, airplanes, ships, and so on. These companies don't make money when there isn't a war going on. But when a war starts, they stand to make millions and millions of dollars. If you think that we are only concerned about stopping the march of communism, you're out of touch, man."

"War is good business?"

"The best."

"What about all the people getting killed over there?"

"Occupational hazard."

I tried to make some sense of Gaston's statement. The marijuana didn't help. "Come on, it isn't that simple," I protested.

"Oh yeah? Are the kids of Dow Chemical executives serving in Vietnam?"

"How the hell do I know."

"Dow Chemical Company makes napalm and sells it to the US Army. And what about the thousands of other government suppliers? They all stand to make millions the longer the war goes on. This war isn't about communism. It's about money, geo-political power, colonialism, and multi-national business."

It had never occurred to me that war was good business. That struck another raw nerve, and I worried that Hoss might die to make somebody rich. I found myself at a mental and moral dead end.

"I don't want to talk about this anymore," I said.

Above-average warm and sunny days blessed the month of May, but the days passed quickly. I continued to buckle down with my studies, and I was sure I was going to graduate with my class in June. Sharman Stromme proved to be a welcome sexual outlet for my increasing concerns about the Selective Service draft. Conversely, my relationship with my father became more strained as the date of my planned San Francisco trip drew closer.

Senior Prom at Riverside High School always took place during the first weekend of May, perhaps to allow the students to recover before the Memorial Day holiday. The prom was always held in the school's gymnasium, the same gymnasium that seniors attended Physical Education classes several hundred times over four years, but you wouldn't have recognized it on prom night. The lavish decorations hid the cracked plaster and the numerous other defects and signs of aging. The stage for the band obscured the entrance to the shower rooms, and the class of 1967 did a marvelous job of decorating the entire gymnasium. It looked like a nightclub, and we knew what nightclubs looked like. Many of us would often go drinking and dancing in bars and nightclubs. Most of the January graduates returned to participate in the prom with the June graduates. Jimmy Gaston arrived with Connie Kelly on his arm and they made a charming couple.

Many parents rented cars for their prom-going kids. The street in front of the high school was lined with large sedans arriving with two or three couples. The young men all wore tuxedos while the girls wore everything from formal gowns to miniskirts. I arrived with Sharman Stromme, who wore a tight, backless black dress that was well above her knees. She looked hot, and I was her proud escort. Unfortunately, she had been drinking all afternoon and was well on her way to getting drunk. Freddy Billford showed up with Donna Read, and we were unusually cool toward each other. Gaston decided that he didn't want to get in the middle so he and Connie avoided both couples.

Milwaukee's hottest band, Twisting Harvey Scales and the Seven Sounds, performed a dazzling array of rhythm and blues songs and everyone had a blast. Sharman and I danced to several songs and then sneaked off to my truck for a quickie. Her sexual performance was energetic, considering she was quite intoxicated. After what was a wrestling match between two hot and horny teenagers, she passed out in the back of my truck. Try as I might, I was unable to revive her so I returned to the evening's festivities alone.

I found Hoss standing by himself in the corner of the gymnasium and offered him my hip flask. He declined and instead pulled out his own hip flask. We both looked around to make sure none of the teachers or chaperones saw us and then we clinked our flasks.

It was a balmy evening and the wind swung to the west, which warmed up the temperature. The prom concluded around eleven, followed by a series of private parties in homes and hotel rooms for the celebrants to attend.

Many of my fellow graduates found themselves hung over on the western banks of Lake Michigan as the sun proudly announced a new day. By five-thirty in the morning, I had already deposited the thoroughly inebriated Sharman Stromme on her front porch and was sitting with Hoss at the George Webb hamburger parlor near the high school.

George Webb hamburger parlors were as much a part of Milwaukee as were the breweries. They were famous for their fifteen-cent hamburgers that were equivalent in size to a silver dollar. It was common for customers to order a bag of fifteen hamburgers and consume them right there at the counter.

The interiors of George Webb hamburger parlors were as austere as the menu. The long and brilliant white Formica counters were fronted by little round stools covered in bright red vinyl that were bolted to the floor. George Webb's restaurants could seat twenty customers at any given time. Six-foot-long fluorescent light fixtures flooded the surroundings in a blinding white light that God on Judgment Day would have trouble equaling. The floors consisted of faded white tile with black grout. The cooks doubled as counter help, as well as cashier and bouncer. They wore white pants, white shirts and pointed little white hats. It was an establishment of white on white–a sanctuary where those with early morning hangovers from alcohol excesses sought refuge in the brilliant white light of redemption. It was also the starting point of another day for thousands of workers.

In contrast to its furnishings, George Webb's coffee was as black as the sky on a new moon. Management knew full well that many of its early morning customers were the rank and file of the city's working class and in need of a touch of sobriety and nourishment before they headed off to their factory, foundry, brewery, or tannery jobs.

Only two counter stools stood unoccupied when Hoss and I entered the hamburger parlor. We both had consumed a fair amount of alcohol but neither of us was intoxicated. We looked out of place, dressed in our disheveled tuxedos, while the other patrons wore soiled work clothes. We disregarded snide remarks hurled our way because we were engaged in an intense discussion.

Hoss was not displaying his usual air of self-confidence and was overly pensive. Perhaps he was more tired than passive. When our hamburgers and coffee arrived, the conversation turned to Hoss' enlistment into the army. He said was leaving for basic training the next day.

"I'm not sure I did the right thing," Hoss confided.

"What are you saying?"

"I don't know, but I got a bad feeling that something bad is going to happen to me."

Hoss' usual radiant smile was nowhere to be found. It was replaced with a furrowed brow, one I had never seen before. I let him do most of the talking.

"I always could do anything I set out to do. I don't remember worrying about much of anything, but I'm worried now. I just hope I don't get assigned infantry duty."

I was worried too.

"It seems odd to me that I have no reservations about serving my country, and a guy like Jimmy Gaston would do anything not to serve. In the Second World War, everybody served. Now it seems like the whole process has become very selective. I serve and somebody my own age doesn't?"

"I don't know the answer," I replied.

"Well, I can't do anything about it now. I ship out for basic training tomorrow. I hope I come back in one piece."

I put my arm around his shoulder to comfort him.

"You'll be all right, man. You'll make it," I said.

The sight of a guy putting his arm around another guy in George Webb's was a bit too much for a few of the more surly and inebriated patrons. Two men at the end of the counter began to taunt Hoss and me.

"What are you, a couple of queers?" one shouted.

"If you like him so much, why don't you kiss him?" another yelled.

I watched Hoss' face tighten in reaction to the comments. Trouble was brewing. Nobody calls Hoss a queer. Hoss stood up and casually took a couple of steps toward the men taunting us and then suddenly stopped a few feet away.

"You know what? You might be right. I could be queer. Why don't you come over here and suck my dick and I'll tell you how much I like it."

Immediately the two men jumped up and charged Hoss and a brawl started. Somebody grabbed me from behind, but I was able to elbow my attacker in the face. I turned around just in time to get clipped by a punch from another guy. Hoss was involved in a furious struggle with the two men, and all three of them were rolling around the floor, punching, grabbing, and kicking. Hoss landed a haymaker punch and laid out one of his attackers cold. The cook tried to separate several of the others who were fighting, but he got knocked to the floor for his trouble. Someone jumped on my back as I was still reeling from a punch that caught me high on the cheekbone. I whirled around and threw the guy directly through the parlor's large plate glass window. The window shattered with a terrific crash, and the man lay on the sidewalk, bleeding.

Hoss subdued his second adversary, and just as he stood up, somebody threw a punch at him. This started another full-scale brawl, and those who had not joined in the initial round of fighting came off their stools and started swinging wildly at anybody and everybody.

I heard police sirens wailing in the distance when someone picked up the cash register and threw it through another plate glass window. Through all the mayhem, Hoss saw that I had fought my way over to the first broken window. Hoss picked up the man he was fighting with and tossed him like a rag doll down the entire length of the counter, which sent plates, glasses, silverware, and hamburgers flying, showering everyone with debris. The police sirens got louder as Hoss leaped over an array of sprawled bodies and grabbed me by the arm. We both jumped through the broken window and ran for a nearby alley.

We hid behind a garbage dumpster and watched as scores of police entered the hamburger parlor, swinging their nightsticks in an attempt to restore order.

We looked like hell, and our tuxedos were ripped and covered with bloodstains and ketchup.

"I guess we just bought these tuxes," Hoss laughed.

We crept away down the alley. A half a mile away, we starting laughing.

As we walked side by side, the dawn's steely rays reflecting off the surrounding office buildings, Hoss put his arm around my shoulder.

"I'm gonna miss you, man," I said in a serious tone.

"I'm gonna miss you too."

"Where's basic training?" I asked.

"I'm going to Fort Hood, Texas, for six weeks and then I get assigned to some army unit."

"Just stay the hell out of Vietnam, man."

"I hope so," Hoss sighed.

I was momentarily at a loss for words.

"I'm truly scared of that place," Hoss said.

"You're gonna be okay."

He just nodded his head.

I tried to lighten up the conversation.

"Don't worry man, cause you're a stone lover, a golden glover, a girl chaser and a money waster. You're so good you should have been twins!" I said, borrowing some shtick from radio disc jockey, Doctor Bop, on WAWA.

We shared another laugh.

Hoss offered me his hand. But rather than shake his hand, I grabbed him and gave him a bear hug.

"You stay out of harm's way, man. I want to see your ass back here in two years. You got it?" I said.

"I'll do my best."

As we parted, Hoss slapped me on the back, just as he had done a hundred times before through our high school years. I walked away with a lump in my throat and wondered if I would ever see him again. I didn't want to turn around and look back at him.

Chapter 11

Just as final exams were about to begin, as always on the first Monday of the first week of June, a very ugly rumor started to circulate, made uglier still when Vice Principal Galding called an assembly, and the students gathered in the school's auditorium. Most of us were unaware of the nature of this hastily called gathering.

Galding took the stage and spoke in a very somber mood.

"Good afternoon. Sometimes we have wonderful news about our school and our students. And sometimes we have very difficult news. I wanted to bring all of us together and inform you of some tragic news before you hear from someone else. This morning, Jim Knudson, Senior Class President, committed suicide. I am cancelling all classes. Teams of student counselors are standing by and available for all those who want to talk to someone about this tragedy or anything else on their mind."

The news was received in stunned silence. Knudson was a very popular student and had an A+ average for his entire four years. He was the head of several clubs, had a steady girlfriend, and was on the school's varsity track team. He was expected to do well at the

University of Wisconsin-Madison, where he had enrolled for the fall semester. Later that afternoon, the Milwaukee Journal reported that Knudson had put a double barrel shotgun in his mouth and pulled both triggers.

Galding dismissed the assembly, but many students sat quietly and did not leave. I was only a casual acquaintance of Knudson's, but I could hardly believe my ears. In my mind, Knudson was a picture of success. My little cocoon as a high school student was becoming unwound. Suddenly I realized that even at eighteen years old, one's mortality can be fleeting. I got up in a daze and walked out of the building. I walked past my parked truck and kept on walking for several blocks. I found myself standing on the North Avenue Bridge overlooking the Milwaukee River. I rested my elbows on the ornate welded railings and watched a flock of ducks swimming in the swift current below.

Was my generation of eighteen-year-olds destined to suffer the same fate as eighteen-year-olds a quarter of a century earlier during World War II? Was death waiting to claim so many of our young lives, lives that would never have the opportunity to grow old, get married, or be blessed with the gift of children? The meaning of success would never be the same for me.

A small motorboat passed under the bridge and I could see several ducklings swimming alone along the muddy, weed-strewn banks. I wondered where their mother was. Was she dead? I thought about what my sister Betsy said about a government lying to its people. I wondered if everything I was taught was just a big lie. I questioned if humans were no more than a lost flock like the little ducklings swimming below me.

I wondered if we were conceived, born, educated, and raised only to end up killing each other. Tears began to well up in my eyes as the ducklings looked hopelessly lost. Another motorboat approached the tiny flock and I was sure that it was about to run the ducklings over. Today, was death going to claim even these young and innocent ducks? I wanted to shout a warning, first to the ducklings and then to the person piloting the boat. However, being fifty feet above the water I knew my voice would not be heard.

My hands grabbed the railings in anticipation as the boat drew closer to the ducklings. It looked like certain death for the little creatures. Suddenly the boat stopped and the boat's pilot reached down inside the craft and lifted a female duck over the side and dropped it into the water next to the ducklings. The duck must have been the mother because the wayward little flock immediately swam over to her and quickly gathered around her. The sight of this family reunion was so touching that tears flowed down my face. I thought about the heartbreak the Knudson family must be experiencing.

I took a deep breath and sighed out loud, "Somebody cares."

I stayed home studying every night for the entire week before final exams. There was a quiet determination in my efforts and I did well on all of my exams. The biggest motivation was the fear of being humiliated at not being able to graduate with my senior class. But after Knudson's funeral service in a stifling hot church, a high school diploma didn't seem that important in the bigger scheme of things.

After my last exam, I met Gaston at a nearby bar known for serving minors. We celebrated the end of my secondary education by getting falling down drunk by three o'clock in the afternoon. We both passed out in the back of my truck, and I didn't make it home until well after midnight.

Finally, graduation day arrived. It was a gloriously sunny day with a gentle breeze. Nothing but blue sky everywhere you looked. The commencement ceremony was scheduled for five o'clock in the school's auditorium and a large number of families, friends, and relatives were expected.

I dressed in my best blue slacks and blue sport coat, and put on a madras tie under my blue mortarboard and gown. My mother, father, and younger sister Susie wanted to accompany me to the ceremony, but I insisted on driving myself in my milk truck. I had made plans to meet Sharman Stromme at a graduation party later in the evening and I didn't want be obligated to go home with them.

As far as graduation ceremonies go, it was not too boring. The guest speaker was John Williamson, from the Class of 1950. He gave an inspirational talk about responsibility in the adult world. Williamson was a pilot for TWA and had served two years in Vietnam as a fighter pilot. He chose not to dwell on Vietnam, but rather talked about what his life had been, and that seventeen years earlier he sat in the same auditorium wondering what he was going to do with the rest of his life. He assured us that if he could do it, we could do it too. I sat there listening to his speech wondering how many people he killed in Vietnam. I wondered how one day you kill or be killed, and the next you're home giving speeches on being a responsible citizen. I concluded that war is a difficult thing to understand.

Riverside High School had a fair amount of tradition. However, there was one tradition frowned upon by the faculty. We were warned not to give the principal a handful of pennies or marbles while receiving our diploma on stage. I had a handful of small cat's eye marbles ready for Principal Rickenwald. When my name was called and I received my diploma, I was all smiles and left Rickenwald standing there, juggling the marbles. I passed through the wings of the stage and Vice Principal Galding gently grabbed me by my arm.

"If I was a betting man, I would have bet you wouldn't have graduated this semester."

"Well, just goes to show you what a guy can do when he is motivated," I replied sarcastically.

"I really believe that my job is going to be a lot easier now that you and Jimmy Gaston have graduated."

"I just want you to know that I never took the hall pass stamp that Mrs. Banks accused me of taking."

"It doesn't matter anymore. Tonight, Robert Ralston, you have accomplished an important milestone," Galding said.

"It hasn't sunk in yet," I replied.

"Good luck to you and give my regards to Mr. Gaston." Galding shook my hand and walked away.

When Jeff Zeal's name was called, a loud cheer went up from the graduates, as we knew he was the last student to receive his diploma. Our high school careers had come to an end. As the last student to graduate, Zeals was given the honor to lead the students in the ceremonial switch of the tassels on their mortarboards. Once the switch was made, another loud cheer went up and four hundred-plus mortarboards were tossed in the air. And with that last formality, it was over. The room was filled with smiles, tears of joy, and plenty of hugs from family members and friends. The auditorium was awash in white light from camera flashes, and even my father gave me a big hug.

It seemed that all the graduation parties had a somber undercurrent. Although alcohol flowed freely and best wishes filled every conversation, there remained an uneasy tension between those going on to college and those not going to college and trying to deal with the Vietnam War and the Selective Service draft.

Sharman Stromme and I spent most of the early evening bouncing from party to party. She stayed uncharacteristically sober, and when we parked along Lake Michigan's Bradford Beach, the conversation in the truck turned serious.

"Are you still going to San Francisco?" she asked.

"I'm leaving Sunday morning."

"Who's going with you?"

"Gaston is going part of the way," I answered.

She swiveled the captain's chair and leaned toward me.

"What are you going to do in San Francisco? Do you know anyone there?"

"I don't know, and no, I don't know anyone," I replied.

"I don't understand why you are going out there, and it sounds like you don't know either," she said sitting back in the chair.

"It's hard to describe. I just feel drawn to San Francisco."

"Drawn to what?"

"The peace movement. The Summer of Love."

"What are you talking about?"

"I didn't think you would understand," I said and turned away and looked out the window.

"Try me," she said leaning forward again.

"It's like the center of the universe. It's the happening place. This country's attitudes originate in San Francisco."

"You feel like you're missing something by not being there."

"Yes."

"So what is so damn important about San Francisco?" she asked angrily.

"I've got to go see for myself."

"See what?"

"Anything. Everything. It's not happening here for me in Milwaukee."

"You don't have to go to San Francisco. You can smoke pot and get laid right here in Milwaukee," she stammered as tears welled up in her eyes.

We were communicating as if we were from different planets.

She put her arms around me and softly sobbed, "I love you, and I'm going to miss you."

"I thought you were just having fun."

"I have fallen in love with you."

"In love?" I stammered.

"That surprise you?" she asked pulling back from me.

I couldn't think of anything to say.

"I have been in love with you for a long time."

"You've been going out with Freddy Billford for over two years," I protested.

"I was just waiting to see what happened between you and Mary Beth."

"That's news to me."

"You're so unaware. You should know me better by now."

I burst out laughing which took her by surprise.

"And all this time I thought you just like talking sexy."

"You don't recognize true affection," she pouted and swiveled the chair facing forward.

I put my arms around her and kissed her softly on her cheek.

"Sharman, I'm sorry. I didn't know you felt this way about me."

"Do you think I'd just go to bed with anyone?"

"No, I didn't mean that."

"What did you mean?" she demanded.

I thought about my answer for a moment and wondered how someone I had such warm feelings for was turning me off so completely. How can people fall from grace so quickly? I only briefly wondered if I was being selfish.

"I am just surprised, that's all," I finally replied.

"We've been making love for the last couple of months and you don't have any feelings for me?"

"Of course I have feelings for you."

But what those feelings were I wasn't sure. Certainly I enjoyed her company. But beyond that, I really hadn't given it much thought. I had more important matters on my mind.

"What do you feel?" she demanded.

"Sharman, I think you are a wonderful person and I'm going to miss you."

"Miss me enough not to go to San Francisco?" she asked.

"What?"

"Do you care enough about me to stay here in Milwaukee so we can be together?"

"Sharman, I've been planning this trip for over a year."

"Can I go with you?"

"No, you can't."

"What do you think you'll find in San Francisco?"

"You don't understand," I said, leaning back from her.

Sharman was falling from grace faster than a comet in the night skies. I found it incredulous that she would ask me to take her on this trip. Here was a girl that almost every guy in Riverside High School would have killed just to have for a date. But at this moment, I would have gladly traded her for the school librarian.

"That's the second time you've said that. I want to know, what's more important, San Francisco or our relationship?" she said, raising her voice.

"I'm going and that's all there is to it."

"So that's it. Bob Ralston gets to do what he wants and he doesn't give a damn about anybody else's feelings," she said raising her voice higher.

"Look, why don't we just call it a night?"

"Call it a night! Why don't we just call it over, finished, done!" She started crying.

"I'm taking you home," I replied.

We didn't speak another word on the way back to Sharman's house. She sat looking out the passenger window, and I just stared straight ahead at the road. I noticed a crescent moon setting over the lake and couldn't help but see the irony in how relationships rise and set.

Chapter 12

On Saturday morning I was busy with last-minute preparations and packing the truck. At the same time, Hoss had just completed basic training in Texas. He was now a private and assigned to infantry duty. Hoss, and one hundred and twenty other men in his company, were assigned to Vietnam.

Several miles away from my house, a civil rights demonstration was starting and the marchers were being led by a white Catholic priest, Father James Grupe.

Gaston arrived at my house with one suitcase, a backpack, and a cowboy hat. The cowboy hat looked rather peculiar on Gaston's head with his long ponytail hanging out the back. When I opened the front door, he let out with his best imitation of a cowboy yell.

"Let's get a move on it, Bobby boy," Gaston said speaking in his best southern drawl.

"I got an idea. Let's paint a peace symbol on the side of the truck," I exclaimed.

"I got a better idea," Gaston replied.

Gaston reached down in a small cardboard box attached to the side of his suitcase and pulled out a set of cow horns.

"Let's attach these babies to the front of your mean machine," Gaston proclaimed.

We both started laughing and agreed to do both, paint the peace symbol and affix the horns. So we spent the afternoon leisurely painting a large black peace symbol on the passenger side of the truck. It was the familiar circle with the upside down *Y* in the center. Unbeknownst to me, and most Americans, the symbol represented the anti-nuclear weapons effort in Britain.

While Gaston and I were enjoying our artistic efforts with the aid of numerous cold beers, Father Grupe and the civil rights marchers were in a showdown with police at the Locust Street Bridge. For generations, it was generally accepted that the Locust Street Bridge over the Milwaukee River was the eastern boundary of Milwaukee's ghetto. Even though Riverside High School was immediately east of the river, very few Black families lived on that side of the river.

As the marchers neared the police blockade of thirty police cars, numerous police dogs, and more than two hundred helmeted riot police officers blocking the bridge, dark thunderheads approached from the west, as if to serve as an omen of the city's impending social troubles.

Police Captain George Klute used a bullhorn to tell the marchers to disperse their unlawful assembly on a public street. Father Grupe, also armed with a bullhorn, begin to taunt the officers and further incite the marchers. Several years later, both men were to be found "grossly negligent in their conduct" by a Federal Civil Rights Commission investigation.

To the marchers, crossing the Locust Street Bridge symbolized the tearing down of old racial and geographical barriers. To the police, the Locust Street Bridge represented law and order. And

Captain Klute, of Polish ancestry, was going to be damned if he'd let those uppity niggers out of where they belonged. When the two men stood face-to-face, tensions on both sides of the line strained to the breaking point.

"Father Grupe, you know that this demonstration is unlawful and the City of Milwaukee has not issued you a demonstration permit," Klute announced.

"Captain Plute."

"That's Klute," interrupted the captain.

"Klute. We don't have a permit because the City Council hasn't the guts to stand up for its constituents and do what is right," Grupe replied.

"I'm not here to make the law, pass the law, understand the law or justify the law. I'm here to enforce the law."

"Look, all we want to do is peacefully march to the Lakefront and hold a public rally there. We don't want any trouble, so just let us do our thing."

"I can't do that. You must disperse this unlawful assembly at once," the captain answered.

"Try to understand the situation. I can't tell these folks to go home. They have the right to walk down a public street just like anybody else."

"If you don't tell them to go home, we'll have to arrest them."

"I don't think you want to do that," Grupe replied.

"This isn't going to be pretty."

"Racism never is."

With that, Captain Klute picked up his bullhorn and announced to the crowd that they were to disperse immediately or face being arrested. His announcement was greeted by catcalls and boos from the crowd of more than fifteen hundred marchers that consisted of a significant number of young children and senior citizens. Many of the older Black marchers had never set foot on the Locust Street Bridge because that was "not their neighborhood."

Things went from bad to worse when Grupe told his followers not to obey the police's unlawful order. The crowd surged forward in a nervous spasm. The police line tightened and one of the officers, without permission, fired a tear gas canister into the crowd. That set off a panic and as the crowd ran in every direction, a fierce hand-to-hand battle broke out on the front line between heavily shielded police officers and the unprotected marchers.

The sign-swinging, bare-fisted demonstrators were no match against the riot-trained police. All but five of the police officers on the riot squad were white. The baton-wielding officers quickly laid waste to the militant portion of the marchers. Only a few marchers symbolically made it over to the east side of the bridge. Numerous people were seriously injured in the melee and the disturbance would become known as the Locust Street Massacre. A couple of hours later, this march would touch off a race riot that would include looting and burning of many ghetto neighborhoods.

Gaston and I just finished our lavishly painted peace symbol when the FM station we were listening to interrupted its programming to break the news about the riot. At first, we misunderstood what the reporter was saying. We thought it was a peaceful rally. But when the news was repeated, we, like many residents of the city, failed to comprehend it was the catalyst that would touch off the worst civil unrest in Milwaukee's history.

"What the hell was that all about?" I asked.

"Sounds like our Black brothers have had enough of this city's quiet discrimination," Gaston proclaimed.

"Quiet discrimination? I don't see any discrimination in this city."

"That's because you're not Black and you don't live in the ghetto," Gaston replied.

"You and I both went to the same high school that is one third Negro, and in four years, I never saw one instance of racial discrimination between students or teachers."

"I think you should start calling them Blacks," Gaston suggested.

"Okay, Blacks."

"If you were Black, you'd see how employers look at you differently than whites. You'd see how hard it is to get a college education. You'd see that crime is almost seventy-five percent higher in Black neighborhoods," Gaston replied.

"So getting the shit kicked out of you by a bunch of thick-headed cops is going to make things better?"

"You got to start somewhere. You got to call attention to your plight," Gaston said while wiping paint off his hands.

Suddenly, the radio station announced that rioting had broken out in several inner city neighborhoods and fires had been set at numerous locations.

All off-duty police officers and firefighters in the city of Milwaukee were ordered to report to their duty stations. The city was about to enter one of its darkest nights. As the afternoon wore on, the situation grew worse. There were more fires and reports of sniper fire directed at firemen responding to the blazes. By five o'clock that afternoon, three firemen had been shot and two were in critical condition.

A somber mood fell over the city, and television news crews, flying over the ghetto in helicopters, had to retreat due to heavy sniper fire.

Gaston and I retreated to the den in my house to watch the events unfold on television. In short order, as my family gathered around the TV set, it was very apparent that this was going to be a major civil disturbance. As the long shadows of afternoon slipped into darkness, Mayor Maier came on television and announced that it was indeed a sad day in the city's history. He said he was asking the governor to call a state emergency in Milwaukee and order the National Guard into the city.

Fires raged through the night and the city's fire chief had no choice and refused to send his men in to fight fires due to the heavy sniper fire. Under the cover of darkness, the snipers were even more deadly. By midnight, a mere twelve hours after the confrontation on the Locust Street Bridge, three firemen were dead, two policemen were dead, twenty-six civilians were dead, and the number of those injured or shot was well over two hundred. Emergency rooms all over the city geared up for a long and terrible night. When the wind picked up from the west, it fanned the flames and soon the glow from the fires could be seen in Brookfield, a town thirty miles away.

Gaston and I decided to spend the night sleeping in the truck. We figured this would be our last opportunity to test out the truck's accommodations before beginning our western trek in the morning. The bedding on the platform was comfortable, but the news emanating from my little portable television set was not.

The governor ordered the National Guard into the city and had imposed a citywide, dusk-to-dawn curfew. Further news updates revealed that Father Grupe and two hundred-fifty marchers had been arrested and were being held in a special section of the city's downtown jail.

Much to Gaston's and my chagrin, it looked like there was no way in or out of the city in the morning. Gaston lit up a joint and passed it to me.

"Not looking good, Roberto," Gaston sighed.

"What is the National Guard, anyway?" I asked as I inhaled.

"They're part-time army guys."

"Why don't they just use regular army guys?"

"I think because it is not allowed under our constitution," Gaston answered.

"What do you mean?"

"I believe the National Guard was created to deal with civil problems within each state. The army is to be used for external problems, like Vietnam. Using the regular army to settle civil unrest in the United States doesn't look good for the government."

"What's going to happen?" I asked.

"I'm afraid it looks like a long, hot summer, and I don't mean the weather."

We finished the joint and rolled over on the large bed and went to sleep. As we slept, the death toll and property damage climbed throughout the night. A light rain began to fall just before daybreak, which gave the city's firefighters a break.

Gaston and I awoke early and busied ourselves with last-minute stowing of personal effects. My mother called us into the kitchen for a hearty Wisconsin breakfast. While the city was in tatters around us, the Ralston family had its usual Sunday morning breakfast of French toast, bacon, rolls, orange juice, milk, and coffee. The conversation waxed and waned between their son's departure and the awful events happening in the city.

Gaston was unusually quiet, choosing not to participate in the discussion of civil unrest. I announced that after breakfast, I was going to the service station near Riverside High School to fill up my gas tank and would return to say good-bye to the family. Gaston quickly agreed to go along, mostly out of fear of being left alone with my family at the breakfast table.

As we approached the high school we were shocked to see several army tanks positioned on the Locust Street Bridge, accompanied by soldiers in full battle dress.

"I didn't think I'd see the day that soldiers had to guard the streets of Milwaukee," I declared.

"Pretty trippy sight seeing tanks aiming their guns at you," Gaston observed.

"How long you think this is going to last?" I asked.

"No idea, man."

Suddenly an army jeep pulled up alongside my truck and a soldier in the passenger seat, with an M-1 carbine rifle, motioned me to pull over. I obeyed, and when the soldiers approached the truck from both sides with their rifles cocked and ready, I rolled down my window.

"What are you doing here?" asked the sergeant in a commanding voice.

"Just going to get some gas," I replied.

"Not today you're not," replied the sergeant, cautiously looking in the driver's side window.

"What do you mean?" I asked.

"All gasoline sales have been suspended within the city limits."

"Do you have enough gas to get out of the city?" Gaston asked.

"Barely."

"Whose truck is this?" the sergeant demanded.

"It's mine," I replied.

"I want both of you to get out of the truck, slowly."

"What for?" protested Gaston.

"Get out of the truck, now!"

"We haven't done anything," I protested.

"Now!" the sergeant shouted.

Gaston and I opened our respective doors and stepped onto the pavement. Several soldiers began to look in the truck and opened the back door to inspect the vehicle's contents.

"Your identification, please," the sergeant asked.

"My driver's license OK?"

"Yeah. Let's see your friend's ID too."

Meanwhile, soldiers began pulling suitcases and other articles from the back of the truck, and I objected.

"What the hell are they doing?"

"Searching your vehicle," the sergeant replied while examining my driver's license.

"Man, we just packed all that stuff and you guys are dumping it out on the street," I said.

"Sounds like a personal problem. Would like to speak to our captain?"

"Sarge, these guys have an American flag in here, and they're using it as a blanket," a voice called out from behind the truck.

"It's only a decoration," I protested.

"It's like freedom of expression," Gaston chimed in.

Several soldiers gathered around Gaston, whose hair was nearing the middle of his back, and me. We were standing directly under the peace symbol we had painted on the side of the truck.

"There are a lot of guys fighting and dying for that flag," the sergeant snarled.

"They're fighting for our right to freedom of expression," Gaston replied.

"Listen, you long haired punk, you keep your fucking mouth shut unless I ask you something. Do you understand?" snapped the sergeant.

Gaston nodded.

I was amazed that we were subjected to this kind of search. In my opinion, it was abuse. The entire contents of the truck lay on the street.

"What did we do to deserve this?" I asked the sergeant.

"We have orders to stop all vehicles that might be transporting those involved in this civil unrest," he replied as he handed back our drivers' licenses.

"What made you think we're one of them?" I asked in an incredulous tone.

"You're driving a suspicious vehicle capable of transporting firearms and large quantities of ammunition."

"What is so suspicious about this truck?"

"For one, your pretty artwork there," the sergeant said as he pointed to the peace symbol.

"Oh man. That's just decoration," I groaned.

"Bullshit. It's an anti-government sign," the sergeant replied.

It finally dawned on me that we were being discriminated against because of the appearance of our vehicle. Luckily, they didn't find the pot Gaston had stored in his backpack.

"Your identification is in order. Go home," ordered the sergeant.

We both stood there silently as the sergeant and the other soldiers walked back to their jeep and drove away. The soldiers were laughing as they drove away. I was more exasperated than Gaston, as we went about putting the truck back together.

"Welcome to America, man," Gaston sighed.

"I can't believe it. We haven't done anything wrong and they do this shit to us," I complained.

"How do you think a Black man feels when he is pulled over for driving through a rich white neighborhood in an old car?"

"But I wasn't doing anything wrong," I protested.

"Are you suggesting that it's wrong for a Black man to drive through a white neighborhood?"

"Come on, man. Of course not."

"Well, welcome to the world of discrimination. How do you like it?"

"Why us?"

"Because of the peace symbol on the side of the truck."

"That's all it takes."

"The city is under martial law and all your civil rights have been suspended. That guy could have shot you and probably nothing would have come of it."

"Great. I get shot for having a peace sign on the side of my truck. Those guys are supposed to keep order not create disorder," I replied.

"Says who?" asked Gaston.

"What?"

"If the National Guard is here to quell civil disobedience, they are in effect trying to restore order of the status quo. By restoring the social order to status quo they are reinforcing a system that discriminates against Blacks. Blacks, therefore, will rise up in protest and create more civil disorder. Do you see a pattern emerging here?"

For the first time in my life I got a taste of what it was like to be discriminated against. For the all-American white boy who always had doors wide open to me, I didn't like it.

It took us an hour to put the truck back together and our enthusiasm for departing the city disappeared. When we returned to my house, everyone was worried that something had happened to us. A fifteen-minute trip to the gas station turned into a two-hour ordeal that would leave a lasting impression on both of us.

It was Monday morning before order was restored in the city and the last of the fires were extinguished. Martin Luther King's television broadcast, calling for restraint, had a pacifying effect on the Black citizens of Milwaukee, and the city slowly resumed business as usual.

Chapter 13

We wasted no time in getting out of town. After last-minute good-byes, we were headed south on Interstate 94 through Chicago and then on to Iowa. After circumnavigating Chicago, we found ourselves crossing the Iowa border in the early afternoon.

As far as we could see there was nothing but a rolling sea of cornfields anchored to a landscape as flat as a marble pool table. I had never been to Iowa and marveled at the acre after acre of corn. There were millions of acres of corn all seemingly at a height of about four feet. It was not corn humans eat, but millions of tons of feed corn for cattle. Traffic on this stretch of the interstate was sparse compared to the congested Chicago metropolitan area when Gaston made a suggestion.

"Hey, man, let's get off the main road and take a county highway. I'll bet it's a lot more scenic that this four lane monster."

"Why not. You got a joint?" I asked.

"For sure, man."

"I'm getting hungry," I proclaimed while passing the joint back and forth.

"Smoking a joint ain't going to help," Gaston replied with a smirk.

"One thing at a time," I answered.

After a quick consultation over the Iowa state highway map, Gaston, acting as chief navigator, made the following proclamation,

"The next right turn is Highway 97. Take it."

As we approached Highway 97, I slowed the truck and eased it down through two gears and rounded the turn in smooth fashion. On both sides of Highway 97 there was nothing but farmhouse after farmhouse with five acres of corn between them. Silver silos rose from the flat landscape like intercontinental missiles taking flight. There was a long silence as the joint was being passed back and forth. I finally spoke as Gaston tossed the roach out the window.

"I feel like I'm going to see the Wizard of Oz," I said.

"Does that mean I'm Toto?"

We both burst out laughing as we approached a steep hill, a true geological rarity in Iowa. When we neared the base of the incline, I noticed an old, disheveled man standing on the side of the road, hitchhiking.

When we passed him, I remarked, "What the hell is that guy doing out here in the middle of fucking nowhere?"

"Let's give him a ride," Gaston replied.

"What?"

"Yeah. Let's give the old guy a ride. He looks harmless."

"I am going to have to turn around."

"Do it. There ain't anybody on the road, if you haven't noticed."

"What the hell, we've got nothing better to do," I chuckled.

I slowly nursed the truck through a U-turn and headed back. When we pulled over on the opposite side of the road, we could see the wrinkled and weathered old man, with tattoos on his arms, sitting on a tattered and faded brown leather suitcase and strumming on a banjo. I executed a slow U-turn on the narrow highway and we pulled up alongside him.

"How's it going, pops?" Gaston asked in friendly tone.

"Just fine," the old man answered.

"Want a ride?" Gaston asked.

"That's why I'm out here, sonny."

"Where are you going?"

"Just over the hill to the next town."

"Get in," Gaston replied.

Gaston reached back and opened the sliding side door and the old man tossed his suitcase in, and with the banjo slung over his shoulder, he climbed into the truck. When he closed the door, we started up the hill.

"What's your name?" Gaston asked.

"People call me Banjo."

"Seems reasonable," I chimed in.

"Where did you get the name Banjo?" Gaston asked.

"Oh, I'm an old Dixieland jazz musician and my buddies down in New Orleans gave me that name many, many years ago."

Banjo wasn't that old, but then again he wasn't that young either. Many years of playing in smoked-filled southern bars and music clubs had wrinkled his face. They were friendly wrinkles. Banjo's demeanor was that of a man who had been through a lot but had emerged through it gracefully. His old plaid shirt was clean but missing a couple of buttons. His silver hair was disorderly but somehow stylish for a man his age. His voice was soft yet sincere. His green eyes were now dimmer and his beard was freshly trimmed. He was not shy.

"Is that marijuana I smell?" Banjo asked.

"You want some?" I asked.

Banjo just started laughing and said nothing. He picked up his banjo and started strumming an impromptu song.

"Driving down a country lane, I began to wonder if life was all in vain. Got a ride on old Highway nine-seven, climbing a hill that just might take us all the way to heaven. They don't know me. I don't know them. Don't crouch; you'll never touch the sky. Don't lie; just look them in the eye. Take what you can get, but don't take too much; that way you'll never have regrets. Dubois, Dubois, take me home, through the vermillion fields of number 403. It's Iowa can't you see. Oh Iowa, oh Iowa you're home to me," Banjo sang out loudly.

"You just make that up?" I asked.

"On the spot," Banjo smiled.

"Can we get something to eat in the next town?" Gaston asked.

"As a matter of fact, my daughter owns the finest eating establishment in Dubois, Iowa."

"Is that close? We're hungry," I asked.

"The next town," Banjo answered.

"How old is your daughter?" Gaston asked.

"Forty-four. Why? You figuring on settling down in Dubois?"

"No. Just curious," Gaston replied.

The truck ascended to the crest of the hill and the view of the valley that lay below was magnificent. Unlike the corn-filled countryside we had been looking at for hundreds of miles, Pleasant Valley was a carpet of green pastures dotted with majestic trees. From the top of the hill, it seemed like one could see a white church steeple every couple of miles. To the north stood an enormous white birch forest. Had it not been summer, one might have mistaken it for a snow-covered forest.

"Pull over here, boys, and I'll tell ya a little about what you're looking at," Banjo said.

I pulled the truck over to the side of the road and all three of us got out and stood looking over the valley. Banjo told us the story of Dubois' founding fathers and interesting historical tidbits about

Iowa's tenth smallest town. He said his great grandfather was the first mayor of Dubois. He bragged that Dubois' biggest claim to fame was it was a major storage location for bootleg whiskey during prohibition. Whether any of his recollections were true didn't matter. Banjo could weave a story and tell it with such richness that it would never occur to the listener to question its veracity.

"So now you have a little history on the town of Dubois. How about getting some good eats at my daughter's café?" Banjo asked.

We both eagerly nodded our approvals and all three of us got back into the truck and headed down into the valley. The center of Dubois consisted of ten commercial enterprises, three of which were bars. All the buildings were the exact same height and were freshly painted. The streets were clean and several children peddled by on their bicycles.

It was hot in Dubois and you could see heat waves rising off the scorched asphalt.

"Pull over here," Banjo barked, pointing to a white building.

The sign over the front door read "Kate's Kafe." I parked the truck in a parking stall, marked with faded lines, just outside the café's front door.

Gaston and I jumped out of the truck with great anticipation of a country-style home-cooked meal. We entered the restaurant walking behind Banjo. The café was crowded with few empty seats to be had. While Banjo was exchanging greetings with several patrons, I spied an empty booth in a distant corner. As we walked over to the table, Banjo was laughing and talking with several people seated at the lunch counter. When we sat down I saw Banjo receive a hug from a slim and attractive woman in her mid to late forties. I assumed she was his daughter. After a brief conversation, Banjo walked over and joined us at our table.

"Where's the bathroom?" Gaston asked.

Banjo pointed across the cafe and Gaston got up and walked to the bathroom. To get to the bathroom, Gaston had to walk past the lunch counter and his long hair caught the attention of several burly men seated there. I was pretending to look at the menu but I was surveying the various patrons in the café. When I finally got around to deciding what to order, I realized that Gaston had been gone for longer than usual. When Gaston reappeared and walked back past the lunch counter, he was accosted by a tall, redheaded, gruff-looking man who stood in his path.

"I got a girlfriend with long hair. I got a horse with a long tail. Which are you, a girl or a horse's ass?" he growled at Gaston.

The entire café broke into laughter that was quickly followed by complete silence. Everyone was riveted on the confrontation. It was so quiet I could hear the hum of the orange juice squeezer motor in the kitchen.

"I'm not here to cause any trouble," Gaston answered.

"I don't give a shit why you are here. Just answer the question. Are you a girl or a horse's ass?"

Banjo stood up and called out as he approached the counter, "Sonny Brighton, that's no way to treat my out-of-town guests."

"You know this lowlife creature?"

"Hell yes. They were kind enough to give me a ride all the way from Highway 97. Now, do we want Dubois to be known as the most unfriendly town in Iowa?"

Laughter again broke out all over the café and I took a deep sigh of relief.

Someone yelled out, "Run for governor, Banjo. You're the best damn diplomat in the state!"

The proclamation was greeted with another roar of laughter. As the redheaded man sat down at the counter, Gaston and Banjo quickly walked back to the table and sat down.

75

"I think you fellas should be on your way after lunch," Banjo stated quietly.

"Gladly," chimed Gaston.

Before we could get a good look at the menu, a sweet looking teenage waitress approached the table to take our orders. She had dazzling blue eyes and turned out to be Banjo's granddaughter. We exchanged greetings and I noticed that she seemed to be grinning at Gaston.

"Gentlemen, I would like to introduce my granddaughter Melissa."

We nodded and she smiled. She was indeed a very cute young lady with a solid build. You could tell she was raised on a farm.

Banjo ordered for all of us, "Give us three blue plate specials. I hope you gentlemen aren't vegetarians, because I just ordered pork chops and mashed potatoes."

Melissa looked as good walking away as she did walking toward us. While I was looking around the restaurant to see if anyone was still staring at us, Melissa returned carrying three plates brimming with food.

As good as the food was, I didn't fully enjoy it. I was uneasy and felt out of place. We were only four hundred-fifty miles from home, but it was like I was in a foreign country.

These were not city folk. They were hard working farming folks who had to fight nature's vulgarities every day to earn a living. I didn't have anything in common with them, nor they with me. Not only did I feel out of place, I looked out of place. I remembered how I felt out of place at the Downer Cafe for Timothy Leary's presentation. Now I was just as out of place at Kate's Kafe.

Banjo walked us out to the truck, shook our hands and wished us luck on our journey out west. He was so down-to-earth, honest, and genuine. I wondered what he knew about the many lessons of life that I didn't. What lessons could he have imparted on me if only we had more time together?

We drove out of Dubois knowing full well we would never return again. Gaston seemed giddy and began whispering louder and louder.

"Melissa, Melissa, Melissa."

"What the hell is with you, man?" I asked.

"Melissa is one fine lady, wouldn't you agree?"

"Probably one of the finest in Iowa," I replied.

"What would you say if she wanted to hitch a ride with us?"

"What are you mumbling about, man?"

Before he could answer, I heard a disturbance in the back of the truck. I looked in the rear view mirror and couldn't decide if the American flag on the bed was moving because of the wind rushing in from the open windows, or something was going on back there. I looked back at the road trying to figure out what Gaston was trying to say. When I turned to look at him, Melissa appeared in his lap like a vision. I was so startled at seeing her that I thought it was the power of suggestion projecting her image. But when she started kissing Gaston on the side of his neck I realized I wasn't dreaming. I returned my attention to the road and discovered I was well over the center yellow line.

"What is she doing here?" I stammered.

"She asked me if she could hitch a ride out west. I told her if it was all right with my friend, she could come along."

Melissa was staring at me and asked, "Well, is it all right?"

"Are you over eighteen?" I asked.

"Yup, eighteen and a half," she replied.

"But how did you arrange this?" I asked looking at Gaston.

"We found we have mutual values," Gaston said.

"When did you have time to figure that out?"

"In the hallway outside the restrooms," Gaston answered.

I said to myself, "This guy doesn't miss an opportunity." Before I could think what to say next, Gaston and Melissa climbed into the back of the truck. They began kissing while sitting on the bed. I never considered myself a voyeur, but I found it very erotic watching them in the rear view mirror. It was only a few heated moments before they were both disrobed and copulating on the bed. I felt my heart rate increase as I glanced into the mirror and watched them thrusting in unison. I fantasized that I was the one in bed with her. But there was a nagging thought somewhere in the back of my mind that said something wasn't right with jumping into bed with someone you only met a few minutes ago.

We crossed the Nebraska border right at sundown and Gaston and Melissa were still locked in a heated union with no sign of relenting. The truck was filled with groans of pleasure. I lit up a joint and turned on the radio to try to drown out the noise emanating from behind me, but I could still hear them.

An occasional semi-truck passed me because I was driving well under the sixty-five speed limit. I was thinking about what Father Zimmer taught me in Saturday Catechism class at Saint Monica Church. I was sure he had never faced the temptations of the 1960s and the sexual revolution that was knocking down most barriers to premarital sex. I felt a strange twinge of Catholic guilt because my best friend was in the back of my truck screwing a girl while I watched.

A brilliant yellow sign flashed in the distance and broke the darkness of the moonless night. After rubbing my tired eyes, I finally made out that it said "Rainbow Acres Trailer Park."

I had enough of driving and pulled into the trailer park and steered toward a small wooden building with a dull, flickering office sign above it. I pulled up to the smartly painted single-story building and parked the truck. Melissa and Gaston climbed back into the cab of the truck with their hair and clothes disheveled.

"Where are we?" Gaston asked.

"Rainbow Acres Trailer Park in Covington, Nebraska," I replied.

I opened the door and stepped out into the evening. The air was filled with wonderful floral smells. I looked to my right and saw flowerbeds awash with night blooming jasmine.

My legs ached from driving all day. I shuffled up to the office door, only to be greeted by a sign that instructed me to take any empty parking space and that the manager would come by at nine o'clock in the morning to collect the overnight fees. I was relieved, because a sign on the office wall stated that you had to be twenty-one years old in order to register for a campsite.

I climbed back into the truck and drove past several recreational vehicles and trailers, all parked for the night in their individual spaces. There were no lights on in any of the vehicles or trailers. I looked at my watch. It was one thirty.

I drove to the far corner of the trailer park and found a parking space under a huge willow tree. As I turned into the gravel parking space, the headlights illuminated the tree's web of hanging branches. I pulled the truck up to the base of the tree and let the branches surround the truck. It was as if the tree was engulfing us in its arms for protection. Melissa and Gaston got out of the truck, and with flashlights in hand, walked a short distance to the bathrooms. They took their toiletries in hopes of finding a shower.

I sat down at a redwood picnic table where I had an unobstructed view of the night sky that was crammed with stars from horizon to horizon. Every two to three seconds, a shooting star would blaze across the starry sky and end its existence.

Watching stars go out in a blaze of glory, I discovered I still had enough energy to ponder my mortality. I couldn't rationalize the purpose of my human existence. Why are we here, I pondered. After ten fruitless minutes, I gave up the quest and the uneasiness in my chest subsided.

A warm breeze rustled the willow tree and I elected to sleep under it. I looked up at this majestic creation and I was comforted by the fact that some things live for quite a while. I shuffled back to the truck and grabbed my sleeping bag. I shook my head while looking at the disheveled bed inside the truck.

I assured myself that it would be much quieter outside the truck than trying to sleep next to Melissa and Gaston. The last thing I remember was listening to the soft rustling of willow branches above me. I slept soundly on my first night away from Wisconsin and I was spared having to listen to Gaston's and Melissa's marathon sexual activities in the truck.

I had a most unusual dream. I dreamed that Banjo was elected governor of Wisconsin. He asked me if I would help him find his granddaughter Melissa, who had been missing since the day we ate at his daughter's restaurant. I was overcome with guilt and kept my head down so I wouldn't have to look him in the eye. Then he told me that I would have to testify in court on anything I knew about his granddaughter's disappearance.

As I was being led into the courtroom, one of the courtroom guards grabbed my arm and directed me to the witness stand. I froze. I didn't want to go on the witness stand and tell them about Gaston and Melissa in my truck. The guard pulled on my arm again. I woke up from the dream to realize that someone was actually pulling on my arm while I lay in my sleeping bag.

At first I thought I had fallen down in the courtroom and the guard was trying to help me to my feet. As I groped to my senses and tried to focus on the figure standing over me, I realized that it was a portly man in a bright red checked shirt and blue jeans. He was not a courtroom bailiff.

"Good morning," he said.

"What time is it?" I groaned.

"Nine-thirty. I'm here to collect the overnight rental fee."

"Okay," I yawned.

I stood up, wearing the exact same blue shirt and blue jeans I had on yesterday, and staggered toward the truck in search of my wallet. I was overwhelmed by the brilliant sunlight. I opened the driver's side door and reached in and grabbed my wallet from its secret hiding place under the steering column.

"How much do I owe you?" I asked.

"For three people, it's ten dollars."

"How do you know I have three people?" I asked, wondering if he looked inside the truck before he woke me up.

"Your two friends are swimming over in the river," he answered.

I nodded and pulled ten dollars out of my wallet and handed it to him.

"Are you going to stay another night?"

"No, we're off to Colorado today," I answered.

"Well, I hope you enjoyed your stay here. Come back another time."

When he walked away, I thought, there is a guy who must like his job. He's friendly and not nosy. I guessed that being nosy is probably not a good idea in the temporary accommodations business.

I grabbed my toiletry bag and headed off to the bathrooms and a hot shower. The trailer park was full of activity. Several children ran around the playground and one child flew a small blue kite that disappeared against the crystal blue Nebraska sky. The smells of breakfasts cooking were everywhere. I disrobed and stood under a warm shower. I heard a radio playing country music, people talking, and a dog barking with joy as it played with its master.

As soapsuds slowly dripped down my arms I thought how wonderful to be able to live in a country like America. On this summer day, in this small park in Nebraska, everything seemed so idyllic, like a Norman Rockwell painting. While toweling off, I wondered how Hoss was doing in the army. By now he would have finished his basic training at Fort Hood. I stood in front of the mirror combing my hair, which was still relatively short. I was hoping, even praying, that Hoss wouldn't get killed in Vietnam.

I walked back to the truck and found Gaston and Melissa sitting at the redwood picnic table smoking a joint. I was surprised at the ease with which Melissa was handling smoking marijuana. I think yesterday was her first time.

"Do you want to get something to eat?" I asked.

"We stayed up all night and walked two miles into town at sunrise," Gaston replied.

"Too bad you weren't awake. The sunrise was beautiful," Melissa added.

"Yeah, too bad," I mumbled, trying to hide my sarcasm. "Let's go. I'm not hungry anyway."

We arranged our personal belongings in the truck and xzdrove off toward Colorado with all three of us in the front seat.

Chapter 14

After several hours of row after row of corn, silver silo after silver silo, red barn after red barn, the landscape began to slowly change. On the distant horizon, the majestic snow-capped Rocky Mountains finally came into view. I had never seen a real mountain. Living in Wisconsin all I ever saw were hills. We crossed the Colorado state line in the late afternoon and the soft, golden light only added to the serenity and beauty of the landscape.

I pulled over at a rest stop to stretch my legs and relieve myself. When I returned to the truck, Gaston and Melissa were on the bed in the back of the truck, locked in their now familiar sexual dance. I grabbed a joint from my white pearl box that I rolled the day before, but never got around to smoking. I was jealous of Gaston because he had found a new sexual partner, but I wasn't interested in listening to their moans and groans, so I got out of the truck and walked several hundred yards to the boundary of the rest stop. When I was far away from the rest of the vehicles and travelers, I lit up the joint.

I stood on a slight knoll that overlooked a rolling pasture where tall grass waved effortlessly in the light westerly breeze. How ironic,

I thought. Hundreds of yards behind me were people all driving somewhere for some purpose, but right in front of me the grass seemed to have no other purpose than to wave some sort of greeting. As I looked at the far off mountains, I wondered if there are hundreds of places on this earth where no human has set foot.

I don't know if it was the magnitude of the natural beauty or the marijuana, or both, but I felt very insignificant. I wondered if I was a very tiny pawn in a cosmic chess game where someone, or something, was calling the moves. Before I could explore this sudden heaviness, a loud horn blast from a semi-trailer brought me back to reality.

Before I could sleep that night, I had the mundane task of finding a place. I walked briskly back to the truck, climbed into the cab, and was determined not to look into the rear view at Gaston and Melissa. I started the truck and was back on the highway, continuing my westward journey to who knows what end.

Melissa and Gaston climbed back into the front seat and he inserted an eight-track tape. The sounds of Eric Clapton and Cream immediately filled the cab. We began our steep ascent into the Rocky Mountains, leaving the Great Plains behind us. The truck's engine chugged along in the thinning atmosphere, but it had more than enough power to pass the countless semi-trucks laboring mightily up the steep grades.

We enjoyed the late afternoon vistas of towering, snow-capped jagged peaks. It was truly awesome. It was getting cooler and cooler as we rose in altitude, so we rolled up the truck's windows. I felt a sense of exhilaration. We entered a majestic white-domed temple of nature.

No one spoke a word for a couple of hours. The Cream tape had ended and no one bothered to select a new tape. We marveled at Nature's raw beauty and were in a state of awe and reverence.

Gaston finally broke the silence. "I guess this will be my last night aboard this rambling milk truck."

"How long are you going to stay at that co-op ranch?" I asked.

"It's a co-op farm."

"Okay, co-op farm."

"I don't know. But I'm not going back to Milwaukee."

"So when will I see you again?"

"Mr. Ralston, that is a good question. Maybe never," Gaston said.

"I'm sure I'll see you back in Milwaukee someday."

"You planning to return to Milwaukee?"

"Well, maybe in a couple of months."

"Once you get to San Francisco, maybe you won't want to go back. You need to open yourself up and let this experience flow through you," Gaston said.

"What does that mean?"

"You're searching for something. If you are not letting experiences happen without prejudice, you will never truly experience them."

"I think I am open to new experiences," I said.

"Let your soul hang out. Be like a piñata."

"What the hell is a piñata?"

"A piñata is a Mexican game where a stuffed animal is hit with a stick. Then it bursts open and releases all the candy surprises held within," Gaston explained. "If your soul is open and receptive, then life's experiences can be accepted and appreciated. This will enrich your life."

I wasn't sure what he was trying to say, but I said, "I don't think I want to go around with my guts hanging out."

Gaston and Melissa burst out laughing.

"Well, just think about it." He paused for a moment and then said, "Anyway, I'm going to miss you, man. I don't know if or when we will see each other again after tomorrow."

I looked at him and understood that I was going to have to pursue this quest for knowledge on my own. No more friends to lean on or ask for guidance. It was going to be a solitary endeavor.

"You make it sound so final," I replied.

"Life is final, man. We only have but a moment. We may have tomorrow, but we're not sure of that until we live it. As every day passes, life becomes a collection of memories. We have only an instant of the here and now, living our lives. Then we get years of memories for having done it."

That heavy feeling of being an insignificant entity in the universe began a slow crawl up my spine. It cast a pall on me as the last remnants of daylight faded into blackness. Melissa was looking at me, waiting for some sort of reply. It was cold in the cab of the truck and my thoughts were equally frigid.

On a dark and lonely stretch of mountain highway, my best friend was telling me good-bye and that maybe we'd never see each other again. He was saying that life was very transient and that in order for me to truly experience life, I had to accept that my fate was beyond my control. This was the law of the universe and I had no choice.

I wanted to say something, but no words would come out of my mouth. Gaston saw that our conversation was having a deep impact on me.

As I ran my hand through my hair, I mumbled in a barely audible voice, "Heavy."

Melissa slipped a Jefferson Airplane tape into the stereo and Grace Slick's raspy voice only deepened my perplexed thoughts. I was so deep in thought that I didn't notice that semi-trucks began passing me. Like a maple leaf being blown across a lawn on a windy autumn day, I realized I had no control over my destiny.

I drove through the night, not wanting to stop. After a few hours in my self-imposed mental exile, Gaston and Melissa tired of my silent company and climbed back onto the bed and began their farewell sexual encounter. They were hard at it for hours, but I didn't pay any attention. I just kept rumbling through a brilliantly star-lit night at sixty miles an hour.

Just before sunrise, I watched that magical moment when gray colors gain brilliance and a palette of color reappears to chase away the night's blackness. I thought about Hoss and his destiny. Hoss believed he was taking control of his destiny by joining the army. It seemed ironic that Hoss, Gaston, and I were all of the same generation, but on totally different paths.

I drove through the Rocky Mountains worrying about the meaning of life while Gaston reaped the fruits of an increasingly promiscuous society, and Hoss was just trying to stay alive. This had to be a new experience for this country. During the Second World War, everyone was in it together, fighting a common enemy. Now it seemed it was every man for himself. Do whatever you have to do to keep Uncle Sam from sending you to Vietnam and getting shot. I wanted to feel sorry for Hoss but I couldn't. Gaston's understanding of the deeper meaning of life made him smarter, hipper, and worldlier than Hoss or I. I felt anyone serving in the military wasn't cool.

I was so immersed in my solitary debate, I didn't notice that Gaston and Melissa had fallen asleep. As the sunrise flooded the valley below, I looked up between two towering peaks and wondered what was to become of Hoss, Gaston, and myself.

I pulled into Meeker, Colorado on a beautiful cloudless morning and I found myself in the center of a quaint, treeless town.

The town consisted of a dozen stores, restaurants, and bars. The blue flashing neon sign over the Meeker Café caught my eye. I parked directly in front of the café's entrance and turned off the engine. As I opened the door to climb out, I heard Gaston and Melissa rustling in the back of the truck. I had driven all day and all night. I was grumpy, tired, and hungry. Frankly, I didn't care if they joined me for breakfast or not.

The café contained a series of small circular tables, and the cook was visible in the kitchen. I chose a table in the front window, which gave me an unobstructed view of the comings and goings on Main Street and my truck. As soon as I sat down, Gaston and Melissa came straggling in the front door. I couldn't help but notice how attractive Melissa looked, even in her disheveled state. I grabbed a menu and pretended not to watch as they approached the table.

"Wow, man, you drove all night," Gaston exclaimed.

"I couldn't sleep," I remarked looking up from the menu.

"You okay?" Melissa asked.

"I'm cool," I said.

"So what's for breakfast?" Gaston asked.

Before I could answer, a tall, slender waitress dressed in a light yellow dress and wearing cowboy boots asked for our order. After ordering, we fell into a brief silence with each of us staring out the window. When the coffee arrived, Gaston finally spoke.

"I guess this is where I get off."

I looked across the table at Gaston as a knot formed in my throat. I nodded and drank from my cup. My hand tightened around the handle as if it were a shield. I put the cup down and looked up to find Melissa and Gaston staring at me awaiting some sort of response.

"I feel sad and confused," I said.

"Sad and confused?" asked Melissa.

"Maybe sentimental is a better word," I said.

"Sentimental about what?" Gaston asked.

"I got this weird feeling that you and I are never going to see each other again," I said.

"That's kinda heavy, man," Gaston said.

"I'm going to the bathroom," Melissa said, excusing herself.

"That's why I drove all night, man. I kept thinking about where we are all going. What made you decide to come to Meeker, Colorado, of all places? What the hell is in Meeker, Colorado?" I asked.

Gaston pondered my question as he picked up his coffee cup. He took a long, slow drink. Just as he put the cup down on the table, the food and Melissa arrived at the same time.

We began eating at once and I kept looking up from my plate, waiting for his reply, but he didn't say anything. He ate in silence and we only exchanged glances. Once the waitress cleared the table, Gaston finally spoke.

"I chose Meeker, Colorado, because there is a communal farm here where they are growing organic food without chemical fertilizers. Everyone works together. There are no bosses and the commune encourages its members to seek spiritual enlightenment," Gaston said.

"I respect you for that," Melissa chimed in.

I didn't know what organic farming was and I had no idea how one pursued spiritual enlightenment. Before I could quiz him again, Gaston got up and walked over to the counter to pay the breakfast tab. He laid some bills on the counter and walked outside as Melissa and I rose from our sun-faded leather chairs. He opened the back door of the truck and unloaded his backpack.

"Do you want me to drive you to the commune?" I asked.

"No, they come into town every morning. I'll just get a ride from them," he replied.

The scene in front of the café felt surreal. Gaston said good-bye to Melissa with hugs and kisses. Then he turned to me with an emotional look I have never seen before. He walked over to me, grabbed me by my coat lapels and pushed me up against the truck's passenger door in a mock show of strength.

"I am going to miss you, man. You've been someone I could always trust," he said.

We embraced in a hug and I said nothing. I was too choked up for words. Gaston picked up his backpack, walked down the street, and sat down on a wooden bus stop bench. He did not look back at me.

Melissa and I got into the truck. I started the engine and got the same nagging feeling that this was the last time I would see Gaston.

Surprisingly, Melissa was not bummed out. She smiled at me and said, "Let's go to Los Angeles."

Chapter 15

The unrelenting rain in Saigon and the persistent humidity foretold of the approaching monsoon season. Fleets of mud-caked US Army jeeps jostled with motorbikes and bicycles for space on Saigon's crowded and deteriorating streets.

Private First Class John Haus walked into Company A's Logistics Headquarters in a putrid alley in the City Center, his green khaki uniform soaked with sweat.

"Private Haus reporting for convoy duty," he announced to a corporal wearing equally sweat-soaked khakis.

"Have a seat, Private. The captain will see you shortly," replied the corporal. "Where are you from, Haus?"

"I am from Milwaukee, a Cheesehead," Hoss answered.

"Cool, my cousin is from Racine," the corporal said.

The door at the far end of the room opened and Hoss watched as a very tall and rugged looking captain walked toward him. Hoss noticed that he was wearing a neatly pressed uniform that was as dry as a bone.

"Private Haus, I'm Captain Rambus and I have an assignment for you. Come into my office." Hoss followed him into his office and was surprised to find it was air-conditioned. He grumbled silently that this is the only guy in Saigon who is not sweating his ass off.

"Private, I understand that you are one of the best jeep wranglers in Company A."

Hoss demurred for an instant and then acknowledged the captain, "Sir, you just got to know how to handle them."

"They call you Hoss. Why's that?" asked the captain.

"Just a nickname I picked up in high school."

"I hear that you're one of the strongest guys in your platoon."

"I know how to handle myself. What is the assignment, Captain?"

"I have to deliver a bunch of field radios to Company B infantry at Bien Hoa, about twenty clicks from here."

"Can't one of the regular drivers handle this?" Hoss asked.

"Probably, but I need to get the radios there tomorrow. The rain is making the roads more difficult. I want someone I can trust not to end up in a ditch. Can I trust you, Private?"

"No sweat, Captain. Where and when do I report?"

"Tomorrow morning 0700 hours. There will be three jeeps here loaded with radios ready to go, and you will leave immediately."

Hoss saluted the captain, did an about-face, and was back on the rainy streets of Saigon in an instant. He walked back to his barracks and wondered why the army would pull him off guard duty at the Regiment's Command Post in Saigon to drive a jeep full of radios. But after almost two months into his one-year duty assignment in Vietnam, he learned that the army did whatever it wanted to do and privates had no say even if the orders didn't make sense.

The next morning the rain fell harder than the day before. Hoss knew his army-issued rain poncho would leak during the daylong drive to Bien Hoa. The temperature was forecast to be in the upper eighties.

As he walked briskly toward his duty assignment with his M-16 rifle slung over his left shoulder, his poncho began to leak and the warm raindrops trickled down the middle of his back. Hoss hoped that the jeep's canvas top would not leak as badly.

Captain Rambus greeted Hoss when he arrived and immediately led him to a jeep full of radios. Two other jeeps, fully loaded with camouflaged field radios stacked in the back, were parked in single file. Two other jeep drivers joined Hoss and the captain. The three men were given a quick briefing by the captain and directions and maps to Bien Hoa where Company B's field headquarters were located. They left immediately after the briefing with Hoss in the lead jeep. They began driving and dodging through Saigon's unruly traffic.

With countless motorcycles and bicycles clogging every intersection, it took thirty minutes to get out of Saigon and onto Route 2A to Bien Hoa. As bad as Saigon's streets were, the conditions on the rural highway were far worse. Rain cascaded across the highway and almost swept the jeeps into a ditch on the side of the narrow road. Hoss understood why the captain wanted hardy jeep drivers for this soggy mission.

The other jeep drivers were just as big and strong as Hoss. Private Mike Andersen, driving in the second jeep, was nineteen years old and from Winona, Minnesota. He had won all-state honors as the top high school defensive lineman. Private Jimmy Landuski from Chicago drove the third jeep. Landuski was nearing the end of his one-year tour of duty in Vietnam, and he had befriended Hoss when Hoss first arrived in Vietnam. His red hair was longer than anyone else in his company. This was a sure sign he was a "short-timer," a soldier nearing the end of his tour of duty in Vietnam.

Hoss, Andersen, and Landuski exchanged radio calls and complaints about how bad the driving conditions were on an unfamiliar road. The delivery was supposed to take about five hours, but the unrelenting bad weather and poor road conditions slowed their pace to less than twenty miles per hour despite the fact the road was completely empty of traffic in either direction. Hoss mumbled to himself that even truck convoy drivers knew when to stay off the rain-swollen roads.

"Make sure we don't miss the junction with Route H, or we'll end up in fucking Timbuktu," Andersen radioed to Hoss and Landuski.

"I am looking for it, but my windshield wipers are for shit," Hoss replied.

"Look for a temple on the left side of the road. The junction is there," Landuski's reply crackled over the radio speakers.

Unbeknownst to the three plodding jeep drivers, they had driven by a small company of Vietcong soldiers that was hunkered down in the pouring rain fifty yards from the road.

Three hours later the rain stopped but a heavy overcast made the late afternoon dour and damp. As the last light of the day faded, the three jeeps rumbled into Bien Hoa with their cargo of radios and drenched drivers. Their arrival was ill-timed. Just as Hoss, Landuski, and Anderson stepped out of their jeeps, a Vietcong mortar attack began.

One incoming mortar round was a direct hit on Landuski's jeep and the exploding shrapnel severed an artery in Landuski's left leg and threw him twenty-five feet from the jeep. Hoss crawled through the roaring explosions and mud to Landuski, face down, moaning loudly, and bleeding profusely from his leg and stomach.

Mortar rounds continued to rain down on the encampment, blowing debris and body parts into the night sky. Soldiers ran from the chaotic scene for any cover they could find. Other platoon members rushed in the direction of the incoming rounds with machine guns and mortars to launch a counter attack.

Hoss rolled Landuski face up to determine his condition. From a large hole in Landuski's pants, Hoss could see blood spurting out and knew instantly that the wound was massive. He grabbed Landuski's pants leg and ripped it all the way down to the ankle so he could determine exactly where the wound was.

The lighting was poor, and the massive amount of blood gushing over Landuski's left leg prevented Hoss from seeing the exact location of the wound. In desperation, Hoss slid his fingers up Landuski's left leg toward his groin. Six inches below Landuski's scrotum, Hoss felt the strong pulsing of blood exiting Landuski's body. He quickly pressed his index and middle finger into the wound in an attempt to stem the bleeding.

"Medic!" Hoss cried out in a hoarse voice.

Chapter 16

Radio stations faded in and out as Melissa and I crossed into Utah and started our descent into Salt Lake City. Two hours passed without a word spoken between us. I was too deep in thought and she was mesmerized by the magnificent view of the Wasatch Mountain Range towering all around us.

"Do you believe there is a God?" I asked without taking my eyes off the road.

"Wow! Where did that come from?" she asked.

"Well?"

"Every time I stop long enough to really consider it, I get all uptight. If there is a God, then who created her? If there isn't a God, then who created the earth and the universe? Everything had to start somewhere. So where did God come from? And if there is no supreme being, then where did everything come from? What blows my mind is the idea of no beginning and no end. Are we just a part of a huge endless loop, no beginning and no end?"

"Far out," I said.

"There is a lot of stuff we don't have a clue about," she said. "We're eighteen-year-olds with no worldly experience. What do we know about anything? For four years, we've been going to football games, holding hands, going out on dates, going to proms, and living in our little teenage worlds."

"That's why I quit the basketball team," I said. "It's all so trivial."

"So what are you going to do now? I mean with your life?"

"I'm going to San Francisco and try to understand what is going on with me and what's going on in this world. I've read some pretty radical books on how we should live our lives, like give up material stuff. Look at The Beatles. Once it was "I Want to Hold Your Hand," now it's "Eleanor Rigby" and "Fool on the Hill." Talk about a quantum leap from "A Hard Day's Night.""

"I've got The Beatles' album. Want to hear it?"

I smiled and nodded. She decided that the glorious orange and yellow sunset that spread across the horizon shouldn't be squandered on a heavy conversation about creation and eternity. After she slid the eight-track tape into the stereo, she reached down into her backpack and pulled out a rolled joint. She lit it and handled it to me.

I realized that I had unfairly compartmentalized her as Gaston's new girlfriend. I had never given a thought to who she really was. Suddenly I felt guilty because she was so good looking and I wasn't mature enough to get past looks to consider substance.

After a couple of tokes on the joint, darkness settled over the mountainous landscape and the faint lights of Salt Lake City could be seen ahead. I could only see Melissa's face when oncoming headlights illuminated it.

"You're pretty cool," I said in a low voice, wishing I hadn't said it.

"You've changed the image I had of you as a dumb, empty-headed, cock hound, jock," she responded softly.

"A cock hound jock?" I protested.

"How many girls did you screw in high school? Can you count them on three hands?"

"A lot less than you think. I let that jock reputation perpetuate itself. Looking back, it was a total waste of time."

"All of it?" she quizzed.

"Let's not go there now. I think John Lennon is trying to tell us something," I said pointing to the dashboard stereo.

She leaned over and softly touched my cheek as John Lennon's voice filled the cab with his song "In My Life." I don't know what possessed me, but I gently grabbed her hand and kissed her knuckles. She laughed.

Chapter 17

The pounding in Hoss's head woke him up. Once he realized he was still alive, he leapt up from the bed he was lying on. A gentle hand grabbed his shoulder from behind.

"Whoa, soldier."

Hoss whirled around to see a wispy, redheaded nurse dressed in green khakis standing face to face with him.

"What happened to Landuski?" he asked in a hoarse voice.

The nurse handed him a steaming tin mug of hot coffee before she spoke.

"Private, sit down over here," she said pointing to a small wooden table at the end of a short row of army cots.

Exhausted, despite a long sleep, Hoss shuffled to the table and sat down in a chair. As he lifted the mug to his lips, the nurse sat down across the table from him.

"You did all you could possibly do to save Private Landuski under extreme fire. But his wound was too catastrophic to stop the bleeding. He's dead. I'm sorry, we just couldn't save him."

Hoss's face contorted in emotional pain that morphed into a totally blank stare as he slowly put the coffee mug down on the table. Without a sound, tears streamed down his scratched and swollen face. He bowed his head and the tears fell into the mug.

Shortly after nine o'clock, Hoss walked across the compound's shell-pocked grounds that were still littered with everything imaginable. He walked up to a tent where inside dead soldiers were zipped up in thick black plastic body bags awaiting transportation back to Saigon. Later that morning, a huge, noisy, green camouflaged Medevac helicopter was scheduled to pick up the dead and wounded from Bien Hoa. Then from Saigon, the bodies would be flown back to the United States to their families for burial.

A team of soldiers was busily preparing for the arrival of the helicopter. When Hoss walked into the dark green tent, a heavy-set sergeant with a booming voice challenged him.

"What are you doing here, private?"

"I wanted to say good-bye to Private Landuski," Hoss replied in a solemn voice.

"Look, private, we ain't got time for that today," the sergeant snapped back.

A stocky, muscular corporal with a crew cut, wearing a Minnesota Vikings t-shirt drenched in sweat, shouted with a heavy Midwest accent from across the tent at the sergeant.

"Hey, sarge, let him say good-bye. He ain't gonna bother anyone in this fucking tent."

The sergeant grunted and the corporal motioned Hoss forward and pointed to a body bag at the end of a long row of body bags.

Hoss trudged reluctantly toward the last body bag in the row. He stood for several moments looking at a bag with a large strip of tape labeled "Private Landuski." He reached down, grabbed the bag's zipper, and lowered it six inches. He recognized Landuski's wavy red hair and then he lowered the zipper another twelve inches where he could see Landuski's complete face.

As Hoss peered down at the body he said softly, "I'm sorry I couldn't save you. We shouldn't have volunteered to drive to this fucking shit hole."

Hoss's anger and sorrow were belayed by the placid and even content expression on Landuski's face. Hoss wondered what he would look like when he got killed in this rotten war. After several minutes of standing over the body in total silence, Hoss zipped up the body bag and walked out of the tent into the blazing sun as the Medevac helicopter approached from the south.

Hoss looked up and shielded his eyes and mumbled, "That's your ride home, Landuski."

The heavy whooshing sounds of the rotor blades echoed off the aluminum barracks. Two-dozen body bags were already lined up next to the helicopter landing pad, but there were still twenty more body bags to be carried out of the tent to the helicopter.

Chapter 18

long line of cars, headed north toward Las Vegas from Los Angeles, stretched for fifty miles on Interstate Highway 15. Melissa and I had spent two star-filled nights camping in the Nevada desert and were headed south toward Los Angeles.

"Sure glad I am going the other way from that traffic," I said.

"You want to go to the Venice Beach boardwalk when we get to LA?" Melissa asked.

"What is it?"

"Pretty hard to explain. I went there last summer and it's a circus. Not a real circus, but a visual circus. You'll see all kinds of people on the boardwalk. It's like no other place in the world. It's very hip."

"What's so hip about it?"

"I'm sure you'll dig the girls roller skating in bikinis."

I looked at her with a grin and nodded yes.

It was about noon when we pulled into a parking lot near Venice Beach. The parking attendant at the entrance of the lot was furiously waving a red flag and motioning people to park for two dollars.

When we climbed out of the truck, Melissa said, "You're going to find this entertaining."

We crossed a street busy with beach-goer traffic and walked about three hundred yards to the Venice Beach Boardwalk. I stood there staring at the Pacific Ocean and Melissa hadn't noticed that I had stopped walking beside her. When she realized I was not next to her, she turned to see me staring out at the waves rolling up on the sandy shore.

She walked back to me and asked, "Hey man, what's happening?"

"This is the first time I have ever seen an ocean," I replied.

She laughed and hooked her arm with mine and dragged me off to the boardwalk.

What an incredible afternoon it was. I saw lots of girls in very skimpy bikinis roller skating; huge, muscular guys lifting weights at Muscle Beach; an incredible array of musicians playing every genre of music; and surfers riding waves in the shore break.

The smell of marijuana wafted through the air everywhere on the boardwalk and I saw dozens of young people openly smoking marijuana. Many of them offered Melissa and me a hit on their joints. We smiled, gave a peace sign, but declined. We were both naturally high just enjoying the comings and goings on the boardwalk and the spectacular ocean view.

A bright pink and reddish sunset capped a perfect day. It did occur to me that Melissa, who I once considered to be Gaston's girlfriend, was walking on a beautiful beach with me in California. Back when I was in Iowa, I would have never guessed that.

"Want to get something to eat?" Melissa asked. "I know a great little taco stand about three blocks from here near the Santa Monica Pier."

"Great. But I have a confession to make."

"All right, man, lay it on me."

"I have never eaten a taco," I replied sheepishly.

"Well tonight's the night. You will no longer be a taco virgin."

"Cool," I said as I threw my arm around her shoulder, not in a romantic way, but in a buddy-buddy way, because that is how I felt about her. She was a new-found friend, albeit a very good-looking female friend, but not a love interest.

Later that night we parked the truck on a side street and climbed into the back to go to sleep. It had been a long, wonderful day, with several firsts for me.

"Thanks, it was really outta sight today," I said as I lay down beside Melissa.

She was wearing a long t-shirt that reached her knees and her tanned face was radiant.

She whispered, "Do you want to make love to me?"

I quickly composed myself.

"You're beautiful, very cool, and your soul shines right through your skin," I said.

"Wow."

"I mean it. I learned a lot of things today. I learned about letting people be who they are. You really have it together. I admire you. You're really cool," I said.

"Okay. Next you'll nominate me for sainthood."

"Today, I saw people and things I had never seen before. I realized that beauty is truly more than skin deep."

She cuddled up to me and pulled me toward her to kiss her. I gently pulled back and then kissed her on her forehead.

"I just want to sleep next to you, nothing else," I said.

"You're not attracted to me?" she protested.

"Quite the opposite. I want to have your friendship in a relationship that doesn't involve sex. Today was a perfect day and I want to keep it that way," I replied.

"OK, I dig it. But you're full of surprises," she stated.

"But, I do want to kiss you good night."

I playfully grabbed her and planted a loud, smacking kiss on her lips. She let out with a giggle and we both cuddled up next to each other and went to sleep. I could hear the waves breaking on the beach three blocks away.

Chapter 19

While looking out his fourth floor office window in the Embarcadero area of San Francisco, FBI Special Agent Crens finished reading the report on the Power Systems fire. He put the report down on his desk and tapped his right index finger on the file folder.

The munitions factory had security fencing around its entire property, a sophisticated motion detector alarm system, and two night watchmen, but not one of these deterrents stopped a determined terrorist or terrorists.

The alarm system was cleverly disarmed and a large hole had been cut in the fencing to gain access to the property in an area far from the security shack. These were telltale signs of the Weathermen Underground group. Arson investigators discovered tire tracks; they suspected a vehicle had waited near the hole in the fence and quickly and quietly whisked the culprits away into the night. Crens' phone rang.

"Agent Crens speaking."

"Crens, this is Agent Andy Wilson," a low and gravelly voice proclaimed.

"Andy, what can I do for you?" Crens replied.

"We just got word that the DuPont headquarters building in Wilmington, Delaware, was just bombed. Director Hoover is on the warpath and you are to go to Travis Air Force Base immediately. Once you get to Travis, a KC-135 will be waiting to take you and the forensic team to Dover Air Force Base. The team will meet you at the plane."

This was the fifteenth bombing in 1967 of companies that were vendors and suppliers to the US Army and the war effort in Vietnam. To date, no one had been arrested and charged.

The FBI had information, gained from paid informants, that the bombings were the work of the radical and violent Weathermen Underground organization. The FBI didn't consider the Weathermen Underground an organization. They were a group of unconnected individuals who only shared a common belief in domestic violence and the overthrow of the US government.

The Weathermen Underground proved to be quite adept at avoiding capture. FBI Chief J. Edgar Hoover, whose health was waning, placed the Weathermen Underground on the top of his Five Most-Wanted list.

Never before in the history of the Federal Bureau of Investigation had a group ever made it onto the Top Five Most Wanted list. The FBI had placed undercover agents pretending to be radicals in numerous cities across the country in hopes of cracking the Weathermen Underground's code.

Agent Crens went to his car quickly and headed home to pack a suitcase. Evening was approaching and dark, heavy cumulus clouds blocked out what little sunlight was left. His thoughts grew equally as dark about the destruction he would be witnessing in Delaware in a few hours.

Chapter 20

a month had passed since that dreadful night at Bien Hoa, but Hoss still hadn't recovered emotionally. Guilt and a sense of loss hung over him like a thick fog bank.

Hoss was reassigned as a driver for Lieutenant Colonel Heins, who was in charge of logistical supplies for the US Fifth Army units in South Vietnam. Heins was responsible for ensuring that everything from bullets to food to gasoline made their way to troops in every corner of the country. Heins was a West Point graduate and a member of his high school ROTC club. He was a quiet and thoughtful man from Georgia, but had no discernible southern accent. He was all army.

After Hoss's heroic drive to Bien Hoa, the army decided that they would use parachute drops for certain needed supplies rather than attempt to deliver them via a jeep or truck convoy.

Many of the American "in country" soldiers and Marines believed that North Vietnamese regular army units, and not the Vietcong, now controlled many of the highways in a great portion of South Vietnam. Any truck convoy would likely be a sitting duck in a shooting gallery, so soldiers in the transport companies were relieved to hear the news about the new airdrop policy.

Hoss's job consisted of shuttling Heins around Saigon from one army logistical center to another. It was an easy and relatively safe assignment. However, Hoss remained sullen, had no real friends, and started drinking heavily at the enlisted men's club. Soldiers who knew Hoss previous to the Bien Hoa incident had never seen him drink so much alcohol before. But ever since Bien Hoa, every evening he was slamming down a half a bottle of Jack Daniels whiskey before staggering back to his barracks.

For centuries, soldiers have believed that some of their fellow soldiers have a special luck because they survive a war almost unscathed despite the death and chaos surrounding them. There were several soldiers in Hoss's company who believed Hoss lived a charmed life, especially after the story of the three-jeep caravan got around.

He looked like hell. His bloodshot eyes, coupled with a two-day beard and his woefully wrinkled green fatigues made him look like a hobo. Nevertheless, he got cleaned up every morning, reported to duty on time, and quickly sped off in an army jeep with Heins in the passenger seat.

If he had spent time reviewing the day's itinerary rather than getting drunk the night before, he would have realized that he was in for a long drive to a remote logistical warehouse in the Mekong Delta, about one hundred-fifty clicks away.

The day started out sunny, but like many days in Vietnam, the sky turned dreary and the humidity and the temperature soared. Then a light but steady rain began to fall.

The jeep didn't have a roof so Lieutenant Colonel Heins quickly pulled on his rain poncho. Hoss seemed oblivious to the rain and soon he was soaked. He just kept driving with a bewildered expression on his face. He stared straight ahead, said nothing, and seemed to forget that his superior officer was a passenger next to him in the front seat. The road had innumerable potholes that caused the jeep to bounce skyward and side-to-side.

At regular intervals, they drove past burnt-out wrecks of US Army trucks and armored vehicles, piled on the roadside, right where they and the soldiers inside them had come to their demise.

Despite these roadside junkyards, the countryside looked almost bucolic. Farmers wore large sun hats and walked slowly behind their water buffalos as they plowed their fields.

Heins looked skyward and recognized the vapor trails of B-52 bombers headed north on bombing missions to North Vietnam; whereas, Hoss remained focused on the road ahead. Occasionally, Hoss would reach down and tap the holster and pistol he was wearing on his belt, just to reassure himself that the gun was still there.

Chapter 21

The DuPont headquarters building was still smoldering when Agent Crens arrived on the scene. Crens was well known and well liked in the FBI. He had graduated third in his class from Stanford University six years ago with a degree in mathematics and statistics. He had risen quickly through the ranks at the agency and was recognized as an analytical and thorough investigator.

Crens quickly sought out the local fire department incident commander, the fire chief, and the department's arson squad captain. He found them standing next to the fire chief's bright red pickup truck.

"I'm Special Agent Crens, FBI," he said as he extended his hand to the fire chief.

"I'm Chief Lawson. We were expecting the FBI."

"Word travels quickly," Crens replied.

"This is no ordinary arson job. Whoever did this knew how to place a bomb so it would have maximum impact on the structure's integrity," the chief stated.

"What was the device?" Crens asked.

"Good old-fashioned dynamite," the chief replied.

"How did you determine that so quickly?"

"Because the motherfuckers who did this had another bundle of dynamite that didn't ignite. The fuse must have failed."

"Are you telling me that old-fashioned, match-lit fuses to sticks of dynamite were the detonating device?" Crens asked.

"Damn hard to believe, but true," the chief replied.

"No sign of any electronic detonating device?"

"No sir. Just dynamite sticks set off with ordinary blasting fuses," chimed in the incident commander.

The chief reached into his truck, pulled out a bundle of six dynamite sticks taped together, and what remained of a long fuse, and handed it to Crens.

Crens took the bundle and examined it for several minutes before speaking. "This type of dynamite is used for hard rock blasting and is sold all over the western United States to mining and blasting companies. This is not the type of dynamite used in the east by coal companies and rock and gravel quarries. This stuff is one step above what a farmer uses to blast out tree stumps."

"Sounds like our perpetrators aren't from Delaware," the chief said.

"I'd say from as far west as Colorado or further west," Crens replied as the red lights flashing from the fire trucks reflected off the perspiration on his forehead.

Chapter 22

When Melissa and I woke up, I opened the truck's back door. We were startled to find the milk truck had attracted a group of admirers. A young man with long brown hair and an equally long beard walked up to me as I was rubbing the sleep out of my eyes.

"Man, this is the grooviest truck I have ever seen."

"Yeah, it's an old milk truck," I replied sleepily.

"Far out. A milk truck?"

"Yep, this truck used to deliver milk all over the city of Milwaukee."

"Wow, far out" he mumbled to himself as he walked away.

From inside the truck Melissa called out, "Hey, let's cruise over to my cousin's house and get some food."

Melissa lived in Los Angeles until she was twelve and then her parents moved to Iowa. It was a short drive to her cousin's house and it was another sunny day in Los Angeles, exactly what you expect in late June.

Her cousin's house was located in a quiet neighborhood of small, single-story ranch style homes. Many of the homes were in need of renovation and a good paint job. Most had been built for returning World War II veterans starting new families.

When we arrived, I followed Melissa in the back door and directly into the kitchen where Bob Dylan's music was playing loudly. The kitchen was crowded with six guys and three girls, all about nineteen or twenty years old. They were sitting around an old wooden kitchen table. It was only nine o'clock, but they were all smoking pot. Melissa had grown up with most of them.

"Hey, Melissa!" her cousin Peter shouted.

He was sitting at the kitchen table, shirtless, and had a great tan.

"You got any food we can have?" Melissa asked.

The kitchen air was so heavy with marijuana smoke that I almost started coughing. It was quite a change from the fresh ocean breeze I had been breathing the day before.

There really wasn't much to eat, and I learned that the house was occupied by Peter and the other guys sitting in the kitchen.

The house was a mess. In fact that would be a gross understatement. The refrigerator was full of beer and had mold growing on the interior walls. Whatever was in the freezer had long since passed the edible stage. Trash was strewn about the backyard.

While she was busily telling her friends about the trip from Iowa to Los Angeles, I walked outside. I decided to check all the truck's essentials, such as the oil, coolant, tire pressure, brake fluid, and even the windshield washer fluid. One of the guys in the kitchen, who was introduced to me as Troy, walked out to the truck and started a conversation with me.

"Melissa's a foxy chick. You're a lucky man," he said.

"I agree, but she's only a friend. She's not my girlfriend."

"She said she was traveling with a guy from Milwaukee. I thought it was you."

"No, she had a boyfriend, who is a friend of mine, but they split up on the trip out here," I replied.

"She said you're going up to San Francisco."

"Yeah, I am leaving later today."

"She's going with you?"

"No, I'm going alone. She's staying in LA."

"I need a ride up to San Francisco, I gotta deliver some dope to some friends in the city. You give me a ride, and I'll give you some great pot and some hashish."

"Sorry, man, I can't do that. I don't want any hassles with the man," I replied as I closed the hood of the truck with a loud slam.

Troy shrugged his shoulders, took a hit off the joint he was smoking and walked back to the kitchen. Just as Troy disappeared into the house, Melissa came bounding out the back door, calling out to me.

"I've got tickets to The Doors concert tonight!" she yelled with delight. "We gotta go!"

"Tonight?" I asked.

"My cousin gave me his tickets as a coming home present. Isn't that cool?" she gushed.

"I was planning to drive up to San Francisco later today," I replied.

"Oh man, we gotta go see The Doors. You don't want to miss this concert. San Francisco can wait another day. This is going to be so far out. The Doors!"

Her eyes were brighter than I had ever seen them before. Her long hair was shimmering in the sunlight, and her excitement was contagious. I agreed to go to the concert. She hugged me and I wondered why the hell I passed up making love to this foxy girl.

The Doors were playing at the Shrine Auditorium near downtown Los Angeles. The auditorium, with its world-famous art deco façade, had hosted many illustrious events, including the Academy Awards.

As we approached the auditorium, the streets were crowded with cars and the sidewalks were full of young people dressed in every imaginable style of clothing. Most of the concertgoers openly smoked joints as they walked toward the auditorium.

After a twenty-minute delay in heavy traffic, we finally reached a parking lot two blocks from the auditorium. The lot was packed with cars and numerous young men and women drinking beer and hard alcohol and smoking joints. The parking lot attendants made no attempt to curtail any illicit activity, despite numerous signs posted around the lot stating that consumption of alcohol was illegal.

When Melissa and I got out of the truck and started walking toward the auditorium, she pulled out a joint, lit it, took a hit, and handed it to me. I hesitated and was reluctant to smoke marijuana in public.

She put her arm around my shoulder and said, "It's cool. Nothing bad is going to happen tonight. It's some really good pot. It's Maui-wowie."

I relented and took a deep hit and immediately started coughing. She broke out laughing and walked over to a group of concertgoers standing around a car and asked if she could have a beer for a friend in need. Meanwhile I was still coughing and sputtering from the pot.

I admired her moxie for going up to strangers and asking for a beer. A short guy with long red hair, thick sideburns, and wearing a Mexican sarape handed her a beer bottle. She thanked him and handed me the beer. I handed her the joint and quickly took a badly needed drink from the bottle. She took a hit on the joint and advised me not to take such a big toke when she handed the joint back to me. This time I took a small drag and chased it quickly with another drink of beer. Then we resumed our walk to the auditorium and quickly became part of the crowd headed to the concert.

I assumed that Mardi Gras must be similar with very colorful groups of people hell-bent on music and a good time. Melissa grabbed my hand as we walked and I started to feel the effects of the Maui-wowie.

People were laughing, singing, drinking, and trudging slowly in the midst of the large crowd headed toward the auditorium's front entrance. A crescent moon hung directly over the Shrine Auditorium for those who took the time to look up. But as we got closer to the auditorium, there was a large contingent of Los Angeles Police officers. There were at least a hundred uniformed police officers, with stern looking faces and billy clubs, standing near the entrance to the auditorium.

Numerous people were milling about the auditorium and overflowing onto the streets. Many were there to party and did not have tickets to the concert. As the throng of people we were walking with approached the auditorium, they began to toss their unfinished joints and beer and whiskey bottles onto a strip of grass alongside the sidewalk. Many of the bottles rolled across the sidewalk and into the curbside gutter. They made a tinkling sound, like a glass wind chime. Since we had tickets, we made our way through the crowd and into the auditorium. We had great seats that were thirty rows back from the stage on the main floor.

By the time I sat down, the Maui-wowie had significantly affected my sensory perception. I had never smoked pot so powerful before, and I began to feel anxious. I squeezed Melissa's hand and she in turn gave me a radiant smile.

The opening act was Norman Greenbaum, who had the recent hit song "Spirit in the Sky." I was okay with taking small hits on a joint that Melissa kept handing me, because everywhere I looked people were smoking pot.

It seemed incongruent to have Norman Greenbaum and The Doors on the same concert bill. Greenbaum was singing about going to heaven and being with God. The Doors' music was dark, hard edge, belligerent, with huge sexual overtones. The angels The Doors sang about didn't live in heaven; they cavorted about in Hollywood bungalows.

Despite never having been in Los Angeles before, I kept seeing faces in the crowd that seemed familiar to me. I wondered if we were all inter-related and our individualism was nothing more than a hindrance to universal order.

I was totally stoned and wondered if I could even stand up if there was an emergency. To gain some reassurance, I squeezed Melissa's hand again, and right on cue, she turned and smiled. We hadn't spoken a word for several minutes, but I was really glad she was there with me.

Greenbaum's performance came and went with the crowd barely paying attention. Everyone in the auditorium was stoned on something. There was a resounding energy building in the crowd in anticipation of The Doors' performance. I could feel it building within me, too.

When the band walked onstage, the audience wasn't sure if it was really The Doors. The auditorium fell into an eerie silence. When Jim Morrison walked up to the microphone and yelled, "LA, let's rock!" the audience went crazy and the sound levels would have broken any decibel meter on the planet.

Morrison was wearing tight, black leather pants and a white linen shirt that was completely unbuttoned. When the band started their first song, Melissa leaned over to me and whispered in my ear, "I'd fuck him all night."

Morrison's performance was riveting. I couldn't take my eyes off him. His voice and body language were so sensual that every word he sang, every note he hit, and every primordial grunt he uttered excited my inner hedonism. His lyrics made sex sound dirty, but enticing. When he took his shirt off and threw it into the crowd, the band began playing "Light My Fire." The excitement and noise elevated to new heights, and so did my sexual desire for Melissa.

How I managed to drive the milk truck back to Melissa's cousin's house from the concert, I will never know. But as the sun's ray began filtering into the back of the truck, I was awakened by a pounding headache. I was fully clothed in the same clothes I had gone to the concert in. I looked at Melissa, who was still asleep, and she was fully dressed too. I was still stoned.

I tried to go back to sleep but my mind was full of visions from The Doors' concert, driving from Milwaukee to Los Angeles, and the beautiful girl lying next to me in the back of my truck. I was silently singing lyrics from "Light My Fire." I wondered what Gaston was doing. I wondered what Hoss was doing.

The late-morning heat made the interior of the truck uncomfortable and I couldn't fall back to sleep. I had a strong urge to get going to San Francisco. I had come all this way to go to San Francisco and summer was slipping away. I leaned over and gently shook Melissa, she wearily opened her eyes and tried to smile at me.

"Time to get up," I said.

"That was a great concert," she said in a barely audible voice.

"Could I take a shower in your cousin's house?" I asked.

"It's cool. I'll go in with you."

I opened the back door of the truck and the bright sunlight jolted our senses. We both grabbed a towel as we got out of the truck and walked toward to house. When we got to the back door Melissa knocked on it loudly, but no one responded. She opened the door, and once in the kitchen, we realized that no one was home. She pointed to the adjacent bathroom and said, "There's a shower in there."

I walked into the bathroom, took off my clothes, and stepped into the shower. I turned on cool water and let it run over my aching head. I stood motionlessly as my thoughts began to race about everything I had seen and heard in Los Angeles. I wondered if I was going to learn anything from this adventure and if I would ever find out what the hippie movement was all about.

I turned up the water temperature and began soaping myself when the shower curtain was pulled back and there stood Melissa, naked. She didn't say anything. She stepped into the tub and drew the shower curtain closed. Her breasts were fuller and more beautiful than I had imagined. I was frozen in place, afraid to move, afraid to say or do anything. She took a step toward me, put her arms around my neck, and kissed me. As she kissed me, I didn't close my eyes. I was still startled by her appearance. I felt a twinge of guilt. I still associated Melissa as Gaston's girlfriend. But if I ever wanted to make love to her, this was my chance.

Chapter 23

The rain came down harder and the condition of the road to the Mekong Delta was deteriorating quickly.

"Fucking rain," Hoss mumbled as he squeezed the steering wheel tighter.

"Corporal, how you doing? Do you think we can get there in one piece?" Heins asked.

"We're okay. I have it in four-wheel drive. We're getting traction," Hoss replied without looking over at Heins.

"Good, I figure we have about another twenty-five clicks to go."

The jeep slogged its way south over muddy roads toward the logistics outpost and Heins picked up the radio microphone.

"Alpha Baker Six, this Alpha Baker One, over."

Heins released the transmission key on the microphone, placed it between his knees to protect it from the rain and awaited a reply.

"Alpha Baker One, this is Alpha Baker Six, go ahead, over," a voice replied over the static radio.

"Alpha Baker Six, do we have Woody Company waiting for us at our destination? Over."

"Alpha Baker One, last I heard all is well and they will be there to meet you. What's your ETA? Over."

"Alpha Baker Six, we'll be there within the hour. Out," Heins replied.

Having to drive a jeep in a pouring rain on a sloppy, muddy road to a distant location brought back bad memories for Hoss. He began tapping his sidearm every five minutes. Heins was busy looking at map coordinates so they wouldn't miss their turnoff.

"Ok, we're coming to the end of the main road; start looking for a turnoff to the left," Heins stated.

The windshield wipers were fiercely trying to provide visibility. Fifteen minutes passed and they still had not found the turnoff on the left. Suddenly a small road, almost obscured by overhanging trees, appeared and Hoss turned the jeep left onto it.

"How far is it from the turnoff?" Hoss asked.

"No more than three or four clicks," Heins answered.

Hoss looked down at the odometer so he could gauge distance to their destination. Ten minutes passed and he looked again.

"Colonel, we have driven five clicks since the turnoff," Hoss said while staring intensely at Heins.

"Stop the jeep," Heins commanded. "Shit, I hope we didn't take the wrong turn-off."

Heins picked the microphone, "Woody Company, this is Alpha Baker One, do you read me?" There was only silence. Heins placed another radio call, and again, he got nothing but silence. Then a barely audible voice came over the radio.

"Alpha Baker One, this is Lieutenant Davies of Woody Company, over."

"Davies, are you at our rendezvous location? Over."

"Alpha Baker One, we are standing right next to the building. Where are you? Over," Davies asked.

"I guess we're fucking lost. We must have made a wrong turn. We should be there by now, over," Heins grumbled.

"Colonel, I suggest you abort the mission and head back north. This area has a lot of VC activity, and they are becoming very aggressive in the daylight hours, over," Davies said.

"Roger that, we're going to abort. Thanks for waiting for us. Be careful out there, out," Heins said.

Heins was resigned to the fact that he screwed up the navigation and failed to complete his mission.

Hoss's mood soured as he spun the jeep around and headed back to the turnoff.

Here we go again, he mumbled to himself.

The rain was unrelenting and the road had turned into a huge quagmire. Nevertheless, the jeep performed admirably in the miserable conditions as Hoss and Heins continued north.

Suddenly a loud explosion struck the right rear quarter panel and the jeep cartwheeled down the road throwing out both Hoss and Heins. The soft mud cushioned Hoss's fall.

It took Hoss five minutes to come to his senses and realize that the jeep had overturned. He sat up and called out to Heins, but got no reply. He struggled to his feet, wiped as much mud out of his eyes as he could, and staggered toward the overturned jeep looking for Heins.

When he neared the badly damaged jeep, he could see Heins lying face up in the muddy road. He knelt down beside him, and even with a heavy layer of mud on Heins' face, Hoss knew he was dead. He had seen death before. He placed his hand on Heins' jugular vein and there was no pulse. He walked over to the overturned jeep and got down on his knees to see if he could reach the radio microphone. He blindly felt under the dashboard and determined that the radio had been crushed in the accident.

He was on his own. It would be at least twelve hours before anyone in the logistics command would determine that he and Heins were missing. Hoss knew that his only hope would be to find Wally Company that was operating somewhere in the area. He cursed himself for not reviewing the charts in preparation for the trip.

He found two water canteens next to the jeep and picked them up. He walked over to Heins' body and unstrapped and took Heins' holster and pistol. He found his rain poncho lying in the mud and slipped it over his head and pulled up the hood. He assumed they hit a mine buried in the road and wondered how they avoided it on the way south. He started walking north in mud up to his ankles. The wind-whipped rain was coming down horizontally and stinging his face. He was scared.

Chapter 24

On the return flight from Delaware, Agent Crens decided that the FBI needed a complete list of suppliers and vendors with whom the US Army was contracting. Then the agency could identify their locations and start sending undercover agents, pretending to be radicals to those locales in an effort to intercept domestic terror plots. He knew it was a fishing expedition, but undercover agents had been successful in infiltrating other anti-government groups.

He found the lack of forensic evidence frustrating. Crens began to worry that perhaps the perpetrators were being aided by external terrorists; however, nothing in exhaustive FBI investigations to date had indicated any external influences or involvement.

The death toll from bombings had reached seventy-five workers and consultants in the United States over the last two years. The FBI ordered security increased by US government-contracted vendors and suppliers that were providing arms, and universities that were providing research. Army bases and National Guard armories were advised to do the same. Several universities decided to drop

ROTC programs to avoid disruptive anti-government and anti-ROTC demonstrations.

Crens sat at his desk, staring out the window when the phone rang.

"Agent Crens," he answered.

"Crens, we just got the lab report from our field office in Delaware, and they identified the company that manufactured the dynamite used in the DuPont building," the FBI agent said.

"Great," Crens answered.

"And we found someone had spray-painted 'Napalm Baby Killers' on one wall of another building. Probably happened the same night. We are tracing where that lot of spray paint was sold."

"Where was the dynamite made?" Crens inquired.

"Reno, Nevada. It's made by a local blasting company that sells to mining companies. The company is SafeTech Blasting. They also do demolition work that involves the use of dynamite."

"I will contact our Reno office and have them pull together a list of all the employees and a list of all their customers," Crens said. "This may be the big break we've been looking for."

He hung up the phone and picked up a folder on his desk that he had been reviewing for weeks. The folder contained a list of recent college graduates who wanted to join the FBI. The agency had conducted extensive interviews and background checks on all of them.

Every individual in the folder had an agency recommendation as a candidate for undercover work, a photograph, a personal history, a background check, and a tape recording from a live interview.

Numerous times before, Crens had carefully reviewed the information on every one of the thirty-five individuals in the folder. He kept gravitating back to one individual: James Logan.

Logan's photo didn't look like an individual trying to get a job at the FBI. He had dark black disheveled hair and a well-trimmed beard. Crens thought Logan would make a perfect undercover agent. Crens picked up the phone and dialed Logan's telephone number in Chicago, where he was living with his parents after graduating with a psychology degree from the University of Indiana. A male voice answered and Crens collected himself before speaking.

Chapter 25

Hoss knew he would have to get off the road; otherwise he would be an easy target for Vietcong patrols. He wondered what it would take to survive this situation. He had learned how to forage for food in the woods as a Boy Scout. He went deer hunting in Wisconsin on two dozen occasions. He was an excellent shot with a rifle, but he only had two forty-five-caliber pistols with forty rounds of ammunition.

Hoss walked slowly into a heavily vegetated area, carefully looking for Vietcong booby traps. After thirty minutes of walking, he sat down and quietly listened for any sounds around him. Other than birds chirping high up in the tall, fully foliated trees, there were no other discernible sounds.

Hoss pondered his fate while he rubbed his sore neck. He wasn't sure if the Vietcong would shoot him on the spot or if they would take him prisoner and torture him. He stood up, took a deep breath, and said softly, "I'm not going to let them take me alive."

He made good progress because of the level topography. He believed he was walking north, based on the sun's position in the western sky. The rain finally let up and he trudged on. He carefully scanned the area ahead and behind him. He saw no one, and only heard the incessant chirping of birds.

Hoss came to a slight rise where he could see a small village surrounded by rice paddies. He knew, from his army training, that Vietnamese villagers were friendly to US soldiers during the day. But when night fell, the Vietcong, known simply as the "VC," would infiltrate the villages and make the inhabitants give them food and any information on US troop movements in the area. Soldiers in the field, who were cut off from their units, who elected to hide with the help of villagers were often turned over to VC troops at night. Every villager in South Vietnam knew that harboring a US soldier meant immediate execution at the hands of the VC.

Hoss figured that if he could make it through the night and avoid detection by a villager or VC troops patrolling in the area, he would have a chance to get far enough north to find Woody Company.

He spent the next hour sitting next to a large tree and watching the village to assess where he could hide. Some of the rows in the rice paddies were not flooded and provided narrow and shallow trenches to walk in. He surmised that these same rows would allow VC troops to quietly approach the village after dark, but VC troops had to be mindful not to surprise an unwary farmer who might whack their heads off with a machete, mistaking them for a wild animal.

Hoss spotted a corral where water buffaloes were penned up. Water buffaloes were very valuable property to farmers and Hoss knew the VC never attempted to kill or take one. VC troops knew that taking a water buffalo would alienate a village's support and cooperation. Forcing the villagers to give them food and information was about as much antagonism as VC troops felt they could impose.

Hoss decided that before it got too dark, he would move over to the area where the water buffaloes were tied up and find a place to hide. He watched two villagers walk their water buffaloes back from the far reaches of the rice paddies and put them into the pen.

As dusk faded, Hoss made his move. Crouching low and moving quietly, Hoss reached the pen area in ten minutes. He was very deliberate and calm as he approached the water buffaloes so as not to startle them. He noticed huge tree branches scattered in piles that a human could hide among and be difficult to see. He decided this is where he was going to spend the night because VC soldiers would not find water buffaloes of any particular interest.

He was exhausted and numerous parts of his body ached from the jeep accident. He nestled himself in between two heavily laden piles of branches. His camouflaged fatigues made him extremely difficult to see and darkness would make him invisible. As he lay there on his stomach, he could raise his head up a few inches and look through a crack between the branches and clearly see the village about a hundred yards away. He put his head down on the soggy ground and immediately fell asleep.

Several hours passed when loud voices coming from the village awoke Hoss. He raised his head, at first, not realizing where he was, but then he saw several figures holding torches for light and talking loudly in Vietnamese. He froze when he saw fifteen men carrying AK-47 automatic rifles enter the village wearing the telltale Vietcong black pajama uniforms. Hoss guessed it was about ten o'clock. Vietcong soldiers were known for waiting three to four hours after sunset before entering a village to make sure American soldiers weren't lying in wait to ambush them. Hoss very quietly smeared mud on his face.

The villagers dutifully carried servings of food to the VC soldiers while torches burned brightly around the village. An individual soldier, who appeared to be the VC squad leader, barked out commands at a villager who hurried off to fulfill his orders.

For several hours, the VC soldiers sat outside the villagers' huts and ate dinner. Only male village elders were allowed to sit and converse with the commander and the VC troops. Hoss was told in basic training that VC troops were a well-trained and highly disciplined group. This was unlike many US soldiers that Hoss observed, who were often drunk, unruly, or high on drugs. Hoss noticed that the VC troops were passing around what appeared to be some sort of bota bag containing a liquid. Two hours later, the VC troops were laughing loudly and several appeared to be intoxicated. Several village elders who had been sharing the bota bag appeared to be drunk too.

Unbeknownst to Hoss, it was an ancient holiday celebrated by the Vietnamese. The VC troops and their commander were drunk. The revelry carried on well into the early morning hours until every VC soldier passed out. The village elders had made their way back to their individual huts–all except one.

An elderly man, hunched over from decades of working in rice paddies, hobbled toward the water buffalo pen. Hoss took a deep breath and held it as the man approached. Hoss hoped he was just looking for a place to urinate. The man fell twice before he managed to get to the pen where the water buffaloes were standing. The animals were unfazed by his presence. Pushing the beasts of burden aside, he stumbled toward the pile of branches where Hoss was hiding. He walked within a couple feet of the branches, pulled down his pants, squatted, and began to defecate. He began grunting and farting, and after a few moments, he reached for a leaf on the ground and wiped himself. When he stood up, he tried to reach down and pull up his pants, but he staggered and fell backwards, knocking askew several branches that Hoss had used to surround himself and landed square on Hoss's back. Hoss lay motionless and waited to see if the drunken villager was conscious. He was not.

Chapter 26

The intercom on Agent Crens' desk rang.

"James Logan is here for his interview," his assistant's voice announced.

"Okay, Amy, send him in," Crens replied.

Crens got up from his desk, walked toward the door, opened it as Logan approached, and held out his hand.

"I've been looking forward to meeting you," Crens said as they shook hands.

"Thank you, sir."

"Have a seat," Crens said, pointing to the chair in front of his desk.

Logan sat down and Crens took his seat across the richly colored mahogany desk.

Crens and Logan spent a few moments exchanging niceties, and then Crens got down to business.

Crens leaned forward, placed his two hands on the desk, and looked intently at Logan.

"James, I am interviewing individuals who have applied to join the Bureau. I have carefully reviewed your application and your psychological profile. I'm specifically looking for recent college graduates who are interested in becoming undercover FBI agents," Crens explained. "Are you interested?"

"Undercover agents? What exactly do they do?" Logan asked, sitting forward in his chair.

"We need agents who can infiltrate radical anti-war and anti-government groups the Bureau believes are responsible for bombings, killings, and domestic terrorist attacks."

"Interesting," Logan said.

Crens stood up and began pacing behind his desk.

"It takes a certain kind of individual with steady nerves and clear thinking to get inside an organization. Someone who understands that everything he says and does will be scrutinized, and any slip up will probably get him killed."

"Why do you think I would be a good candidate for the job?"

Crens walked around the desk and sat down in a chair next to Logan.

"Your psychological profile indicates that you possess many of the traits necessary for a successful undercover agent. You're smart, analytical, and resourceful. For twenty years, I have recruited undercover agents and you have many similar traits that our most successful agents possess. There is no such thing as a natural in this business, but you seem like you're well-suited for this line of work," Crens stated.

"I am very interested in doing this," Logan stated.

"First, you have to let your hair and beard grow and look like a hippie," Crens said.

"When do I start?"

"We'll send you to Los Angeles, to our terrorist training facility, where you'll get special training and briefings. I want you to start immediately, so go home and say good-bye to your family, but do not tell them you are joining the FBI." Crens stated. "Tell them you're going to take a trip to the West Coast."

"This sounds exciting," Logan gushed.

"This is dangerous work. If you or someone blows your cover, you will get yourself killed," Crens warned.

They both stood up and by shaking Crens' hand, James Logan agreed to transform himself from a bright eyed, handsome college graduate into a hippie and an undercover agent.

He would have to start hanging out with people who wanted to destroy or radically change the United States government. As Logan turned to leave, Crens slapped him on the back and said, "Welcome to the FBI."

Chapter 27

I was arranging my clothes in the back of my truck when Melissa came out to say good-bye. She made a sandwich for lunch and handed me a brown paper bag.

"What lies ahead is the road to your future and enlightenment. Whatever you're looking for, I hope you find in San Francisco," she said softly with a smile.

I looked into her eyes and saw someone who cared about me. Someone I barely knew a week ago had touched me with her strength of character and her confidence in the ability of young people to find their way in life.

"You're a really together person. I hope I can gain some insights on life, like you have. Sometimes I think I'm just a ping-pong ball in the cosmos," I said.

I hugged her and stepped back to look into her eyes again. She had a radiant smile and she said, "You'll find your way. You're a good guy."

She stepped forward and hugged me. We were locked in a tight embrace. She let go, kissed me on my cheek, and walked back into the house. I climbed into the cab of the truck, started the engine, and headed north on Pacific Coast Highway for San Francisco. I was excited to finally be on my own.

Driving along the coast through Malibu and Ventura, the prevailing southwest breeze filled the truck and took the edge off the ninety-degree day. I drove the first fifty miles in a daze thinking about nothing but Melissa. I was greatly tempted to turn around and go back to her cousin's house and hang out with her again.

I looked out at the Pacific Ocean and I tried to imagine its immenseness, its depth, its power, and the distant islands and civilizations thousands of miles away. I imagined myself as a Spanish explorer, sailing north along the California coast in search of something valuable, something unknown. Soon Melissa became a memory, as I was anxious about what awaited me in San Francisco.

Another one hundred miles rolled under my wheels and I remained deep in thought. Suddenly I was filled with an immense sense of loss. I was convinced I would never see Gaston, Hoss, or Melissa again. I reflected on the meaning of life, love, friendships, and growing up. My heart grew heavy.

I wondered what people sixty-five years old were thinking. I wondered about my mortality. Would I ever make it to sixty-five? I wondered how Hoss was doing in Vietnam. Mom told me on a recent phone call home that Hoss had not written to his parents in more than a month. She read his last letter to me over the phone after I left on my trip west.

Pacific Coast Highway continued to snake north, gently twisting and turning through small cities and even smaller towns. Leaving Morro Bay, I saw a bearded man with a backpack hitchhiking on the side of the highway. I pulled over and motioned him into the cab. He opened the passenger door, climbed in, and dropped his heavily soiled backpack at his feet.

"Where are you headed?" I asked.

When he turned to speak to me, I got a good look at his matted, dirty long hair and filthy ragged clothes. When he opened his mouth to speak, I could see he was missing most of his teeth, and the few teeth he had remaining were disgustingly yellow and brown. I wondered if this is what eventually happens to hippies.

He mumbled that he was going to San Jose, which gave me great relief. I didn't have to take him all the way to San Francisco. He reached into his shirt pocket and pulled out a joint and asked if I wanted a hit. After seeing the condition of his teeth, I didn't want to share anything orally with him, so I made up a quick excuse.

"I don't like getting stoned while I'm driving."

He just nodded and lit the joint and inhaled heavily. His exhale filled the cab, and after a few moments, I was getting a contact high from the smoke. He just stared out the passenger window and didn't say another word for an hour, until I asked him where he was from. Without looking at me, he mumbled, "Boston." I noticed he never spoke in complete sentences.

"How did you end up in California?" I asked.

Again, without looking at me he responded, "Hitchhiked."

Now I regretted picking up this guy. If this is what hippies turn into from smoking too much pot and cruising around the country, I wondered what was so cool about being a hippie. I was totally turned off by his personal hygiene. And after an hour in the truck, I could smell his body odor. I stepped on the accelerator to get to San Jose as soon as possible so I could discharge my smelly passenger. I was delighted to finally see the San Jose city limit sign in the distance.

He turned and said, "You can drop me at Pleasant Valley Road, about a mile ahead." It was his first complete sentence. The late afternoon was flooded in sunlight when I pulled over at Pleasant

Valley Road. He climbed out, slammed the door shut, and walked away without saying a word. I was delighted to see him go.

I pulled back onto the highway and drove on toward San Francisco. I knew I would not make it to San Francisco before it got dark, so I pulled over at a highway rest stop and scoured my California road map for a place to park my truck for the night. I wanted to arrive in San Francisco in the morning so I could see it clearly. I found a county park fifteen miles north that was about five miles off the highway.

I arrived at the park as dusk faded, paid my five-dollar camping fee, and parked in a camping spot next to a small stream. Then I realized that I had completely forgotten about the sandwich Melissa made me because I was so distracted by the disheveled and filthy hitchhiker. I ate the sandwich for dinner while I reminisced about making love to Melissa in the shower that morning.

When I walked to the shower facilities, the giant constellation Scorpio was high in the eastern sky. I remembered in Science class at Riverside High School we had a section on astronomy. Our Science teacher, Mister Burrow, told us about Greek mythology and the names of the constellations. Burrow said that Orion, the great warrior and son of Zeus, wanted to marry all seven sisters of the Pleiades. Zeus strenuously objected to Orion marrying more than one of the sisters. Zeus, according to Burrow, sent the giant bull Taurus to stop Orion. But Orion, being the mighty warrior he was, instantly dispatched the bull. According to mythology, once you are dead, you are placed in the sky for eternity and that was Taurus's fate.

Orion's lustful desires for all seven sisters continued unabated. So Zeus decided to call on the giant Scorpio to stop Orion. Scorpio accosted Orion and they fought fiercely, with the scorpion trying to sting Orion, and Orion trying to behead the scorpion with his all-powerful sword. During one of Orion's mighty swings of his huge silver sword, his ankle was exposed and Scorpio stung him on his Achilles tendon. Orion succumbed to the poison and died. But when a scorpion stings something, it dies too. Well, at least that is what Mister Burrow said.

Another cool thing he said was that Orion and Scorpio were enemies for eternity and their constellations never appear in the same sky. If you are in the northern hemisphere, Orion appears in the winter and Scorpio appears in the summer. I later read a book on astronomy and found out that Mister Burrow's stories were totally made up and inaccurate.

Scorpio's timing was perfect as it was now the second week of July. As I walked back from the bathrooms, I looked up at the sky and wondered what my fate would be. I bid Scorpio a good night while looking at its long tail pointing due south. Then I looked at the seven sisters of the Pleiades and tried to recount how many girls I had made love to. I quickly admonished myself for acting like an immature kid.

Chapter 28

Hoss knew he couldn't wait much longer for fear that someone might come looking for the missing village elder. Besides, the villager was a strain on his back. All the Vietcong soldiers were passed out from drinking what must have been rice wine, and only one fading torch was still visible.

Hoss guessed that it was about two o'clock. That meant it would be about three hours before the Vietcong soldiers got up and moved out before daybreak. If he could get the old man off his back without waking him, he could slip away quickly and quietly and continue north in hopes of finding Woody Company. It was a perfectly clear night with a waxing moon that would provide Hoss with just enough light to see where he was walking.

Hoss knew a lot about chokeholds from his varsity wrestling days, although chokeholds were illegal in matches. He decided that if the old man woke up, he would have to strangle him quickly. Hoss arched his back up six inches to see if the old man would stir. He didn't. Hoss slowly turned on his left side and the old man gently slid off his back and remained out cold next to Hoss. Hoss crawled forward, like an inchworm, until he was ten yards away from the woodpile. Then he took off walking briskly in a semi-crouched position.

His back ached from the drunken villager and the semi-crouched position only aggravated it. He initially followed the path the villagers used to lead the water buffalo to the rice paddies. He walked quickly but carefully to avoid fallen branches that would cause noise. After twenty minutes, he could no longer see the village or any light coming from it.

His body was racked with pain from the jeep accident. He had to take a break after walking more than an hour. After a five-minute rest, he stood up and did some stretches and deep knee bends. Then he resumed walking. He knew he had about an hour and half before the Vietcong troops in the village would be on the move. He had no idea what direction they would take. He pressed on for another hour until he reached a small rise that was thick with trees and vines. He took the pistol out of his holster and approached it slowly.

A heavy cloud layer displaced the clear skies and obscured the moon. Hoss stood at the base of the rise and listened for any noise. He heard nothing. Cautiously, he walked up the rise with the pistol in his right hand, his uniform and face covered with mud, helping him appear almost invisible in the darkness. When he reached the summit of the rise, he heard a very faint noise that he could not discern. He froze next to a group of trees and got down on the ground. He strained his ears and listened for the noise again. The unusual sound was growing slightly louder. Hoss looked in the direction he was headed and even in the darkness he could see that the topography leveled off. It appeared to be a valley, but with the heavy cloud cover, he couldn't be sure. A discernable rumbling noise was getting louder. He wondered if a thunderstorm was approaching.

Suddenly, there were thundering explosions that shook the ground and overpowering flashes of light in the valley ahead. The ground began to shake so violently that Hoss couldn't stand up. He grasped some vines to keep from bouncing up and down on his stomach.

Then he realized that he was on the edge of a US Air Force B-52 bombing mission that was carpet bombing suspected Vietcong and North Vietnamese troop concentrations. Hundreds of incendiary bombs rained down on the valley floor, so much so, that the night was turned into day. With every brilliant explosion, Hoss could see figures running in all directions to get away from the bombing attack.

"Vietcong," Hoss muttered.

He looked around for small branches and leaves that he could hide himself under. Over the noise of exploding bombs, he could hear voices, yelling in Vietnamese, getting closer. He grabbed leaves off nearby vines, scrounged up several branches, dragged them over to a cluster of three trees, and covered himself. The bombs were exploding closer to the rise as the B-52 bombers, flying at 35,000 feet, dropped their bombs in a calculated pattern. As he had done in the village woodpile, Hoss made a small slit so he could see out.

The noise from the exploding bombs deafened him. The ground shook more violently. Hoss was sure he was going to die right there and then. He gritted his teeth and muttered, "What a fucking way to go. Killed by our own B-52s."

Every second seemed like a minute. Every minute seemed like an hour. Bombs continued to rain down, but the pattern veered to the west, sparing the small rise where Hoss was hiding. Then suddenly the night fell silent. Hoss raised his head and listened. There were no voices. He heard only the wind in the trees above him. He could see numerous fires burning on the valley floor from the bombing, but nothing else. He laid his head down, closed his eyes, and fell asleep out of sheer exhaustion.

A light breeze rustled the leaves in the trees above Hoss when he opened his eyes and saw a bright, sunny day. He raised his head and looked down upon the valley. It was difficult to discern what exactly he was looking at as the valley had been transformed into a mass of jumbled trees, and tangled vegetation and there were countless bomb craters.

He climbed out from under the small brush pile and crawled forward to where the rise started to descend toward the valley. He didn't see anything moving. He stood up and his body ached worse than the day before. He was thirsty and terribly hungry. But most of all, he was afraid. He found himself in a world that he had never experienced before. Life was always just an instant away from being extinguished in Vietnam.

Nothing he had learned or seen prepared him for what he had experienced in his two months of duty in Vietnam. Life was at best a day-by-day proposition. No one planned more than a day ahead. But this was neither the time nor the place to ponder the future, a future he might never realize. He knew that forty percent of the men who arrived in Vietnam with him, sixty days ago, were either wounded or dead.

Hoss looked off to his right and he could see the sun rising. He knew north lay straight ahead. He started walking into the valley and was surrounded by immense environmental devastation. He carefully navigated the numerous bomb craters. Some were five feet deep, and some were fifteen feet deep.

He came upon an incredible scene of human carnage. First, he saw a severed leg. A few yards ahead, there were body parts strewn all over. Then he saw the upper torso of a Vietcong soldier wedged in a splintered tree trunk. The soldier's entire lower body was missing and his face was twisted in total horror. Hoss stared at the body and began vomiting. His mind began to go numb at the sight of dismembered bodies everywhere. He stumbled onward and had to step over more and more severed body parts.

Hoss switched into mental survival mode. His mind shut down; he just walked and walked. He no longer worried about being cautious and keeping a sharp look out for Vietcong soldiers. He just walked to escape the grisly valley of death in which he found himself.

His ears still rang from the bomb explosions. He remembered how much his body ached and how hungry he was, but he just kept walking, looking for anything or anyone in the distance.

Despite the ringing in his ears, he heard a noise. His survival skills reengaged and he crouched to listen. He could hear someone moaning twenty yards ahead. He drew his pistol and crept slowly toward where the moaning came from. As he approached, the moaning became louder. Hoss had heard this type of moaning from soldiers wounded in action. He remembered the awful night after delivering the radios when the base came under a deadly mortar attack that killed his friend Landuski and dozens of others. He advanced several more yards and found a Vietcong soldier lying on his back with a massive, bloody stomach wound.

Stomach wounds are a soldier's worse fate. Often they do not kill the victim for many hours or even days. During the US Civil War, troops from both the Union and Confederate armies would lie on a battle field with stomach wounds and cry out for their mothers, wives, and siblings for a day or two before finally succumbing.

Hoss walked up to the wounded soldier, who was barely conscious and was delirious. He looked up at Hoss and moaned loudly. Hoss stared at this pathetic human being and let out an anguished sigh.

Hoss remembered the first time he went deer hunting with a rifle in Wisconsin, when he had spotted an enormous twelve-point buck and tracked it for hours. Then late in the afternoon, he spotted the buck again. A small clearing afforded Hoss a clean shot at the deer.

Hoss drew a bead on it in his rifle's scope and he squeezed the trigger. The shot rang out loudly across the forest and the buck turned his head just as the bullet struck its neck. The animal seemed to hesitate for an instant and then began to run, but it only took two steps before collapsing. It took five minutes for Hoss to reach the fallen deer.

When he arrived, the first thing he saw was the buck's wide-open eyes, as it lay there quivering near death. Hoss recognized what a majestic animal it was just as it died. With the thrill of the hunt over, the thrill of the kill was not equally as enjoyable. He dutifully field-quartered the deer, just as his father had taught him. That wasn't a particularly enjoyable experience either. After that deer hunting trip, Hoss realized that he didn't like killing animals, and he never went hunting again.

The soldier's moaning brought Hoss back to his present reality. He knew the soldier had been suffering terribly since the bombing attack. Hoss had never killed another human being, but his sense of mercy told him to put the poor guy out of his agony. His hand was trembling as he pulled his pistol from the holster and pointed it between the soldier's eyes. He put the pistol six inches from the soldier's head and fired a round. The soldier stopped moaning.

Hoss stepped back and knew that anyone in the area could have heard the shot and that he had possibly given away his position, but he didn't care. He would have wanted someone to put him out of his misery if he had been so mortally wounded. He put the pistol back in the holster and started walking again, but this time without worrying if someone saw him.

He spotted a VC canteen lying on the ground, picked it up, and found it had water in it. He eagerly drank from it. Death was now his partner, and if it was to come upon him, so be it.

The further he walked, the devastation from the bombing diminished. By midday, he was fifteen miles north of the valley and dense foliage returned. By late afternoon, his soldiering and survival skills returned, and he began to think about where to seek shelter before dark to avoid Vietcong patrols.

As dusk approached, Hoss trudged on. He saw a small pool of fresh water and knew that Vietcong troops would stop to fill their canteens there. He wanted to get as far away from the pool as possible before dark. He remembered seeing a movie when he was a boy about a soldier who climbed a tree to avoid detection. The soldier tied himself to a lofty tree branch to avoid falling out while he slept.

There were plenty of trees all around him, so right before dark, Hoss climbed up a tall tree with heavy foliage. He climbed higher and higher until he was about twenty-five feet above ground. There, he found co-joining branches where he could actually lay across the branches and not be seen from below. He took off his belt and lashed his waist to the branches and quickly nodded off to sleep as darkness and silence engulfed everything around him.

Chapter 29

I was so excited to finally get to San Francisco, the mecca of the hippie movement. I overflowed with sky-high expectations on what a cool place San Francisco was going to be. San Francisco had become my quest to find a deeper meaning of life.

I walked to the restrooms, combed my hair, brushed my teeth, and returned to the ever-faithful former milk truck, anxious to get on the road. The truck started up immediately and away I went to meet my destiny.

When San Francisco came into view, I was stunned. In the distance, I saw the Golden Gate Bridge while the tall downtown buildings glistened in the sunshine. I had my windows rolled down and a local FM station played a song by Big Brother and the Holding Company. I felt so giddy that I didn't notice that my truck was drifting into the next lane. The motorist in the adjoining lane let me know her displeasure with a long blast of her horn.

Months prior to departing Milwaukee, I wrote down the directions on how to get to Haight-Ashbury; nevertheless, I almost missed my turnoff. Thanks to light traffic, I was able to quickly move into the exit lane.

After wandering through a city maze, I found Ashbury Street where once-proud Victorian mansions were showing their age. Despite the lack of maintenance, these architectural gems retained their majesty if one could look past the peeling paint and falling-down rain gutters. Unlike Milwaukee's duplexes, where there is space between buildings, the Victorians were tightly fitted side by side.

I arrived a few minutes before noon. Bearded men with long hair and young women in tie-dye tank tops and shorts, with every imaginable hairstyle crowded the sidewalks. A sea of humanity, a human tide, flowed in every direction. I slowed the truck to take a good look. Many of these pedestrians appeared to be about my age.

Suddenly, my truck caught the attention of several people as I drove very slowly down the street. Two girls and a guy with a bushy black beard ran alongside of my truck throwing flower petals and shouting "Peace and love, Brother!" I stopped the truck out of fear I would run over one of them. I hopped over to the passenger seat and slid the door open and asked, "Are you okay?"

The girls were laughing and jumped into the cab of the truck and held up two fingers, giving me the peace sign. I quickly learned that there was a correct way and an incorrect way to give the peace sign. The index finger and middle finger had to be presented with the palm facing forward. By holding those two fingers up with the palm facing inward only indicated the number two.

When the girls got a glimpse of the interior of the truck, they gushed with praise.

"What a cool truck, man."

"This is so outta sight, man. Did you fix this truck up?" the other girl asked.

"I love this truck. It's taken me from Wisconsin to San Francisco, and I'm having a blast," I blurted out.

"You're on a cross country trip? That's really far out," the redhead said.

While I was stopped, a crowd surrounded my truck and more people began throwing flower petals and giving me the peace sign. It turned into a parade of sorts, with people hanging off the side and back of the truck and several more girls clamoring into the cab as I resumed driving down Ashbury Street. I giggled and wondered if I was being received as some sort of conquering hero. As I approached a stop sign, two beat patrol police officers walked in front of the truck and started shooing people off and away from the truck. Two delivery trucks behind me starting beeping their horns. I worried that I was going to get in trouble with the police.

The two officers approached the driver side of the truck. One was rather plump and had white hair. The other, a much younger man with strong looking shoulders and a crew cut, walked up to the open driver side door and spoke. "What's going on? Let me see your license."

"Officer, people just started jumping into the truck. I really didn't do anything."

I nervously handed him my driver's license.

"So you're from Wisconsin. How long have you been in San Francisco?"

"I just arrived about thirty minutes ago. I'm looking for a room to rent," I replied.

I noticed the nametag on his uniform read Schlaeger.

"Do you have relatives in Wisconsin?" I asked.

Handing my license back and pointing to a green painted curbside about fifteen feet ahead on the right, he said, "Pull your truck into that loading zone so you're not blocking traffic."

I moved the truck over to the curb while he walked slowly behind the truck and waved the two anxious delivery trucks forward.

Officer Schlaeger walked up to the passenger side, where the sliding door was open, and stepped in and sat down in the passenger seat. I thought for sure I was going to get a ticket for blocking traffic.

"I'm actually from Milwaukee like you," he said.

"Wow, far out."

"In fact, my youngest sister went to Rufus King High School and she played softball against your sister Betsy," he said.

"Wow, small world," I blurted out.

"Look, there is a little coffee shop and restaurant about three blocks straight ahead. Turn right on Haight Street; it's called My Karma. It's a neighborhood-gathering place and they have a bulletin board where people post rooms for rent. Check it out. They have good food too."

"Thanks, that's a great tip. How long have you been in San Francisco?" I asked.

"I've been on the police force four years now. And here's another good tip. Not everything and not everyone in San Francisco are what they appear to be. Don't get involved in the heavy drug scene. There are some bad dudes selling heroin."

"I have no interest in doing smack," I said.

"Keep away from the Hell's Angels motorcycle gang and stay out of the Tenderloin District. Nothing but bad shit goes on down there. And find a place where you can park this truck because parking is very, very scarce in this city."

Before I could thank him for his good advice, he gave me a friendly slap on the shoulder and stepped out of the truck and started walking toward his partner, who was waiting for him at the corner.

I pulled out of the loading zone and motored to the corner and stopped at the stop sign. As I pulled forward into the intersection, Officer Schlaeger yelled at me, "Go Packers!"

He smiled and gave me the two-finger peace sign. He was the coolest cop I had ever met.

"Wow, even the cops are cool in San Francisco," I said out loud.

I followed Officer Schlaeger's directions, and by sheer luck, I found an on-street parking space about ten feet from My Karma's front door. A brightly colored mural depicting American Indians riding horses on a grassy plain covered the front of the building, along with Hindu figures, their hands raised toward the sun with planets circling in the background. I quickly determined that San Francisco was a city where free expression was welcome and abundant.

I walked into the restaurant and a thick plume of marijuana smoke obscured many of the patrons who were sitting on the floor at Japanese style tables. There was no hostess and no one greeted me. I noticed the bulletin board that Officer Schlaeger mentioned, covered with notes, slips of paper, flyers for musical concerts, and invitations to special healing events.

Since no one offered me a table, I walked up to a long cork bulletin board and noticed that the upper part of the bulletin board contained all the room for rent offers. After scanning thirty different rental offers, I wrote down only those offered on Haight or Ashbury streets. In my opinion, these were the two most famous streets in San Francisco. There were only two rooms on Ashbury Street, and one on Haight Street. Since no one ever came to see if I wanted any food, which I didn't, I didn't feel obligated to buy anything; so I walked back outside to my truck.

I decided to go to the two addresses on Ashbury Street first since they were relatively close to each other according to their street numbers. When I got back into the truck, I pulled out my San Francisco city map from the glove compartment and studied it carefully. Once assured that I knew where I was going, I started driving.

I arrived at Ashbury Street, turned left, and found 635 Ashbury. I stopped the truck and noticed a dozen people sleeping on mattresses on the front porch of this very weathered Victorian. Several more people were hanging out on the front porch or milling around the small front yard.

I was so put off by people sleeping on mattresses and the motley group in the front yard, I continued on to the second Ashbury Street address without bothering to inquire about the room for rent.

The second house was only four blocks further north. But upon arriving there, I could not find a parking space. I drove around the block four times in a fruitless effort to find parking. So I went to the Haight Street address, which was only a few blocks away, and hoped that my prospects for parking would be better there. Officer Schlaeger was right, and I was learning quickly that parking a milk truck in San Francisco was going to be a challenge.

When I arrived at 806 Haight Street, something happened that doesn't happen very often in San Francisco: someone pulled out of a parking space. I was delighted and started to back into the vacant spot. It was going to be a very tight fit, but I was determined to get that parking spot.

After a series of tight back-and-forth maneuvers, and without banging either the car in front or the car in back, I finally squeezed the truck into the space. I felt very proud of my parking job. The numerous pedestrians on the sidewalk paid no attention to my accomplishment or glee.

The two-story Victorian appeared to be in somewhat better condition than other Victorians on Haight Street, although the multi-colored paint was all faded and peeling. I was relieved to see that no one was sleeping on the front porch. I walked up the stairs to the front door and noticed that all the porch railings looked like they were ready to fall off at any moment.

The front door was open and there was a wooden screen door. I knocked on the screen door as loudly as I could. I waited patiently, but no one answered the door. I knocked again, this time a little louder.

Still no one came to the door. I put my face up to the screen mesh to see if I could see in, but the sun's afternoon rays were bouncing off the screening, making it impossible to see anything inside. I assumed that no one was home, and apparently, leaving a front door open was acceptable in the coolest city in the world. I gave it one last try, knocking very loudly for a third and final time.

After waiting about thirty seconds, I turned to walk away. Suddenly I heard footsteps and a gravelly male voice call out, "What do you want?"

"I'm inquiring about the room for rent," I said facing the screen door.

A male with a shabby beard and disheveled, long jet-black hair pushed the screen door open, almost striking my forehead. He frowned and squinted his eyes in the sunshine trying to get a better look at me. Finally he grumbled, "There's no room for rent here."

"I saw a note at My Karma there was a room for rent at 806 Haight Street. Am I at the wrong house?" I asked.

"Right place, but wrong information. No room for rent here," he snapped back.

"Sorry, man, didn't mean to bother you," I said slumping my shoulders.

He pulled the screen door shut and walked away. In the hallway behind him I heard a woman's voice.

"John, I put the room for rent notice back up at My Karma. We agreed that some extra bread around here would be a good idea."

"I don't want a renter in this house," John replied.

"We are all renters, man. We don't own this house," the woman replied.

She walked up to the screen door and asked, "What's your name?"

I couldn't see her facial features because the sun was still reflecting off the copper screening.

"Bob Ralston. I want to rent a room for two or three months, and then I may go back to Wisconsin."

She pushed the screen open and stepped out onto the porch to check me out. Her beauty stunned me. She had long silky black hair down to her mid-back, dazzling green eyes, a flawless complexion, and luscious, full lips.

"Is there a room for rent or not?" I asked with a furrowed brow.

"Yeah, there is a room for rent," she said. "We're charging fifty a week, two hundred a month. Can you afford that?"

"Yeah, but can I see the room?"

"Sure, come in."

I followed her down to a very dimly lit hallway with scuffed and faded hardwood floors. She opened a door and showed me into a large bedroom with a ten-foot high ceiling. The room had a large window with faded white lace curtains. There was a queen-size bed with a black wrought iron headboard and a small closet opposite the window.

"What do you think? she asked.

"I like it.

Truth be told, I was looking more intensely at her than the room. She was the most beautiful woman I had ever seen in my life. Anne Nitche had just fallen into second place.

"I'll take it for two months for sure," I replied, with a broad smile. "I have a truck. Where do I park it?"

She walked past me to the window and pointed down to the alley below. "You can park it in the alley. There are no parking restrictions. But park at this end of the alley and stay away from the farthest end. There are some really bad-ass motorcycle gang members living in a house at the end of the alley."

"Can I bring my stuff in from the truck right now? I asked.

"Give me two hundred dollars and it's your room."

"What's your name?" I asked.

She turned around slowly in the hallway and the late afternoon sunshine, flooding in from the bedroom window, illuminated her slender body in a golden sheen, which made her look even more stunning.

"Maryanne Cetio," she said.

"What kind of name is Cetio?" I asked.

"It's Sicilian."

Wow, no wonder she's so gorgeous. She's an Italian babe, I thought.

"Who is the guy who answered the door?"

"John Robinson. He's actually a nice guy, but he gets a little nervous and that makes him grumpy. Just don't bug him and you'll get along fine," she said.

As we walked down the hallway she said, "You can use the kitchen and share the refrigerator. But under no circumstances are you to go down into the basement. It's probably impossible anyway because John always keeps the basement door locked."

I didn't bother to ask why.

I spent the rest of the afternoon moving clothes and personal items into the room. I didn't have that much stuff so everything fit neatly in the old oak dresser and the small, musty closet.

I went out to the truck and drove it around the block to the alley behind the house. Just as I was beginning my turn into the alley, four loud Harley-Davidson motorcycles, ridden by long-haired, leather-clad, and very unfriendly looking Hell's Angels, roared out of the alley right in front of me. One of the riders gave me a very dirty look even though I was stopped and did not impede their exit.

I'd seen Hell's Angels before in Wisconsin, riding their "hog" motorcycles, but these Hell's Angels looked hardcore and I took to heart the warning about staying away from their end of the alley.

I found a small patch of concrete next to the garage and that's where I parked the truck. A path led to a gate that opened into the backyard. When I walked into the backyard, I knew I would be able to see my truck from the kitchen window, as well as my bedroom window.

Chapter 30

The day turned into a warm summer night, and Haight Street was crowded. Lots of young people sat on porches that lined both sides of the street. At first, I thought that a street festival was taking place, but I came to learn that there was a lot of activity every night in the Haight-Ashbury district. The smell of marijuana was everywhere, and acoustic guitar music echoed from street corners well past midnight.

On my first evening strolling around the neighborhood, I felt intimidated by all the activity and the numerous people milling about. The vast majority of local residents were young men and women between eighteen and thirty years old, and most of them smoked grass. With my relatively short hair, I stood out in this sizable crowd of long hair and bearded men, but wherever I went, people were friendly to me. While walking around the neighborhood, young men and women offered me a "hit" on a joint or offered to sell me marijuana or LSD. I politely declined because I was trying to get a feel for what was going on at ground zero of the hippie movement. I didn't think I could do that if I was stoned. As the night wore on, I felt out of place, so I didn't interact with many people.

I wanted to try a different place for dinner every night. On my first night, I chose an Indian restaurant named Gandhi and ate authentic Indian food for the first time. The restaurant stood in a former bank building and I saw the big gray bank vault on the back wall. Two hours after leaving the restaurant, the spicy food gave me a churning upset stomach. As I headed home, I vowed never to eat Indian food again.

On my third night walking around, I decided I was never going to meet or get to know anyone or make new friends, unless I made an effort to be more friendly and engaging. I didn't have to go far. Three houses down the street from where I was staying I saw a small crowd of people sitting crossed-legged on the front porch. They were listening to a tall, slender, bearded man who stood in front of the gathering. I walked onto the porch and squeezed into a small open space and sat down. With everyone listening intently, the speaker declared that a new cosmic order was being created by harmonic vibrations due to an alignment of the planets. He rambled on about how this new cosmic order would create great forces of good and evil and it was up to every individual to decide what path in life they wanted to follow. He, like Officer Schlaeger, warned that things were changing and would not be what they appeared.

After ten minutes, I lost interest and my attention turned to a blonde girl in a blue tank top seated near me. At that same moment, she glanced at me. She had a very pleasant appearance but there was a curious look on her face. When I smiled at her, she turned her attention back to the speaker.

I sat there trying to figure out how I could gracefully exit without looking like I was bailing out on the presentation. I decided it was impossible and resigned myself that I would have to stay until he finished speaking. The presentation droned on for another ten minutes and then–mercifully–concluded.

When I stood up to leave, I realized that I was not used to sitting crossed-legged for any length of time. My knees ached, so I waited a few moments until several people left the porch.

I watched this interesting mix of people depart. Some were teenagers and some had white hair and long beards. I half-heartedly wondered if there was an age limit for being a hippie, and if so, how young and how old were the limits. I started walking toward the porch stairs when I felt a tap on my shoulder. I turned and there was the blonde girl in the blue tank top.

"Hi, I'm Autumn. I've never seen you at these presentations before," she said.

"Hi," I said, "I'm Bob Ralston. I just moved here a few days ago."

"I live at 807 Haight."

"Far out, we're neighbors. I live across the street at 806."

"I'm going to meet some friends at the Sunshine Café. You want to come along? You'll get to meet people there and make new friends."

"Cool," I said.

We began walking to the Sunshine Café.

"Where are you from?" I asked.

"I grew up in a southern California beach city called Hermosa Beach."

"Do you have family in San Francisco?"

"No, my parents and my older brother and younger sister still live in Hermosa Beach."

"How long have you been in San Francisco?"

"About a year. I graduated from high school two years ago." I determined that she was very much at ease with someone she just met and that she was not a whole lot older than I.

"So you rented a room at 806?" she asked.

"Yup."

"There's always a bunch of people coming and going from that house, sometimes at very odd hours of the night," she said.

"I moved in a few days ago, and I really haven't spent any time with my roommates yet. There were some folks in the living room late last night talking about something I couldn't quite make out from the kitchen."

"Is Maryanne Cetio still living there?"

"She is. Do you know her?"

"She is a well-known Sociology professor at the University of San Francisco. She has a reputation for very fiery speeches about America's involvement in the Vietnam War. The University voted to censure her once."

"Did they?"

"No. The American Civil Liberties Union stepped in and sued the University over denying her free speech rights. The school backed off. She still teaches there," she replied.

"Do you know the guy who is her roommate?"

"Not really. His name is John Robinson. I met him at an anti-war rally on Market Street a few months ago. He's a professor at Berkeley, but he's not a friendly guy."

The Sunshine Café was located in a cavernous former warehouse. Dozens of circular tables and wooden chairs were scattered about the stained and cracked concrete floor, and brightly colored tapestries hung from the ceiling. The air was heavy with marijuana and hashish smoke.

When we walked in, Autumn recognized several individuals and they exchanged greetings with a peace sign. Others came up to her and exchanged hugs while I stood quietly by. It seemed that Autumn knew a lot of people in Haight-Ashbury.

Tuesday Morning, a folk-rock group, played on a rickety plywood stage supported by an array of plastic milk crates. Their acoustic music gently wafted above the din of conversations and provided a musical pulse to counteract the lethargic effects of the pot and various drugs being consumed.

We walked up to three tables that had been pushed together and occupied by a dozen people Autumn knew. All the guys and girls had long hair. I felt self-conscious because my hair was considerably shorter than everyone else's. I still looked like a high school senior.

"Look who is here: Miss Autumn," shouted out a young man with blond curly hair and a broad smile. He wore a tie-dye t-shirt and a bandana around his forehead.

"Far out, Autumn said. "I haven't seen you in a while, Lightning."

Later I was told that Lightning got his nickname because he was once Georgia's high school cross-country champion.

"Brothers and sisters," Autumn announced, "let me introduce my new neighbor, Bob Ralston. He just moved in across the street from me."

"Welcome to the center of the universe, brother," said a young man with a red beard and glassy eyes just before he took another toke on a large joint.

After a quick round of introductions, I sat down next to a young lady wearing a long white saree and she asked me where I was from.

"I'm from Wisconsin," I replied.

"There are several other new Midwest arrivals here," she said, pointing across the table. "Jimmy is from Indiana, Crystal is from Chicago, Billy is from St. Louis, and sweet little Violet Somsen is from New Ulm, Minnesota." They all acknowledged their names with a nod, or a peace sign, and smiled at me. I nodded back in recognition.

The evening continued with fascinating and intense discussions about the Vietnam War, the upcoming presidential election, self-awareness, spiritual enlightenment, and the meaning of existence. I sat there totally enthralled just listening to the exchange of ideas. On regular intervals, a joint worked its way around the tables and I took a few tokes. The pot added a degree of surrealism to the diverse opinions being expressed. I purposely limited the amount of pot I smoked because I didn't want to get stoned and miss any of the cross-table conversations. I also didn't want to come across as a stoner to Autumn and all these people I just met.

Everyone sitting there threw a few dollars on the tables to buy several rounds of beer. Unlike Wisconsin, no one asked to see my ID card or verify my age. At two o'clock, with the band long gone, the café owner announced "last call" and turned on harsh overhead spotlights, indicating it was closing time and everyone had to leave.

Autumn and I walked home together. Even at two o'clock, young people still crowded the streets and played music on the sidewalks and on front porches while others listened and smoked marijuana.

As we approached our respective houses, I felt the effects of the pot, the beer, and a long day. "I had a great time," I stammered. "Thanks for such a cool night."

"You're going to hear, see, and learn a lot in San Francisco," she said with a smile.

"Good night," I said, standing awkwardly next to her, not knowing what I was supposed to do. I wondered if I should hug her like her other friends did or kiss her good night?

"Good night, Mr. Ralston from Wisconsin."

She kissed me on my cheek and turned around and walked across the street.

I watched her walk away and thought what a pleasant person she was. I walked around to the back of the house to avoid coming in through the front door. That way I wouldn't have to go through the living room. I could see a dim light on in there and I didn't want to disturb anyone. A few minutes later, lying in bed, I thought about what a wonderful and interesting night I just had and then quickly fell asleep.

Chapter 31

If Vietcong patrols had passed Hoss in the night, he never heard them. Daylight filtered through the green canopy above and every muscle in Hoss's body ached, including his stomach from a lack of food and water. It took him a few moments to come to his senses and remember that he was up a tree, lashed to two branches. Before he dared move, he listened carefully for any noise that would indicate enemy soldiers nearby. He heard nothing other than birds going about their daily chores. Unbuckling the belt that had secured him tightly during the night, he worked his body into a sitting position. For five minutes, he sat motionlessly looking and listening for any sign of Vietcong troops. When he was convinced that it was safe to move, he gingerly climbed down the tree and remembered what his father had told him, climbing down was a lot harder than climbing up.

When he stepped on the ground he could tell that his legs were growing significantly weaker. Getting back to US Army lines was an imperative if he was going to survive. He put his helmet on and began walking north where he thought US Army outpost positions would be.

Heat from the early morning sun was moderate and the breeze was refreshing. The birds chirping overhead provided a serene effect. Hoss slid his right hand down to his holster to ensure his pistol was still there.

Hoss figured he could walk another ten miles before collapsing. He also guessed that ten miles might be just enough to reach American front line soldiers in the field. As he trudged forward in a stooped and weary position, he told himself that he didn't want to die in a field in Vietnam.

For three hours he walked through a heavily vegetated bamboo forest that led onto a rolling plain, covered in six-foot-tall, lush grass that waived gently in the light breeze. The grass was so high that a man could walk through it totally undetected, but Hoss knew this was both a blessing and a curse, because a man could walk right into a gathering of soldiers and not know it until it was too late. He had no choice; he had to keep pushing on until the very last ounce of strength and willpower left his body. He kept telling himself, "I am not going to die in Vietnam," energizing his will to live.

Two more grueling hours passed before Hoss got the sense that something was going on around him. He wasn't sure what it was, but a sixth sense told him that danger lay ahead. In the tall grass, he couldn't see or hear anything other than the sound of the blades of grass rubbing against each other. Suddenly, gunfire burst out all around him as countless rounds of ammunition whizzed over his head and into the grass. Hoss dove for the ground. He thought he was caught in the middle of a firefight between US and Vietcong troops. As he lay there, he heard voices yelling instructions about twenty yards in front of him. Because of the gunfire, he couldn't tell if the voices were speaking in English or Vietnamese. He decided that he was going to run with all his remaining strength straight ahead, convinced the men in front of him were American soldiers.

He drew his pistol from the holster, jumped up, and began running straight ahead. He ran about three yards and gunfire erupted again. The bullets mowed down the grass all around him. Suddenly, his left leg slipped out from under him and he tumbled to the ground, dropping his pistol. He tried to get up and grab his pistol, but his left leg would not respond. He rolled on his back to look at his leg and saw a gaping wound on the inside of his left thigh. Blood gushed down his leg. Uncertain how serious the wound was, he tried to get up and run. And again, his left leg would not support him. He lay there cursing as the bullets continued to fly all around him. Then excruciating pain enveloped his lower body and he lost consciousness.

When Hoss opened his eyes, he saw US Army medics lifting him onto a stretcher. They said something, but he couldn't comprehend a single word. He wondered if he was dreaming. He tried to move but couldn't. He raised his head and realized he was strapped to a stretcher, and saw one of the medics holding an IV bag over his head. He tried to speak but no words came out. He heard the medics shouting something as they carried him on the stretcher, but he still couldn't make out what they were saying. He was puzzled why he was on a stretcher because he felt no pain. Convinced this was all a bad dream, he closed his eyes.

Chapter 32

I awoke to a bright, sunny and warm Saturday morning and got out of bed. A bit disheveled, I walked into the kitchen and saw Maryanne sitting at the breakfast table. She was wearing a tight fitting white t-shirt and black shorts, while reading the *San Francisco Chronicle.*

"Good morning," I said.

"Well, good morning to you," she asked, looking up from the newspaper. "Are you enjoying San Francisco?"

"It's really outta sight. A lot of very interesting people with a lot of interesting things to say."

"Made any friends yet?"

"I'm not sure I would call them friends. How about acquaintances?"

"All right, acquaintances then," she smiled. "Want a cup of coffee?"

"Thanks, but caffeine makes me very jumpy."

"Okay, how about some fresh squeezed California orange juice for our Midwestern boy in residence?"

I smiled and nodded, sitting down across the table from her. I was thoroughly convinced she was the most beautiful woman I had ever set eyes on. I longed to touch her long dark, silky smooth hair.

As I watched her walk over to the sink and start squeezing the oranges, I said, "I saw a flyer at the Sunshine Café that said you are the featured speaker at an anti-war rally tonight at the University of California-Davis. Is that true?"

She had her back to me and didn't answer right away. I thought she didn't hear me so I started to ask her again, but she turned and said "Yup, at seven." She walked back to the table and handed me the glass of orange juice and sat down. "I have some friends coming over about one o'clock. You're welcome to join us. It'll give you a chance to meet some more people," she said.

"Groovy," I replied.

"We're going to sit on the front porch and gab," she said. "I have to go to the farmers' market. I'm almost out of food. See you later."

She got up, grabbed her purse, and walked out the front door. I sat there drinking the orange juice and eating a banana and some yogurt.

Suddenly, the basement door that adjoined the kitchen swung open and in walked my other roommate, John.

"Good morning," I said somewhat sheepishly.

"Yeah," he grumbled without looking at me.

He turned toward the open basement door and I thought that he had forgotten something in the basement. He pulled out a set of keys, closed the door, and locked it. He gave me a fleeting glance as he walked out the front door.

"Friendly he is not," I whispered.

There was a knock on the front door. I got up and opened it. Jim, a fellow I met when Autumn took me to the Sunshine Café, was standing on the front porch.

"What's happening, man?" I asked.

"I was walking down the street when I remembered Autumn said you just moved into 806, so I thought I'd stop and pay you a visit."

"Cool, man," I said, pointing to the two rattan armchairs on the porch. "Sit down."

Jim's hair wasn't much longer than mine, and I could tell that he had recently migrated to San Francisco. We were both letting our hair grow out for the first time and I sensed some kind of bond. Shortly into our conversation he told me that he had recently graduated from Indiana University, and he liked to follow various sports.

We spent an hour talking about our favorite sports teams and bantered back and forth on which was the best major league baseball team. We spent the next hour talking about professional football teams. Jim agreed with me that the best team was my favorite team, the Green Bay Packers.

I heard footsteps and saw John Robinson walking onto the porch. He stopped in his tracks when he saw Jim and me sitting in the chairs. He was wearing a faded black t-shirt and ragged jeans. His long black hair was scattered in all directions and he looked menacing. He walked forcefully toward us and began admonishing me for having a visitor at the house.

"You are not to have visitors here!" he said.

I was so stunned I didn't immediately reply.

"You are going to have to leave, now!" he shouted, pointing at Jim.

"We're just sitting here talking," I protested.

"I don't care. No visitors, no guests, period!"

Jim stood up. "It's cool, man," he said. "I'm leaving."

John turned around and walked into the house and slammed the front door. I walked with Jim to the sidewalk and apologized.

"I'm sorry. I don't know what's up with him," I said.

"No big deal," he said. "Hey, you want to go see a Giants game on Monday night at Candlestick Park?"

"Who are they playing?"

"The hated Dodgers."

"Yeah, that sounds like fun," I said, relieved that I didn't have to make more excuses for John's rude behavior.

I walked into the house and didn't see John so I assumed he was in the basement. That's where he spent an inordinate amount of his time. I walked outside to the alley to check on my truck and opened the doors to give it some fresh air. I stepped out into the alley and looked toward the Hell's Angels' domain. Numerous motorcycles were parked at the end of alley where loud music was blaring. Although I couldn't get a real good look, it appeared that there were several women and men, all dressed in motorcycle leathers, partying in the backyard of the house. I decided to grab my binoculars from the truck and go up to my bedroom, where I would have an unobstructed view of their backyard.

I walked into my bedroom, pulled back the curtains, and raised the binoculars to my eyes, focusing them on the motorcyclists' backyard. A large keg of beer stood in the middle of the yard while a barbeque grill belched out white smoke. The smoke obscured some of the party, but on the back porch, I could see what appeared to be a naked woman. I zoomed in and was startled by what I saw. She was giving one man a blowjob while another man was humping her doggy style.

I momentarily put the binoculars down in disbelief. I picked them up again and scanned the backyard. Near the barbeque grill another naked woman was sprawled on a picnic table having sexual intercourse with one man while several other men stood around her in a circle watching.

"Wow," I mumbled to myself. "They're having a gangbang."

I watched for a few moments, excited by my voyeurism, but I became disgusted when three men urinated on the woman lying on the picnic table.

Suddenly, I remembered that I hadn't called home in quite a while. I went into the kitchen and grabbed the wall phone and placed a collect call to my parents in Milwaukee. While the phone rang on the other end, I couldn't shake the image of the men urinating on the woman.

My mother's voice answered and she told the operator that she would accept the collect call.

"Hi Mom, it's Bobby. I'm in San Francisco," I said.

"Oh, Bobby! We've been so worried about you."

"Well, I made it to San Francisco safe and sound."

"Congratulations. That was your goal. What's it like?"

"Wow, it's a very unique place with some very exotic people, and I've heard some pretty intriguing ideas."

"Have you made any friends?"

"Sort of," I said. I'm going to a Giants baseball game on Monday with a new friend."

"I just got a call last night from Hoss's mom," she said.

"Did she have any news about Hoss?"

"Hoss has been shot."

I felt stunned. My legs trembled, and I wanted to make sure I understood her correctly.

"What happened?"

"I don't know all the details but she said Hoss was shot in the leg and the army was flying him back to the Naval Station Great Lakes' hospital in Illinois for an operation. It sounds like a serious wound."

"Is he going to live?" I asked as my throat tightened.

"I don't know, but I assume they wouldn't fly him from Vietnam to the United States if he was in a life-threatening situation."

Just then I heard the front screen door and could hear Maryanne speaking with someone.

"Mom, I gotta go. I'll call you tomorrow night. Can you find out more what's going on with Hoss?" I asked while covering the mouthpiece with my other hand.

"Yes, but please call tomorrow night. Your dad and I want to know what is going on with you."

I hung up the phone and stood staring out the kitchen window wondering if Hoss was going to die. Maryanne broke the spell when she walked into the kitchen with a bag of groceries. A very tall black man followed her with another bag of groceries. He wore his hair in a huge Afro and covered his muscular frame with a tight tie-dye t-shirt.

"Oh, you're here," she said upon seeing me.

"I'm going to take you up on your invitation," I said.

"Cool. This is my friend Abraham. Abraham, this is my new roommate, Bob."

"How old are you, man?" he asked.

"Eighteen going on nineteen," I replied.

"He's checking out San Francisco. He's from Wisconsin," she said.

"All right, my man," he said, extending his right hand. I extended my hand but instead of clasping each other's hand, he curled his four fingers and grabbed my hand, causing my fingers to curl around his and our thumbs across each other. Since arriving in San Francisco, this was the fourth different way of shaking hands I had experienced.

"Can I help you unload the groceries?" I asked.

Maryanne nodded.

While I was putting the groceries away, three more people arrived. One was a short, bald professor from Berkeley who wore thick black-rimmed glasses and a long, white shirt over his faded jeans and Birkenstock sandals. With him were two girls in their early twenties, wearing tank tops and blue jean shorts. I assumed they were Berkeley students.

As we all walked out onto the front porch, a tall and handsome priest, wearing his vestments, walked up the sidewalk and shouted a greeting to Maryanne. She responded with a wave and a broad smile. When the priest reached the porch, he gave Maryanne a warm hug and she greeted him by kissing him on the lips. I was stunned. I had never seen anyone kiss a priest on the lips before. As the group was exchanging greetings and introductions, I walked up to the priest and said, "My name is Bob, father."

He laughed and said, "You can call me Patrick."

"Okay, Father Patrick."

"Just Patrick will do," he said. "Drop the father thing."

For the next two hours the conversation centered on what Maryanne was going to say at her presentation that evening. Stanley Glass, the Berkeley professor, took an aggressive position, asking her to address the profit motives of the military-industrial complex in support of the Vietnam War. He had reams of statistics on the amount of money being made by companies supplying everything from bullets to aircraft.

I listened intently, but I had a hard time taking my eyes off Maryanne. Patrick was sitting next to her and eventually he took off his priest collar and outer vestment revealing a t-shirt with a brightly colored peace sign. Maryanne occasionally reached over and put her hand on his knee. The two college girls didn't say anything but were as attentive as I. Patrick chimed in that war was immoral and the United States was grossly exercising its colonial powers. You could tell that he was well versed in giving sermons, as his words were forceful and carefully chosen for maximum effect.

When there was a slight lull in the conversation, Maryanne turned to me and asked, "What do you think I should say tonight?"

I was stunned that she would ask for my thoughts. I took a moment to compose myself and said, "Let me preface my comments by saying that a year ago my high school World History textbook still called Vietnam, French Indochina."

Members of the group shook their heads in disbelief.

"It's very hard to understand why we are there fighting a war in the first place. I believe that America still has political leaders who believe in the communist domino theory. It's a carryover from the Korean War and the Dulles brothers' view of foreign policy and goes back through several administrations. I think most Americans don't understand what we are doing in Vietnam or why we went there in the first place," I said.

I hoped that I didn't say something stupid, especially in front of Maryanne, but my fears were quickly allayed.

"Well, well, our high school friend isn't a Cheesehead after all," said Maryanne smiling broadly at me.

I think I impressed her and that gave me a great deal of satisfaction.

"Okay, Bob, I want you to come with me tonight to hear my presentation," she said.

Without hesitation, I answered, "Absolutely."

At two thirty, the discussion group broke up and everyone departed. Patrick was the last to leave and gave Maryanne another big hug and again kissed her on her lips. I stood watching and wondered what was going on between the two of them. I went into the house and into my bedroom.

The sun streamed through my bedroom window, making the room warm and comfortable. I took off my t-shirt and laid down on my bed with my hands behind my head. The sun's rays bounced off the circular glass knobs on the old wooden dresser, creating a series of mini-rainbows. I thought about how different San Francisco was from Milwaukee. In the short time since I arrived in San Francisco, I had met interesting people, some very weird people, and a lot of very nice people. For an instant I felt like a traveler on a foreign planet, and yet, I had not gotten any closer to figuring out what being a hippie was all about.

It was about three hours before we would have to leave to go to Maryanne's presentation, or speech, or whatever it was going to be. I started to drift into a nap when there was a light tapping on my open bedroom door. Much to my amazement, Maryanne walked in wearing a brightly colored bikini. At the sight of her stunning body, I froze. She walked into the room and very nonchalantly sat on the edge of the bed.

"I'm going to Tahiti with Patrick next month, and I hope I look okay in this bikini," she declared.

I fruitlessly groped for a reply, but was overwhelmed by her beauty. I muttered silently, "Oh my God."

She stood up and modeled the bikini for me and twirled in a stream of sunlight from the window.

"What do you think?" she said as she stopped twirling and faced me.

"I think you will give the lifeguards a heart attack," I replied.

She laughed and sat on the edge of the bed again, this time much closer to me.

"I like you, Bob Ralston from Wisconsin."

"How's that?" I asked. "You hardly know me."

"You are intelligent. You are seeking greater knowledge and enlightenment. You are young and open-minded."

She reached over and began to run her index finger up and down my bare chest.

"And you have rock-hard abs, and you're kinda of sexy."

I lay there with my arms still behind my head, mesmerized by this beautiful woman. I was afraid to move or say anything that might ruin the moment.

She leaned forward and kissed me gently. Then she French kissed me. I took my arms from behind my head and pulled her gently onto my chest as we continued in a long kiss. I ran my fingers through her long hair and then unhooked her bikini top. She arched up and let the top tumble down her arms onto my chest. Her breasts were supple and her skin was fair.

"Do you like my breasts?" she asked softly.

My throat knotted up so I could only nod.

She slid off my chest and while sitting next to me, she reached down to unbuckle my belt. My full erection was pushing tightly against my bellbottom pants. She unbuckled the belt and unzipped my pants. She reached in and began stroking my penis gently. I was so aroused I feared I might have a premature ejaculation. She stopped and stood up and dropped her bikini bottoms to the floor. I reached down and slid my pants and underwear off. I stood up because I wanted to kiss her while she was standing there totally naked, but she playfully pushed me back onto the bed and climbed on top of me.

We began kissing gently, but quickly began kissing vigorously. Our breathing became heavier and louder. While arching her body, she reached down and grabbed my penis firmly and began rubbing the tip on her clitoris. While she was arched up, I held her right nipple between my left index finger and thumb and began gently twirling it. She let out with a deep, soft sigh as my penis penetrated her vagina.

For forty-five minutes we were locked in a passionate struggle. First she was on top, then I was on top, and then we changed to doggy style. Finally, I was on top again thrusting as quickly and deeply as I could while her soft eyes looked up at me. She let out a scream of ecstasy when she reached her climax. I was startled by the scream but found it extremely sexy causing me to ejaculate forcefully. As much as I tried not to, I moaned loudly with every pulse of sperm leaving my body. When we stopped, she laid down next to me. We were both breathing heavily and our bodies were soaked in sweat. She looked at me and said, "I'm glad you like my bikini."

Before I could answer, she bolted to her feet, picked up her bikini, and while walking out of the bedroom said, "Got to get ready for tonight."

As I lay there in the afterglow, I felt very proud of myself. I made it to San Francisco. I lived in the grooviest part of the hippest city in the country. I met new friends like Autumn and Jim, and I had just made love to the most beautiful woman in the world.

In my wildest dreams about San Francisco, I never thought it would turn out this good. My joyful thoughts mingled with the cool breeze coming in the window. Then I realized that I had forgotten to call Hoss's parents to ask how Hoss was doing.

At the exact same time Maryanne and Bob were making love, an explosion rocked the corporate offices of Parnell Resources in San Jose, California, killing twelve people. Parnell was a defense contractor that manufactured tracer bullets for the US Army's M-16 rifles being used in Vietnam.

Chapter 33

Hoss squinted at the harsh fluorescent lights above him. He was being moved on a noisy gurney from his room into the surgery center at the Naval Station Great Lakes' hospital and rehabilitation center. As he listened to the gurney's wheels clatter on the tile hallway floor, he felt angry that he had been wounded by friendly fire. He had been shot by another US Army infantryman when he stood up and ran forward in the tall grass.

Despite his anger, he knew he was lucky to be alive. The bullet from the M-16 rifle struck his upper left leg, just missing the femoral artery by a quarter of an inch. The bullet shattered six inches of his femur. If the bullet had severed the femoral artery, he would have bled to death within minutes.

The orderly wheeled the gurney into the operating room where Hoss's surgeon, Doctor Gene Sorensen, stood at the entrance in an operating gown. Sorensen, an accomplished surgeon and an army major, would operate on many of the wounded soldiers, Marines, Air Force, and Navy personnel that arrived with Hoss.

Sorensen met with Hoss the day before and counseled him that he would have to do a bone graft. He told Hoss he would take part of Hoss's left hip and graft it in a splint-like device that would eventually allow the graft to join the shattered femur back together. He said that if the operation was successful, Hoss's left leg would be about one to two inches shorter than his right leg. It was likely that Hoss would have to wear a specially designed shoe for the rest of his life. He went on to say that there was a good chance that Hoss would get arthritis later in life. Sorensen also told Hoss that after rehabilitation was completed, Hoss would probably walk with a slight limp.

"Are you ready to do this, soldier?" Sorensen asked Hoss.

"Let's do it, Doc. I want my left leg in one piece, not two," Hoss replied in a soft voice.

Hoss knew that even if the surgery went extremely well, he was in for a long and painful rehabilitation. Orderlies had told him that, at a minimum, he would be in the hospital for six months after the surgery.

When the orderlies lifted Hoss from the gurney onto the operating table, Hoss saw the entire surgical team of four nurses and two doctors putting on their blue surgical masks and surgical gloves. Moments after the anesthesia began dripping into his right arm, Hoss faded into unconsciousness.

Just as Hoss' surgery began, a massive explosion obliterated the National Guard Armory in Tracy, California, sixty-three miles east of San Francisco, seriously injuring fourteen National Guardsmen sleeping in the armory's barracks and killing two.

The FBI investigated the incident but made no comment. A preliminary report, obtained by a *San Francisco Chronicle* reporter, indicated that a large satchel of dynamite was the probable cause. *The New York Times* quoted FBI Special Agent Crens that the FBI would not rest until it caught the perpetrators and brought them to justice.

When Hoss woke up in the recovery room, he saw his parents standing beside his bed. Hoss felt groggy when he heard his mom's voice.

"The surgery went very well," she said. "Doctor Sorensen expects the bone graft will be successful."

Hoss just nodded and then drifted back to sleep.

His mother broke down sobbing to see her son so pale and gaunt. His father knew Hoss was in for a long and tough road to recovery and wiped a tear from his eye as he grasped his wife's hand. Both of them knew they had to be as supportive as possible and not let Hoss see their concerns. They made plans to drive down from Milwaukee every weekend to visit Hoss, no matter how long it took. Next Saturday would be his nineteenth birthday and they planned to bring him a birthday cake with vanilla frosting, his favorite.

Chapter 34

Maryanne and I climbed into my truck and drove off toward the University of California, Davis, about seventy-five minutes east of San Francisco, for her speech. She looked striking, which aroused my desires to have more sex with her.

Her jet-black hair swept down her back and over a black t-shirt with a picture of Huey Newton on the front. She was not wearing a bra and her breasts and nipples were eye candy for me, a horny eighteen-year-old. As I drove, I kept glancing over at her, but she took no notice of me. She intently studied the notes for her speech.

When we pulled into the auditorium parking lot at UC-Davis, I was surprised to see so many people milling around the auditorium entrance. There were at least three hundred people, probably more, waiting to get in. I was able to squeeze the truck between a light standard and a fence in a poorly marked parking spot.

While we were walking toward the entrance, I noticed a significant number of African-American men and women waiting to get in, and most of the men had large Afros. As we approached the crowd, numerous people recognized and greeted Maryanne with hugs. Maryanne turned and nodded to me, and then walked into the auditorium talking to several individuals that crowded around her.

I found a seat about three-quarters of the way back from the stage and I was surrounded by college students. Virtually all the students, men and women, had long hair. Although my hair had grown longer in the forty-five days since graduation, it was considerably shorter than any other male in attendance. I felt self-conscious and inferior. I wanted to fit in, not stand out. When people looked at me, I felt a strange vibe. I wondered if they wondered who I was, and what I was doing there.

The auditorium was filled to capacity. I looked at the fire marshal's sign on a wall near the stage and determined that at least four hundred and fifty people were in attendance. Suddenly the house lights went down and a tall, thin Caucasian man, wearing a long flowing silk shirt with African patterns, approached the podium and spoke in a fiery baritone voice, instantly commanding the audience's attention.

"Good evening, comrades," he said. "America is staggering under the weight of greedy capitalism and choking on its colonialist ambitions. Whether it's in Argentina, Vietnam, or Panama, America has spread unrest, deception, death, and despair. This corrupt foreign affairs approach has created a deep distrust of the US government. Capitalism has abandoned working families, here and abroad, all to line the pockets of rich industrialists. Those who profit from death and destruction have led America down a path from which we will never return. Thousands of young American men have died in a war in Vietnam that only benefits members of the military-industrial complex. Under the flimsy guise of stopping communistic aggression, America has propped up corrupt dictators across the globe. Dictators are only interested in self-gratification and the accumulation of enormous amounts of wealth at the expense of their fellow citizens, but they will reap what they sow.

"Tonight, it is my pleasure to introduce a woman who is teaching and enlightening young people on the evil ways of the American government and the decadent principles of capitalism. Because she speaks the truth, the government harasses her and tries to silence her voice. Twice, FBI thugs broke into her office at the University of San Francisco. Thankfully, the ACLU has prevailed in court to defend her free speech rights. There are probably FBI undercover agents sitting in this audience tonight. But nothing ever silences or replaces the truth. And nothing will stop her from continuing on the righteous path she leads others on. Please welcome Professor Maryanne Cetio."

The audience rose to its feet with robust applause. Maryanne walked onto the stage with a captivating smile and she waved to the crowd. Suddenly I realized, that although I just had made love to this woman, I had no idea who she was. I looked at the flyer, given to me as I entered the auditorium, and quickly read her biography. I was more than surprised to read that she was a prominent member of the American Communist Party, and that earlier in the year she had led a faculty and student occupation of USF's chancellor's office for seven days. Her father was a famous member of the Italian Communist Party who fought alongside the partisans during the Second World War in occupied Italy. Her mother was a published poet, and Maryanne was an only child. She and her parents had moved to San Francisco in the early 1950s. She walked to the podium and began her speech in a commanding voice.

"When you look at President Johnson's blood-stained hands, and the bloody hands of profiteers, it's hard to be proud of America. It's difficult to walk the back roads of Tennessee and West Virginia and see the extreme poverty and squalor while our government spends hundreds of millions of dollars fighting a war in Vietnam. Vietnam is where an indigenous population is trying to break the centuries-old chains of colonialism and servitude to foreigners. It's difficult to be proud of a country that ignores the plight of homeless citizens in every city within its borders. It's difficult to encourage women and blacks to strive for a higher education and meaningful professional careers when there is a smothering veil of discrimination that prevents advancement. And this country's leaders are not interested in its citizens, they are only interested in getting reelected. Their priorities are not aligned with the aspirations, needs, and desires of the American people. They want to suppress discourse, meaningful discussion, and disagreement that don't promote their narrow capitalistic goals. Government should serve its citizens, not enslave them."

Maryanne's speech enthralled the audience. As her anti-American rhetoric and voice rose, so did the fevered pitch of the audience's cheers and applause. Maryanne continued to denigrate virtually every American ideal, institution, and political leader.

"Next year, America goes through its ritual of electing a new president. It's a cruel hoax perpetrated on the needy citizens of this country. Every year, the number of people living below the poverty line increases. Every year, the number of millionaires serving in the US Senate and Congress increases. These people are nothing more than lackeys for the industrialists who make millions upon millions of dollars making weapons, bombs, airplanes, and bullets for an unjust war in Vietnam."

The crowd rose to its feet with thunderous cheers and applause. I stood up and clapped. Anti-American slogans echoed throughout the auditorium. It appeared for a moment to be a well-rehearsed theatrical presentation until I saw the deep convictions reflected in the eyes of people sitting around me. Maryanne's speech lasted forty-five minutes and she worked the crowd into a lather.

I had never been exposed to so much anti-American rhetoric. Although I was disturbed by the war in Vietnam, I didn't want to tear down and dismantle America. That thought never entered my mind. I always believed in improving, reenergizing, rebuilding, not tearing down, discarding, and destroying. It was now abundantly clear that I was in a gathering of communists, socialists, and social anarchists and that made me feel very uneasy; plus the menacing looks I was getting from some individuals made me paranoid that I was suspected of being an undercover FBI agent. By the end of Maryanne's speech, I felt totally uncomfortable and out of place.

When the crowd filed out of the auditorium, I remained in my seat. For ten minutes I watched Maryanne greet and talk to admirers as she walked down from the stage. I felt ashamed that my mind quickly shifted from contemplation of discrimination and societal and international issues to lusting after Maryanne. I didn't care if she was communist, I wanted to make love to her again, and again, and again.

I finally walked toward where Maryanne was talking with a small group of people. She saw me and motioned me over. I walked up to her and she greeted me with a smile as we stepped aside from the small gathering of people.

"What do you think?" she asked.

"Wow, my head is spinning. That's a lot to digest," I replied.

I reached out and grasped her and asked, "Do you want to go get a drink or something to eat?"

The smile instantly disappeared from her face and was replaced with a pained expression. She pulled me farther aside and spoke in a firm, but hushed voice.

"What happened today was a fling. It may happen again, or it may never happen again. Stop acting like you are back in high school. We aren't going steady and I am not your girlfriend. I'm going out with Patrick. So go home."

I stood there dumbfounded, unable to respond.

She returned to her well-wishers, which included Patrick, the Catholic priest. I was devastated. I had never been put down or so summarily dismissed by a woman like that in my life. I felt two inches tall. She totally eviscerated my manhood.

I shuffled out of the auditorium with a hangdog look. My pride was vaporized. I felt like I was just kicked in the gut and I developed a stomachache as I walked to the truck.

Suddenly a loud explosion rocked the parking lot and I almost fell to the ground. A large group of people leaving the event began running in all directions. Huge flames erupted from the roof of the nearby Science building. The scene instantly turned chaotic. I careened off people as I tried to make my way to my truck at the far end of the parking lot. I was knocked to the ground by the surging crowd but got up quickly out of fear of being trampled. My left arm was cut and bleeding. As I turned around to get my bearings, another person ran into me and knocked me down onto the asphalt. That person also fell to the ground. We both stood up and looked at each other. I was startled when I recognized it was my grumpy roommate John. Just as I spoke, he turned quickly and ran off in the opposite direction.

I made it to my truck and climbed in the back looking for my first-aid kit. My left shirtsleeve was soaked in blood. Upon examining the injury, I realized it was a long but minor laceration, nothing serious. I wrapped cotton gauze around my arm and climbed into the driver's seat.

There were still quite a few people running near the area where I was parked. I backed the truck out of the stall and headed for the parking lot exit. I could hear numerous wailing sirens. When I pulled out onto the street, a parade of six fire engines and a series of ambulances went screeching by in the opposite direction.

After all the commotion, the drive back to San Francisco was quiet and uneventful. When I pulled into the alley behind the house, I could see that the Hell's Angels were having a large party. Motorcycles were parked all over the alley. Some were even parked near our garage. I was grateful that no one parked their motorcycle in my parking spot. The last thing in the world I wanted to do was to have to confront a Hell's Angel.

I went inside, quickly got undressed, and took a shower. I called out for John to see if he was home, but there was no reply. Since Maryanne was out with Patrick, and John wasn't home, I sat down and ate some yogurt in the kitchen in my underwear. I began thinking about all that had transpired over the last few hours.

I climbed into my bed and tried to analyze everything that I heard, saw, and experienced. My left arm ached and I discovered that my right hip had a large bruise. The bruise ached more than my left arm. As I started to nod off to sleep, I thought about Melissa. I missed her company. When I heard a mournful foghorn wailing on the bay, I felt lonely. Then I wondered how Jim Gaston was doing. I wondered how Hoss was doing. Then I got angry with myself because I hadn't called Hoss's parents. At last sleep came, but not before a final question entered my consciousness. Did I belong in San Francisco?

Chapter 35

I finally got out of bed and puttered about my bedroom getting dressed in shorts, a white V-neck t-shirt, and sandals. I heard some noise coming up from the basement and knew that John must have come home late last night. There was no sign of Maryanne so I assumed she must have spent the night with Patrick. The thought of her with Patrick made me jealous. What the hell was a priest doing fornicating with a woman? Then a devious thought raced through my head.

"I ought to call the Archbishop of San Francisco and report him," I muttered quietly.

I walked across the street to see if Autumn was home. I wanted to ask her to join me for breakfast. She was standing on the sidewalk in a jogging outfit and talking with a group of three men and three women.

"Autumn," I called out.

She turned and smiled when she recognized me. "Good morning," she called. Then she noticed the bandage on my left arm. "What happened to your arm?"

"I went to see Maryanne speak last night and there was some kind of fire which caused a huge panic. I got knocked down in the stampede," I replied.

"No way!" she shouted and grabbed my uninjured arm. "That wasn't a fire. It was a bomb that blew up the Science building. Three people were killed and a dozen more seriously injured!"

"What?"

"It was a bomb purposely set off to destroy the Science building. The story is all over today's *Chronicle*. The FBI said they believe many of the bomb attacks in the western United States were committed by the same group or same individual," she said.

I pondered what she just said and asked, "Do want to go to Breakfast?"

"I can't today. I'm running in the Bay to Breakers Race."

"What's the Bay to Breakers Race?"

"It's a very cool race. People get dressed up in elaborate costumes and run in the race. It's a lot of fun. You should do it one day."

Before I could reply, one of the men Autumn was talking with called out that it was time to go to the race.

"Gotta go. See you later," she smiled.

The rest of Sunday was a blur. I wandered around Golden Gate Park and sat on benches, people-watching. I saw a rare sight: families with children in San Francisco, playing in the park. There was a local rock band, Moby Grape, playing in a dilapidated band shell in the east end of the park. They attracted a large crowd and I heard they had a strong local following in San Francisco.

There were lots of girls in bikinis and short halter-tops, bounding about the band shell and waving brightly colored ribbons on long sticks, blowing soap bubbles, and dancing merrily.

Normally, girls in skimpy clothing attracted my attention, but I was in a funky mood. I felt sorry for myself; Maryanne had burst my bubble. I was no longer the happy-go-lucky high school graduate adventurer, and my mood soured further because I didn't like Moby Grape's music. They sounded like the Grateful Dead, a band I just didn't get. I never understood why people liked the Grateful Dead and their music, but I had to admit they had a very large and loyal following.

Out of boredom and a depressed mood, I went for a cold beer at a small bar near my house. The bartenders there always accepted my fake Wisconsin ID card. I didn't want to go home for a while. I didn't want to run into Maryanne there. I wasn't sure how we would interact from now on. Despite the sting of her rejection, I was still very attracted to her. I was willing to forgive a lot, including her being a card-carrying communist, fooling around with a priest, and putting me in my place. I just wanted to be intimate with her again.

I spent the late afternoon sitting on a wooden bar stool at the Market Street Bar drinking a few beers and chatting with fellow bar mates. There was very little talk of political ideology in the bar. The conversation was dominated by San Francisco Giants fans who were talking about the tight pennant race with the hated Los Angeles Dodgers. When I mentioned that I was going to the Giants game the next day, my announcement was greeted with envy. By the time I left the bar, I had consumed eight beers, more than I normally drank. I had to ask the bartender directions on how to get back to Haight Street. When I got home it was dark. I just flopped down on my bed and passed out.

The sunlight flooding in my bedroom window cruelly reflected off the dresser mirror and onto my face. I was hung over. I rolled over and looked at my alarm clock; it was eight thirty. Fortunately I didn't have to meet Jim and go to Candlestick Park for the Giants game until about noon. It was going to take me that long to start feeling better.

As we had agreed, I met Jim in front of his house, got into his faded blue 1963 Chevy Impala sedan and headed off to the ballgame.

The game had a one o'clock start time and there was light traffic on the 101 freeway south out of the city. Jim had purchased the tickets in advance, so we went to the will call window and then strolled into the stadium.

I was delighted that from our seats on the second level, I could see the southern reaches of San Francisco Bay, but I soon learned that there was a price to be paid for seats with a view. By the second inning, there was a strong, damp, and foggy breeze blowing in from left field that forced me to put on my jacket. Jim warned me to take a jacket to the game despite my objection that it was a sunny summer day in the City. I realized that Mark Twain was correct about summers in San Francisco.

Jim was chatty about baseball and the Giants through the first several innings. Then he began asking me questions on my political views: what I thought about the Vietnam War, the unrest in America, including the recent riots in several cities across America. I gave him half-hearted answers because I was more interested in watching two very good baseball teams play.

In the seventh inning with the Giants losing 4-2, he asked how I felt about the bombings by revolutionaries, including the blast that I experienced at UC Davis. His tone was quite serious and his persistence was beginning to annoy me.

"I think I was in the wrong place at the wrong time at Davis. I guess I'm lucky I didn't get killed. That's probably true for my roommates."

"Your roommates were at Davis at the time of the explosion?" he asked.

"Maryanne was giving a speech there."

"Was John there too?"

I put my beer down and turned to Jim and said, "I came to see a ballgame to get away from all the trouble and strife in the world for a few hours. I don't want to talk about the Vietnam War and bombings and revolutionaries. I'm sorry, I'm still hung over, so give it rest, okay?"

He immediately lightened up and said, "Okay, that's cool. The only way to fight a hangover is to get some hair of the dog. I'm going to get a couple of beers."

I was puzzled why a recent high school graduate's views on important national and international issues would be of any interest to a graduate of a Big Ten university.

When he returned with the beers, the Giants were coming to bat in the bottom of the seventh inning. When the public address system began playing "Take Me Out to the Ball Game," dozens of protesters in the left bleachers unfurled a banner that read "Stop the War!" Dozens of ushers rushed in and tried to grab the banner. A scuffle ensued and scores of police officers intervened and hauled off several longhaired, bearded protestors. There was a mixed chorus of cheers and boos as the protesters were led out of the stadium.

"Can't even get away from a fucking anti-war protest at a baseball game," I complained.

The game went into extra innings and in the bottom of the twelfth inning, the Giants scored the winning run.

Chapter 36

$\mathfrak{a}$ gent Crens poured his third cup of coffee of the morning and looked at his watch. In ten minutes, he had a high-level meeting with the FBI's forensic laboratory team on domestic terrorism. He raised the coffee cup to his lips and looked out the window in the spacious conference room on the third floor of the FBI headquarters building in Washington, D.C. He wondered if the forensic team had finally collected enough evidence to identify the individual, or individuals, responsible for the bombings in California.

The forensic team already knew that the dynamite used in the University of California Davis bombing was purchased at the mining and farming supply store in Lodi, California. They contacted the manufacturer, Cummings Chemical Company of Reno, Nevada, and the general manager stated that there had been no unusual activity in dynamite sales in California or Nevada, but he did say that it wouldn't be hard to steal dynamite from the numerous mining sites in Nevada due to the lax security of the mining companies. This quandary befuddled investigators. Were the perpetrators buying the dynamite in California or stealing from Nevada mine sites, or both?

For more than three years, the FBI had assembled a list of suspected terrorists across the country and put them under close surveillance. The Bureau convinced a federal judge in Chicago to grant permission for dozens of telephone wiretaps. The FBI also had more than two hundred undercover agents infiltrating suspected terrorist organizations. In a few moments, Special Agent Crens would learn the results of this aggressive and comprehensive domestic surveillance effort.

The conference room door opened and a group of ten individuals walked in. They carried large dossiers that contained laboratory results, photos, audiotapes from wiretaps, and undercover agent reports. Crens turned away from the window and joined them at the long oak conference table.

Special Agent Mike Melser, a handsome forty-two-year-old graduate from Columbia Law School, led the procession of agents into the room. He was in charge of the domestic surveillance program and reported directly to FBI Director J. Edgar Hoover. Melser, who was in his twentieth year at the agency, got right down to business.

"Richard, I have some good news. We have identified the guy who is responsible for at least six or seven of the bombings in California. We also have identified two groups in New York and Connecticut responsible for the Dow Chemical and five other bombings on the East Coast."

A broad smile came across Crens' face as he spoke. "What do you have?"

Melser opened a large dossier folder and said, "The type of dynamite used in California is all the same. It was purchased in Lodi by an individual using a fake State of California Explosive Ordnance Operators license. We placed a surveillance team at the mining and farming implement store in Lodi and were able to photograph the individual and trace the vehicle he used."

"Who is he?"

"A white male, thirty-one years old, named John Robinson, who lives in the Haight-Ashbury District of San Francisco. He has no previous record, but has been photographed with known members of the Weathermen Underground."

"Do we have a positive ID that he purchased the dynamite?" Crens asked reaching for the folder.

"We were able to get his fingerprints from the counter at the store in Lodi and get into a garage that he rents on Haight Street where he parks his car. We have his matching fingerprints and a chemical analysis that dynamite was present in the trunk of his vehicle, the same dynamite sold at the Lodi store."

"Great. What's our next move?"

"Well, as of now we could only arrest him on an accessory to a crime since we have no evidence that he actually detonated any explosive device. If we arrested him now he probably gets charged for having a fake explosive operator's license and buying dynamite illegally. Although those are both felonies, he'd probably get some liberal San Francisco judge to give him probation," Melser answered.

"We sure as shit don't want that. If he is the bomber, we have to positively tie him to a bombing. We need a witness, or someone who can rat him out, or catch him red-handed in the act," Crens replied with a stern face.

"We've had a wiretap on his phone and have been following his every move," Melser said.

"What's the story on this guy? Is he married, single? Where does he work"?

"He is a professor at Berkeley and appears to be a real loner. He is single and shares a house on Haight Street with a couple of people. We are getting information and background checks on them."

"Any chance he could be storing dynamite at his residence? That is potentially very dangerous. That motherfucker could blow up a whole city block. I don't know how much longer we can wait because there may be a bunch of dynamite sitting in the basement of a house in the heart of San Francisco. If that shit blows up and it comes out that the Bureau suspected there was dynamite there and did nothing about it, all hell is going to break loose," Crens said.

"Okay, here's what we are going to do. Tomorrow, we are going to send a forensic guy dressed as a PG&E serviceman to his residence and see if we can get access to the house and the basement. Then we will see if there is any indication of dynamite present. He'll take an explosive detector with him and if we get any real indication that dynamite is present, we'll send out the bomb squad and arrest the guy the minute he comes home from Berkeley," Melser said.

"I really wish we could play this out a bit more to see if he is connected to any group or is acting alone, but I don't think we have a choice here. This is too big a public safety risk," Crens said rising out of his seat.

Chapter 37

Tuesday morning started like most San Francisco summer mornings, foggy and cold. I could barely make out the top of Coit Tower as I started on a two-block walk to Raymond's Deli for breakfast and coffee. When I locked the front door and turned around, a man in dark blue overalls wearing a baseball cap with the letters PG&E, and carrying some sort of equipment, walked up onto the porch. He had a plastic identification badge hanging on a tether around his neck that indicated that he worked for Pacific Gas & Electric.

"Good morning," he said. "I'm with PG&E and we are responding to a possible gas leak in the neighborhood."

"Good morning," I said.

"Could I go inside and check your stove and furnace to make sure there is no gas leak?"

"I guess, but I'm not the owner. I just rent a room here."

"That's fine. We just have to make sure that this house doesn't have a gas leak that could be explosive," he answered.

I stepped back in front of the door. "Do you have some identification that you are a PG&E employee?"

He held out his identification badge, and I stepped forward to examine it. The badge had his picture, his name, a PG&E logo, and looked perfectly authentic, so I opened the door and followed him in.

Once inside, he walked into the kitchen and examined the stove.

"No gas leak here," he declared. "Where is the furnace?"

"I don't really know. I guess in the basement," I answered.

"Can you show me where the basement is?"

"Yeah, but one of my roommates always keeps the door locked. I've never been down there."

"Is your roommate home?" he asked.

"No, he's at work. He teaches at Berkeley."

"Show me where the basement door is. I may have to remove the lock in order to inspect the basement," he stated.

"I don't think he's going to like that. He doesn't let anyone go down into the basement."

"This is serious business. If there is a gas leak in this house, it could cause a major explosion. If I have to, I will call the police and they will force you to open the door," he said with an intense stare.

"Look, it's cool with me, but I don't have a key to the basement door," I replied.

"That's okay. I have tools that can open a lock. We have to do it all the time when we get locked out and there is a gas leak," he said.

I showed him the basement door and watched him pick the lock in about a minute. He turned on the basement light, which I thought was a bit odd since a gas leak can be ignited by an electric switch. He carried his equipment down the stairs and I decided not to follow him for fear I would incur my roommate's wrath.

I could hear him rummaging around the basement. He spent fifteen minutes in the basement and came up and closed the basement door and re-locked it.

"Okay, I did a complete inspection of the furnace and the incoming gas lines, and there is no leak," he declared. "Sorry for the inconvenience."

I followed him out the front door and then headed off to the deli wondering if I should tell John that someone had violated his secret sanctuary.

On the way back from the deli I saw Autumn coming out of her house and waved to her. She responded by skip-stepping toward me with a broad smile, her hair flowing in the breeze.

"Good morning, Bob Ralston of Wisconsin," she said gleefully.

"Good morning, Autumn of Haight Street."

"Are you doing anything today?"

"Just the usual. Trying to decide what to do with my life. No big deal." I chuckled.

"Have you ever been to Angel Island out on the bay?"

"No. Remember I just got here a couple of weeks ago."

"We can catch a boat out to the island, hike around, and have lunch. Want to go?"

"Angel Island. Hmm, maybe I can get some divine intervention in my quest for the meaning of life," I said with a smirk. "Sure, let's go. Sounds like a blast."

"Cool. Get a pair of shorts on, some shoes for hiking, and a hat. It'll be sunny and hot on the island. I'll pack a lunch for both of us. See you out here in forty-five minutes," she said.

"Hot and sunny on the bay–is that possible?"

"You'll see. Angel Island is a far-out place. Oh, bring a jacket for the boat ride to the island. Once you get there, you won't need it," she said as she walked away toward her house.

The boat for Angel Island left from Pier 32 on the famous San Francisco Embarcadero, which is right next to Pier 33 where the boat to Alcatraz Island was moored. Pier 33 was swarming with tourists trying to get tickets for the tour of the infamous prison. Unfortunately, many of them were disappointed because prison tours boats were normally sold out weeks in advance.

Conversely, Pier 32 only had about two-dozen people queued up for tickets to Angel Island. When Autumn and I arrived, I wondered why there was such a great disparity in the two destinations.

"Are you sure about going to Angel Island?" I asked.

"You'll see. It's a special place," she said.

Autumn wore a pair of white shorts, a tight maroon tank top, and a San Francisco Giants' baseball cap. Her blonde hair, tied in pigtails, was very cute. Her complexion was radiant, her blue eyes glistened, her smile was infectious, and her kind personality was endearing. Autumn was sweet, kind, and sexy all at the same time.

The boat ride to Angel Island, near the Sausalito side of the bay, provided a unique view of Alcatraz Island and a stunning view of the San Francisco skyline. We spent the early afternoon hiking, and she was right: it was sunny and hot.

We hiked to the peak of the island, about four hundred feet above the bay, and sat at the summit to eat lunch. Our perch high above the water furnished us with an exquisite view of San Francisco. It seemed as if we could reach out and touch the buildings across the bay.

"So what do you think?" she asked. "Pretty cool place huh?"

"Wow. Very far out. The view from up here is incredible."

"It's such a great place to get away from everything."

"Sometimes I wonder what I am doing here, why I came to San Francisco and where I am going to end up?" I said rubbing my forehead.

She leaned over and put her arm around my shoulder in a comforting manner and spoke softly. "There is a Greek philosopher who said it is difficult to see or understand what's going on when you are deeply involved in something. It's equally difficult to see and understand when you are outside looking in, because you're not really in it or really experiencing it. We choose to follow paths in our lives that often end up in much different destinations than we planned or expected.

"So what are you saying? We mostly don't know what the hell we're doing or where the hell we're going?"

"That gets into the debate about fate and destiny. I believe that we influence our destiny by the choices we make in our lives. Our fate is controlled by circumstances and forces beyond our control. If you're a religious person, then you believe that God controls your fate."

"I enjoy studying world religions and they all believe in some sort of a supreme being. It's just so hard to understand how God, if there is a God, would let the world become such a screwed-up place," I said.

"Those are intensely personal questions that only an individual can answer. I believe that your time on earth is the most important. What you do, what you say, how you treat people, how you live your life with honor and integrity is, in the end, all you can really control," she said.

"I thought I would find something in San Francisco that would give me a greater meaning of life. So far, I have seen a lot of pretty spaced-out people with some pretty bizarre ideas. I'm running out of time. Either I decide to go to college in a month or two, or I'll get drafted and sent to Vietnam when I turn nineteen."

"You could go to Canada or Mexico and hang out there for a while."

"I don't speak French or Spanish, so I can't see myself doing that for the rest of my life."

"Well, you're going to have to decide for yourself what you want to do. No one can do it for you. Even your friends can't help you make an important personal decision"

"Yeah," I grumbled in a pensive mood. "Of all the people I have met in San Francisco, you're the only one I would consider a friend," I said.

"A friend who would like to be your lover too," she replied taking my hand.

I turned and looked into her eyes. I knew that I would use her only for sexual gratification because I really wanted to be Maryanne's lover. I didn't want to jeopardize Autumn's friendship, which meant much more to me than jumping into bed with her. Nevertheless, she was very attractive and there was a sincere sweetness and honesty about her.

My brain momentarily flashed the idea that she was not born with original sin. She was just too honest and too sincere to be burdened with that, but now I had to turn away her amorous advance without offending her.

"Autumn, there was a time when I would have been all over you. You are a babe and a deeply spiritual person, but I don't want to complicate our friendship, a friendship I truly value. I can imagine how sweet making love to you would be, but my head just isn't there. Please don't take this wrong. You mean a lot to me. I really mean that, but let's just be friends for now, okay?" She nodded, smiled, and kissed me on the check.

"Let's smoke a little hash. That'll brighten up your mood," she said.

We smoked a tiny hash cube in a small hash pipe. When we stood up, I gave her a big hug. We spent the rest of the afternoon hiking all over the island, laughing, joking, and chasing after one another. It was the most pleasant day I had spent in San Francisco. On the boat ride back, we talked about our childhoods and our families. She told me she went steady with her high school boyfriend for two years until she caught him dating another girl from a neighboring high school. I listened to her voice and questioned why I didn't want to make love to this darling and incredible young woman. When the boat docked, I gave her a kiss on her cheek.

Chapter 38

When Autumn and I rounded the corner onto Haight Street, we saw numerous fire engines, police cars with red lights flashing, and unmarked police cars on the block in front of our houses.

"Holy shit. Maybe there was a gas explosion," I exclaimed.

"Gas explosion?"

"Yeah, a gas repairman came to my house this morning before we left and said that there might be a gas leak on our block."

"Wow, I hope no one got hurt."

As we approached the police barriers, we could see that numerous first responders were walking in and out of my house at 806 Haight Street. We looked at each other and I grimaced. When we reached the police barrier, I called out to a police officer guarding the perimeter.

"What's going on?"

"Not sure, but I heard it has to do with explosives in the house," the officer replied above the din.

With all the noise and excitement going on, I wasn't sure I understood him correctly.

"What? Was there an explosion in the house?" I yelled.

"No explosion. I think there are explosives in the house," he replied in a loud voice.

I asked Autumn, "Did he say explosives in the house?"

"Yeah, he said explosives in the house," she answered while reaching out and grabbing my arm.

I walked up to the officer and said, "I live in that house."

The officer stared at me intently and grabbed his handheld radio and called for additional officers to come to his location. Suddenly Autumn and I were surrounded by a dozen police officers.

A short stocky officer approached me and said, "Do you reside at 806 Haight Street?"

"Yes, I live at 806," I replied.

"What's your name?"

"Bob Ralston."

"Do you live at 806 too?" he said, pointing at Autumn.

"No, I live across the street," she answered.

"What's your name?"

"Autumn Thomas."

The officer turned to me and said, "You'll have to come down to the station house. We have some questions for you. Put your hands out. I am going to handcuff you."

"Handcuff me? I didn't do anything," I protested.

Then two police officers standing behind me grabbed my arms and the officer slapped a set of handcuffs on me. Autumn and I exchanged worried looks as the officers placed me in the back seat of a dark blue unmarked police car. Two plainclothes officers climbed into the front seat. My hands were handcuffed behind my back so it was a terribly uncomfortable ride.

It took fifteen minutes to get to wherever they were taking me to be questioned, and my wrists ached. When the car pulled up in front of a four-story gray building, I noticed an FBI logo on the front door intercom system.

"I thought we were going to the police station. Why does it say FBI on the front door?" I asked.

The officer in the front passenger seat turned and said, "We're FBI agents and you are going to be interviewed by the FBI," he stated.

"FBI!" I said in astonishment.

I was led into an interview room, where I could tell there was a one-way mirror on the wall facing me. Four FBI agents, dressed in suits and ties, came into the room, and one unshackled my wrists.

"Mr. Ralston, my name is Special Agent Crens, and we would like to ask you a few questions about where you live and about your roommates and your friends," he stated.

"Why the hell am I being questioned by the FBI?"

"We'll ask the questions, Mr. Ralston," Crens quickly replied. "Do you know an individual named John Robinson?"

"Yes, he is one of my roommates in the house where I rent a room."

"Have you ever traveled anywhere with Mr. Robinson?"

"No. I barely know the guy. He's not very friendly or talkative."

"Have you ever associated with any of Mr. Robinson's friends or relatives?"

"No, I have only lived in that house for a few weeks."

"Do you know a Maryanne Cetio?"

"Yes, she is my other roommate at 806 Haight Street."

"Mr. Ralston, who is Hoss?"

"Hoss? Hoss is a high school buddy of mine from Milwaukee. What does Hoss have to do with any of this?"

"Does Hoss have any connection to John Robinson?"

"What the hell are you talking about? Hoss was in Vietnam in the Army," I sputtered while slamming my hand on the table. "He has nothing to do with John Robinson."

It occurred to me that the telephone at the house was tapped when I finally called his parents to find out how Hoss was doing, that's how his name came up.

"Mr. Ralston, where were you last Saturday night?"

"I went with my roommate Maryanne to the University of California-Davis," I replied. "She was giving a speech there."

"Did John Robinson go with you to Davis?"

"No, I drove Maryanne in my truck."

"Is that your truck parked in the alley behind the house?"

"Yeah, it's my truck. Do you mind telling me what this is all about?"

"John Robinson has been arrested and charged with murder and bombing several buildings and businesses, including the blast at UC, Davis last Saturday night," Crens said.

I was dumbfounded. I sat back in the chair and rubbed my eyes with both hands. I looked at the floor for a moment trying to make sense of what Agent Crens said and everything going on around me.

"What makes you think John Robinson is responsible for the bombings?" I finally asked.

Crens became even more annoyed with my question.

"We don't have time for fifty questions, Mr. Ralston. John Robinson purchased dozens of dynamite sticks, and today we found that he stored two dozen of them in your house. Did you know he was storing dynamite in the house?"

"Are you out of your mind? I haven't said five words to the guy since I moved in, and I have never been in the basement."

"How do you know he was storing the dynamite in the basement?" Crens pressed.

"I don't know. I just assumed that's where he would store them."

Then it struck me. "Wait a minute. Was the guy in blue overalls that came to the house this morning and went down in the basement an FBI agent?" I asked.

"I can't answer that. That is part of an ongoing investigation," Crens snapped back.

"Probably was," I quipped.

"Mr. Ralston, have you ever been involved in a bombing or assisted those who have set off bombs in the United States?" Crens asked standing over me with an intense stare.

"Are you out of your mind?" I leaned forward in my chair. "I was a high school senior in Milwaukee up until about a month ago. I just arrived in San Francisco a couple of weeks ago. I haven't been involved in any bombings!" I said raising my voice.

Crens motioned to one of the agents standing by the door. The door opened, and to my astonishment, in walked Jim Logan, the guy Autumn introduced me to. We had gone to the Giants game together the week before.

"What the hell are you doing here?" I blurted out.

Jim nodded to Crens and sat down at the conference table directly across from me.

"Did they arrest you too?" I asked Jim in bewilderment.

Before he could answer, Crens spoke up. "James Logan is an FBI special agent."

"You're kidding! You're a fucking FBI undercover agent?" I blurted out.

"Watch your language," Crens said.

"Bob, I am an FBI special agent assigned to San Francisco," Jim said.

"And here I thought you were my friend."

"I am your friend."

"No, you're not! You're paid to make friends and spy on people."

"This is about people killing fellow American citizens and trying to start a revolution to bring down our government," Logan replied leaning toward me with a serious expression.

"Save the patriotic shit. I'm not some naïve kid," I replied while clenching my fists.

"On one hand you say you're just a recent high school graduate, and on the other hand you say you're a sophisticated individual. Which is it? Are you hanging around with declared communists and members of the Weathermen Underground because you think it's cool?" Logan asked. "Look, we could charge you for being an accessory to a crime because virtually every jury in this country is going to believe you knew there was dynamite in the basement. When I went to your house, I wiped several surfaces, like the front door knob for samples and there were chemical traces of dynamite all around the porch. Meaning that someone in that house, you, were handling or storing dynamite."

"Okay, I can see where this is going. Let's scare the kid," I said sitting back in the chair with a disgusted look. "What do you want from me?"

Agent Crens sat down next to Jim Logan and spoke. "Bob."

"So now it's Bob instead of Mr. Ralston," I interrupted.

Crens continued undeterred, "John Robinson is a cold-blooded murderer. He is a member of the Weathermen Underground and an avowed anarchist. We've had him under surveillance for almost two years and he has been very ingenious in covering his tracks. But we have witnesses that can place him at the University of California, Davis last Saturday night when the blast took place. We have proof beyond a doubt that he purchased the dynamite used in the Davis explosion, the same dynamite that was stored in the basement of your house. What we need is a witness that actually saw him on the Davis campus shortly before or after the blast."

"You said you have witnesses. So what's the problem?"

"The problem is all our witnesses are paid informants that work for the FBI," Crens replied.

"Like my buddy Jim here?" I asked sarcastically.

Crens continued undeterred again. "Robinson is going to have at least twenty people testify that he was fifty miles away from the Davis campus on the night of the explosion."

"At the Giants game, you said your roommates were at Davis," Logan interjected.

"You mean roommate, Maryanne."

"No. You said roommates," Logan replied.

"Slip of the tongue, I guess."

"Did you see John Robinson on the Davis campus last Saturday night?" Crens asked.

"If I did happen to see John Robinson last Saturday, then what?" I asked.

"We would subpoena you to testify as a witness for the government against Robinson," Crens said.

"If John Robinson is such a bad dude, he must be hanging out with other bad dudes. Where is he now?" I asked.

"He's in federal custody," Crens answered.

"If you charge him, aren't these other bad dudes going to come after me to get rid of the only witness that can help get him convicted?" I asked.

"Normally I would say that is a reasonable assumption and we would put you in the Federal Witness Protection Program. But in this case, I don't have to declare who the witness, or witnesses, are until the preliminary hearing in about three weeks to a month. So until you walk into the courtroom, no one but the FBI is going to know you are a witness," Crens stated.

"Wow, that's real reassuring. Either I hide out in a log cabin in the Nevada desert until the trial, or I walk around San Francisco for a few weeks wondering who knows that I am the key witness. And wonder who would like to get rid of the key witness," I said grabbing the arms of the chair.

"Bob, you would be doing your country a great service. You'd be doing the right thing," Logan said.

"Don't I have a right to an attorney? I want an attorney now!" I demanded.

"You have a right to an attorney, but not during the first twelve hours of interrogation. Let's cut to the chase. Did you or did you not see John Robinson on the Davis campus last Saturday night?" Crens demanded.

"I don't know," I said. "I saw a lot of people. Almost got trampled by a lot of people. I still have the cuts and bruises to prove it."

"Bob, if it turns out that you did see Robinson and you deny it under oath, that's perjury and you'll go to jail. You'll be a convicted felon, never get a good job, and never get into a decent college. It will pretty much seal your fate for the rest of your life," Logan stated.

"Look, there was a lot of chaos, not to mention a lot of smoke. I got knocked to the ground twice. I'm not sure who or what I saw. I was just trying to avoid getting trampled," I said.

"Did you see him or not?" Crens said standing up and pointing a finger at me.

"I'm not sure," I replied.

"That was a yes-or-no question. Did you see him or not?" Crens demanded.

"Not sure."

As an experienced interrogator, Crens knew he had pushed me as far as I was going to go in this initial interrogation.

"Okay. Why don't you go home and think about it. We'll be in touch," Crens said.

"I'll give you a ride home," Logan offered.

"No thanks, I'll take a cable car," I replied.

I stood up and walked right up to Logan and was standing nose to nose with him. "Stay away from me and my house. And stay away from Autumn. She has nothing to do with any of this," I said in a harsh tone.

"You don't tell a federal law officer what to do," Logan replied.

"How would you like it if all the folks at the Sunshine Café and My Karma were to find out that you are an undercover FBI agent?" I asked still in his face.

"You do that and you're going to be in big trouble," he replied.

"I'm already in big trouble," I replied in a heated voice.

I purposely brushed against him as I walked out of the conference room in a huff.

Logan yelled out to me, "You haven't done anything wrong yet! Keep it that way!"

Chapter 39

Night descended on San Francisco and a heavy fog rolled in off the bay. As I stood waiting for a cable car, I felt like my world had just imploded. I couldn't believe that destiny had called me to San Francisco only to find myself in a big mess when I hadn't done anything wrong.

When the cable car arrived, the smiling faces of the tourists scrambling to get onboard didn't brighten my mood. The fog was as dank and dark as my thoughts. There was only one person I could trust now: Autumn.

As the cable car rumbled on, I decided that a drink at the Market Street Bar would do me good. But when I walked into the bar, I suddenly got a paranoia attack. I really didn't know anyone there. I began to wonder if the friendly bartender was really an undercover FBI agent. I immediately turned around and walked out of the bar. As I walked home, the fog and my mood turned progressively gloomier. I couldn't believe that my best day in San Francisco suddenly turned into my worst.

When I approached the house, I could see Maryanne talking to someone on the front porch. I decided to go in through the back door to avoid her and to check on my truck in the alley. I took a few steps into the alley when a big Harley-Davidson motorcycle came screeching around the corner and turned into the alley at a high rate of speed. I had to leap to my left to avoid being struck. The female passenger, dressed in tight black leather clothing, flipped me off as she sped by and I stumbled to regain my balance.

Upon reaching my truck, I could see that the right rear side door was partially open. I approached slowly, not knowing what to expect. The interior was in shambles. The mattress on the wooden platform was pushed to one side. All the storage drawers were pulled out, their contents strewn about the bed.

All the contents in the glove compartment were dumped on the passenger side floor. I assumed it was the result of an FBI search. I locked all the doors and left everything just the way I found it. I would deal with the mess tomorrow and I went inside.

I entered the kitchen via the back door. I assumed if Maryanne didn't see me, I could go into my room, close the door, and pretend I wasn't home. I did not turn on the bedroom light and disrobed in the dark and then climbed into bed. Fifteen minutes later, there was a knock on the bedroom door.

"Bob, are you in there?" Maryanne's voice called out from the hallway.

She knocked on the door again. I didn't answer. I hoped she wouldn't open the door. She didn't.

I lay there for hours staring at the reflections of light flickering across my bedroom ceiling. Finally I drifted off to sleep.

I woke up at eight and knew that Maryanne would already be off to work. While showering, I decided that I was going to the airport, buy a ticket for Chicago, and go see my friend Hoss at the Naval Station Great Lakes' hospital. I still had plenty of money to pay for the ticket.

When I left the house, I ran across the street and pinned a note on Autumn's front door that said I would be back in a few days. An hour later I was sitting in the San Francisco International Airport at the gate for a United Airlines flight to Chicago.

I was happy to be getting out of San Francisco. While people watching, I wondered if there were FBI agents watching me. And I wondered if there were members of the Weathermen Underground watching me too. I also wondered what Hoss would look like.

The plane climbed smartly through the heavy marine layer and once above the clouds, I felt a sense of relief. I was going to get a respite from the calamity that had befallen me in San Francisco. When the stewardess offered me lunch, I shook my head. I was in a window seat and this afforded me a panoramic view of the northern California coastline before the plane turned slowly east.

I spent the next four hours oblivious to everything and everyone around me. I just stared out the window. I wondered what was happening to all the members of the Class of 1967 across America who had decided not to go to college, at least not right away. Three people I knew, Hoss, Jim Gaston, and I, had taken widely divergent paths, and our choices had yielded significantly different results. Hoss almost got himself killed in Vietnam. Gaston, for all practical purposes, was dropping out of society. And I found myself in a very dangerous situation.

The plane bounced on the runway with a hard thud and snapped me out of my trance. Since I was sitting in a window seat, I elected to wait until everyone had exited. I wanted to see if anyone looked like an FBI agent. I was the last one to deplane.

I jealously watched families reunite in the terminal. I saw grandparents hug their grandchildren and their children. I saw young lovers embrace and kiss. I saw old friends shake hands and greet each other with hardy back slaps. I longed for someone to hug me and tell me that everything was going to be all right. However, that was not to be.

When a nurse dressed in a crisp white uniform approached me with an imitation rose and asked for a donation for a local children's hospital, I immediately pulled out my wallet and gave her five dollars. I watched her walk away and admired her for really caring about someone. I could feel there was a void in my life. I didn't really have strong feelings for anyone. There were feelings of infatuation, lust, admiration, but certainly not love.

I stepped outside the terminal in search of a cab to take me to the naval hospital, when a hot and humid blast of August air reminded me that I was back in the Midwest. The thirty-minute cab ride took me through the prestigious northern suburbs of Chicago. Large homes with lush, green front yards indicated wealth and success, a far cry from the crowded metropolitan area of the country's third largest city. The cab passed Northwestern University and shortly we were at the front gate of the Naval Station Great Lakes, home to the second-largest military hospital in the country.

In my haste to get out of San Francisco, I forgot to take into consideration that hospitals have visiting hours. By sheer luck it was five o'clock when I arrived and the sentry asked me where I was going. I explained I had come to visit US Army Private John Haus, who was a patient in the hospital. The sentry reached into his booth and pulled out a clipboard and handed it to me to sign in as a visitor. He instructed the cab driver that the hospital was four blocks to the west and not to attempt to enter the actual naval training base, which was off limits to non-military personnel.

The cabby found the hospital without a hitch. I found myself, with a backpack hanging over my shoulder, standing in front of the medical building. I stood there preparing myself for what I was about to see. I had no idea what to expect. I took a deep breath, got my courage up, and walked through the entrance doors.

I never liked the smell of hospitals. I don't know if it was the clinical smell, the bedpans, or old people dying. I was fortunate and healthy enough to avoid hospitals since my tonsillectomy at six years old.

The hospital staff was extremely busy because a US Air Force C-141 cargo plane had just delivered two hundred-fifty wounded, some seriously, soldiers and Marines coming from Tripler Army Medical Center in Hawaii. I asked the heavyset admissions nurse where I could find John Haus. She told me he was in room 328, which was down the hall, and I was to take two left turns.

I walked down the hall and took the first left turn. The hallway was crowded with wounded young men on gurneys lined up against the walls. As I walked by, I looked at their dazed faces and many of them looked up at me without any expression. I tried to keep a pleasant face even when I came upon several that were missing limbs. My stomach was tied in knots. Most of the wounded appeared to be my age or just a little older. I felt my throat tightening as I lamented why such an awful fate had befallen them.

I reached room 328 and the door was closed. I peered into the window and I could see Hoss lying in a bed with his left leg raised in a mechanical sling. He stared blankly at the ceiling. I took a deep breath, opened the door, and walked in.

For a moment, Hoss didn't realize that I had entered the room.

I called out to him as I approached the bed.

"Hoss, it's good to see you, my friend."

He turned his head slowly and his eyes opened wide when he realized it was me.

"Bob Ralston! What are you doing here, man?" he said in a raspy voice.

I grabbed his arm as I spoke. "I heard you were vacationing here so I thought I'd come and check it out," I replied.

"Your fucking hair is getting a little long, isn't it?" he kidded.

"When in San Francisco you gotta do what the locals do," I said. "How are you doing, man?"

"I got shot in my upper leg and damn near bled to death. But, I'm alive."

"How long are you going to be in here?"

"Hard to say. My femur is shattered and I have to go through several more bone graft operations. Shit, I could be here for another year," he sighed.

"I hope it doesn't take that long."

"The doctors tell me I may have difficulty walking again without a cane or a leg brace. Hell, there is even a chance it may need to be amputated."

Suddenly I grasped the severity of his situation. Hoss sensed that by the expression on my face.

"Why don't you tell me what you've been doing since I last saw you in Milwaukee," he said.

"I drove from Milwaukee to San Francisco right after graduation, and Gaston went part of the way with a girl named Melissa." I said.

I told him about the various adventures along the way, the beautiful scenery, and the interesting people like Banjo and Autumn. He was enjoying the gritty details and a smile came across his face when I told him that I had sex with Gaston's girlfriend Melissa. It was his familiar smile that I hadn't seen in a while.

He kept interrupting me with questions and the minutes turned to hours. I spun my tale of travel across half the United States in a retired milk truck. A nurse came in and informed me that visiting hours were over and I would have to leave.

I'll come back in the morning to see you again before I fly back to San Francisco," I said.

The nurse was kind enough to call a cab for me. When I walked out the door, Hoss called out to me, "Get a haircut while you're out there."

I chuckled and held up the two finger peace sign without turning around.

I didn't know where to stay so I asked the cab driver to take me downtown to the Loop. I walked for several blocks and found a medium priced Holiday Inn Hotel and got a room for the night. It was only nine thirty when I checked in, so I decided to take a walk to the famous Navy Pier along the lakeshore. On a warm summer evening it would probably be very busy.

The clear and starry sky, along with a gentle breeze off Lake Michigan, made for a very pleasant evening. I guessed correctly: Navy Pier was crowded with throngs of people. I wanted to get lost in the crowd because if anyone was following me, I could ditch them.

I walked out to the end of the pier and stood there for quite some time, just gazing out onto the dark waters of the lake. While walking back deep in thought toward Lake Shore Drive, I literally bumped into several people, two guys and three girls, all wearing various University of Wisconsin paraphernalia. I apologized and one of the girls, who had long red hair and wore a black cotton blouse and a red mini skirt, spoke to me.

"Don't worry about it. Where are you from?"

"I live in San Francisco now, but I grew up in Milwaukee," I said.

"What are you doing in Chicago?"

"That's a long story."

"You here by yourself?"

"Yup."

"We're heading into Antonio's. Want to join us?" She pointed to a bar and grill several yards away on the pier.

I looked to see what the reaction was from her friends to the offer she just made. It was clear they were both couples and the girl who invited me was the odd person out.

"Cool, I think will," I replied.

"I'm Kara, and that's Margie and Rebecca and Carl and Danny," she said pointing toward each individual.

They nodded and I said, "I'm Bob."

Antonio's was very crowded. We managed to grab a table in the bar that was big enough to accommodate six. We delved into small talk as we waited for a waitress to take our drink orders. All five of them were incoming freshman at the University of Wisconsin-Madison and were to begin college classes in about a month, right after Labor Day. I felt inferior because I was not going off to college, but I enjoyed their company. I wasn't expecting anything and I wasn't trying to make any moves on Kara. Kara was quite attractive and very physically fit. Her arms were well-defined and her miniskirt showed off the tight calf muscles on her great looking legs. I wondered if she lifted weights.

I could tell she was checking me out as much as I was checking her out. While the other two couples drifted off into their own conversations, Kara and I started up a private conversation.

"Chicago is very different from San Francisco," I said.

"What's it like to be in San Francisco in the 'Summer of Love'?"

I chuckled. "It's pretty far out. There's a lot of pretty interesting people and a lot of weird people that are tripping out."

"Is everyone getting high out there?"

"Yeah, a lot of people are using drugs to help them look for the meaning of life and answers to the universe," I said. "In San Francisco, it's easy to get any drug you want: LSD, pot, hash, speed, magic mushrooms, and heroin."

"I heard that the Haight-Ashbury district is overflowing with hippies and free love. Where do you live in San Francisco?"

"Haight-Ashbury," I answered with a smile as our drinks arrived at the table.

"Are you living in a commune?"

"I live in an old rundown Victorian with two other people, a guy and a woman, but the Victorian next door has about twenty people living there. There are a lot of people crammed into Victorians and apartments all over the city."

"What are magic mushrooms?"

"Psilocybin. It's a hallucinogenic mushroom."

"So tell me why you are in Chicago?"

"Hoping to meet beautiful red-headed girls that are going to University of Wisconsin," I said with a broad grin.

She laughed, took a drink, leaned toward me and said, "No, you're not."

"Okay, busted," I said, dropping my shoulders.

"Girls with red hair are smart. You can't take advantage of us," she said, sitting up proud and straight and smiling.

"I'll keep that in mind."

She leaned back in her chair and waited for me to reply to her question while the two other couples were smooching.

"I have a friend who is in the Army and he was seriously wounded in Vietnam. I came to visit him at Naval Station Great Lakes' hospital, where he is recovering," I said while drinking my Schlitz beer.

"Is he going to be okay?"

"I think so," I answered.

"What do you think about the war?"

"I don't understand what we're doing there. It looks like a very big mistake and a lot of people are dying."

"It is a very big mistake and our government is not telling us the truth about what's really going on in Vietnam. In the little town of

Silver Lake, where I grew up, we have had four young men killed. It's such a waste of young lives," she said looking down at the table.

"If I don't get my shit together soon, I'm going to end up in Vietnam," I said.

"What do you mean?"

"I have three months to decide if I am going to college before I have to take my draft physical. If I don't sign up for college, I will get drafted on my nineteenth birthday in February and most likely get sent to Vietnam."

"Is that what happened to your friend?"

"No, he volunteered because he knew he wasn't going to college. But, that was almost a fatal decision."

She looked directly into my eyes and asked, "Why did you go to San Francisco?"

"I wanted to see what the hippie movement is all about, and what better place than San Francisco's Haight-Ashbury district in the 'Summer of Love'?" I replied. "I drove from Milwaukee in an old milk truck that I fixed up."

"So, what's the hippie movement all about?"

"I really don't know. I had some ideas what it was about, but those ideas and ideals have pretty much been dispelled," I sighed.

"I've never been outside of Wisconsin before tonight" she said with a shrug.

"I hadn't either, until my road trip to San Francisco."

"We're going to a famous steakhouse on LaSalle Street for dinner. Want to join us, since you're all alone in Chicago?"

"I'd love to, but I'm going to pass. I'm going to visit my friend tomorrow morning and then I am flying back to San Francisco early tomorrow afternoon."

She held her glass up for a toast and said, "Good luck to you. I hope you stay out of harm's way."

We touched glasses and I finished my beer.

"I wish we could have met under different circumstances," I said as I stood up.

"Me too," she said.

I walked along Lake Shore Drive toward the hotel and felt like a rat in a maze with no way out. I wanted to get into my truck and drive too far and never come back again. Maybe I should go to South Dakota and work on a ranch where no one would come looking for me. For a brief moment, I thought about moving to Canada and hiding among the hordes of draft-evaders there.

When I arrived back at the hotel, I knew I had to stop worrying about my situation and get prepared to visit Hoss in the morning. He was scheduled for his third bone graft surgery in the afternoon and I wanted to be as positive as I could to buck him up. While locals and tourists partied the night away all around my hotel, all I wanted to do was go to sleep. I was physically and emotionally exhausted and sleep came quickly.

I awoke at seven o'clock, showered, packed my stuff, and checked out of the hotel. The bellman hailed a cab for me. The traffic coming into Chicago was very heavy, but I was headed in the opposite direction. I struck up a conversation with the cabbie, a heavyset man of Polish descent in his late fifties. He rattled off tales of his twenty-five years plying the streets of Chicago as a cabbie. He told me about the time he had to take the parents of a deceased Army soldier to a special area of O'Hare airport to claim the body of their son. That provoked me to ask him his thoughts on the Vietnam War.

"Are we winning the war in Vietnam?" I asked.

"Hell no, we are not winning the war," he answered.

"Why do you say that?"

"I have a son who is a corporal in the army in Vietnam and he writes home every week and says that the war is a mess and most of the Vietnamese don't like us and don't want us there. He says the South Vietnamese Army is a joke and every night the Vietcong control most of the countryside. The only safe place is Saigon, but now even Saigon gets attacked about every night. He told me not to believe a word that Robert McNamara or Lyndon Johnson have to say about the war's progress," he replied.

"That's pretty heavy," I said.

"We're praying every day and every night he makes it home alive."

When the cab dropped me off, I said, "I hope your son makes it home all right."

I checked in with the nurse at the admissions desk and walked down the hallways to Hoss's room. Again, the hallways were crowded with wounded soldiers and Marines lying on gurneys. This time I avoided looking at their pained faces. When I arrived at Hoss's room I found the door was propped out and a nurse was helping Hoss into a wheelchair so she could change the sheets on the bed. She also had to prep him for surgery.

"Cool set of wheels, man," I called out.

"I can do zero to sixty in four point five seconds," he replied with a big smile, hiding the pain from his wounds.

"You can take him outside for some fresh air. You don't have to stay in here," the nurse stated.

I grabbed the handles on the wheelchair and followed the nurse down to the end of a hallway where she pointed to an exit sign and a door that led outside. I wheeled Hoss down the hallway toward the exit and right next to the door a gurney was parked with a sheet that covered the body of a dead soldier.

"Unlucky bastard," Hoss grumbled.

We decided to park the wheelchair under a sprawling chestnut tree that provided shade from the sun. It was going to be a very hot August day in Illinois. Hoss wasted no time in pursuing his questioning of my intentions.

"What are you going to do? Go to college, go to Canada, or let them draft you?" he asked.

"I'm in big trouble," I replied.

"No shit, Sherlock. You have a draft physical breathing down your neck."

"I have more immediate problems."

"What? Did you knock up some babe in San Francisco?"

"I unintentionally got involved into some very heavy shit," I replied.

"You dealing drugs?" he asked his face contorted into a grimace.

"No, it's not that."

"What the fuck is it?"

I took a deep breath and started telling him about renting a room in the wrong house in Haight-Ashbury.

"I found a place with a room for rent on Haight Street. I have two roommates, one is a member of the American Communist Party and the other is a member of the Weathermen Underground."

"No shit!" he replied with a laugh.

"No, seriously."

"Come on!"

"One roommate, the communist, is an absolute babe. Probably the most beautiful woman I have ever seen and certainly the most beautiful woman I have ever made love to."

"You dog!" he exclaimed.

"Unfortunately, the other roommate has been going around California blowing up buildings with dynamite."

"No shit." he replied in a serious tone.

"So one night I go to see the Communist babe give a speech at a local university and my other roommate blows up one of the buildings there and kills some people."

"Oh man, this is too far out," he said. "Are you hosing me?"

"I wish. It turns out that the FBI has been following this crazy bomber guy and they need a witness that saw him at the university the night of the bombing. They want me to testify against this guy in court. They think I saw him there and they want me to be their star witness."

"Did you see him?"

"Look, there could be FBI agents following me who have a listening device pointed at me right now. I think it would be better if you didn't know," I answered.

"What difference does it make if I know?" he asked in a hushed tone leaning forward in his wheelchair.

"The bomber is a member of the Weathermen Underground and if they think I saw him there and I'm a witness, they're going to off me. And if they think I told someone else, they would probably off that person too," I said in a hushed tone.

"No wonder you're all uptight."

"I don't know who knows that the FBI brought me in for questioning. But if the FBI has undercover agents everywhere in San Francisco, I gotta believe that the Weathermen have a bunch of spies too. I am constantly looking over my shoulder every minute."

"Answer my question another way," he said.

"Huh?"

"Do you remember on the freshmen football team when we were contemplating faking a punt and the punter would hold up one finger, if yes, for running or passing the ball. Or hold up two fingers for no, that meant he was going to kick the ball?"

I stood there silently for a moment. Then I started singing, dancing, and delivering a silly rendition of a black gospel song belting out the lyrics, "There is only one way to heaven, my friend. There is only one way to heaven, my friend." While singing, I was holding up one finger and waving it wildly in the air. When I stopped, Hoss nodded his head while I caught my breath.

"What's it like in Vietnam? Do you feel like talking about it?" I asked as I sat down on the ground next to the wheelchair.

"The worst part is seeing your friends getting shot or blown up. One minute they are there, the next, they're gone. It's hard to make real friends because you don't want to get too close to anyone."

"Did you see a lot of Americans get killed?"

"I saw a lot of our guys, a lot of Vietcong, and a shit load of civilians get killed."

"Are we winning the war?" I asked.

"Total bullshit! The South Vietnamese Army is worthless. The Vietcong control virtually every village in the south. They hide all day when we go looking for them, then they come out at night and do whatever the fuck they want. The Vietnamese have been fighting ever since the Second World War and they kicked France's ass out of the country. I think historically they have been fighting foreign invaders for a thousand years, so they are pretty damn good fighters."

"What's going to happen?" I asked.

"We're beginning to seriously bomb North Vietnam and McNamara thinks this is going to make them settle for a truce like North Korea."

"Is that going to work?"

"I don't see how. It may prolong the time before the North Vietnamese Army regulars attack the south, but it won't stop them."

"Are we're going to lose the war?"

"The big difference is they live there and they will not give up. We have a lot of guys over there hyped up on booze and drugs who are only trying to stay alive. The only people who want this war are the people and companies who make a lot of money from it. They are the good old military-industrial complex, the corrupt South Vietnamese government officials, and the prostitutes. Our enemy believes in a cause. Our side believes in money, getting high, and getting laid once in a while. We're no match for them. Believe me, they are tough and they are determined."

"Why does President Johnson keep saying we are winning the war?"

"He's full of shit like the rest of them," he growled.

"I don't know what to do about this situation in San Francisco. One part of me says I have to do the right thing. People are getting killed," I said holding up one finger in the air.

"We're killing lots of people in Vietnam. Is that the right thing?" he asked holding up two fingers in the air.

"So your answer is don't do it?"

"Damn straight. Don't do the government's dirty work. They are masters of dirty work. They can clean up their own messes without your help."

"I never thought I'd hear something like that from the all-American boy Hoss."

"You can see what you get for supporting misguided ambitions," he said pointing to his injured leg.

I stood there reflecting on Hoss's comments when a nurse walked up and said it was time for Hoss to come in. He had to get ready for surgery.

She grabbed the wheelchair's handles and began wheeling Hoss away.

"I hope the next time I see you, I'll be in much better shape," he said.

I shook his hand and held it tightly and said, "I hope there is a next time."

When Hoss reached the entrance door he held up two fingers and then disappeared inside. I got the same bad feeling that I had at Billford's farm when Hoss told me he was going to join the Army. I wondered if we would ever see each other again.

Chapter 40

When my United return flight approached San Francisco, I dreaded seeing Maryanne at the house. I had no idea what she knew and I had to play it very cool and pretend that I knew nothing. If she asked what happened to me that night at Davis, I was going to tell her that I got into my truck and drove away before anything happened. Then I was going to tell her I spent the night at a girl's house that I met at the Sunshine Cafe. I was also going to tell her that I went to see my wounded buddy in a hospital near Chicago. I hoped that would prevent her from thinking I was running away or hiding.

The cab whisked me from the airport to the house and I walked in the front door and didn't see Maryanne. I opened my bedroom door, dropped my backpack on my bed, and headed to the bathroom.

As I walked down the hallway I heard a noise. I stopped and listened. I heard soft moans coming from the end of the hallway in Maryanne's room. I took a few steps toward her bedroom and stood silently listening. I could hear Maryanne moaning while she was having sex with someone. I listened for a moment, which brought back erotic memories of making love with her. I turned and walked into the bathroom, undressed, and stepped into the shower. I decided that I wasn't going to be intimidated by Maryanne. While I scrubbed my scalp with shampoo, I wondered if Maryanne was in cahoots with John. I interrupted my thoughts and mumbled jealously, "Patrick, the holy Catholic priest, is banging her brains out."

I finished showering, toweled off, wrapped the towel around my waist, grabbed my clothes, and opened the door. I took a few steps down the hallway toward my bedroom and Patrick came out of Maryanne's bedroom. We met in the hallway just outside my bedroom.

"Where have you been?" he asked. "I haven't seen you in a while."

He was all cheery and smiley and I could see the afterglow of sex in his face. That made me even more jealous of him. I thought he was a fraud. He was supposed to be a priest. Priests don't go around screwing women. I didn't like priests in general because I had heard rumors that they like to molest altar boys. I don't know how true that was because I had been an altar boy and a priest never molested me.

"I've been out and about," I replied.

"Maryanne has been looking for you," he said.

"I'm here," I replied and walked into my bedroom and closed the door.

While I was getting dressed, I could hear Maryanne walk down the hallway and she and Patrick were talking in the living room. Then I heard the front door open and close and knew Patrick had left. I took a deep breath, opened my bedroom door, and walked toward the kitchen to get some food. When I entered the kitchen, I could see Maryanne, dressed in a light blue robe, standing over the kitchen sink with her back to me.

"Good evening," I said in a friendly voice.

She turned and said, "Well, good evening to you. I haven't seen you for a few days. Do you want some coffee?"

Her skin was radiant and her hair was still wet from showering. She was beautiful as ever and her robe did more to show off her cleavage than hide it.

I was both hopelessly attracted to her and angry with her because she had just finished screwing Patrick. But most of all, I didn't trust her.

I grabbed a yogurt container from the refrigerator and sat down at the kitchen table. She carried two cups of coffee to the table and sat down across from me.

"I assume you know what happened to John," she said.

"I heard that he was arrested for blowing up buildings," I answered.

I lifted my cup to take a drink and watched Maryanne's eyes to gauge what her reaction was to my statement. Before she could speak, I asked in a naïve tone, "Is it true?"

"No, it's not true. The charges will be dismissed," she stated flatly.

"What about the dynamite in the basement?" I asked and then regretted bringing the subject up.

"How do you know about the dynamite?"

"The rumors are swirling around the neighborhood. I heard it at Sunshine Café," I replied quickly, trying to cover my tracks.

"Really?"

I nodded. Her eyes narrowed in on me but she kept a smile on her face.

"I heard that you were taken in for questioning by the FBI," she said, staring into my eyes.

"Where did you hear that?"

"At the Sunshine Café," she replied with a stern look.

I knew that couldn't be true because I was originally picked up by the San Francisco police and then transferred to the FBI for questioning. I realized that she must have some connection to the Weathermen Underground and their spies told her. I decided that I wasn't going to deny it and risk my credibility with her. I wondered if she knew that John was blowing up buildings and killing people.

"I was picked up by the San Francisco police when I arrived home because I live in this house. The police transferred me to the FBI for questioning. They wanted to know if I was involved in bombing buildings. I told them absolutely not and that I had just recently arrived in San Francisco. They asked me if I knew what John was doing and that he was storing dynamite in the basement of this house. I told them I had no idea what he was doing."

"Then what?" she asked.

"I didn't do anything so they let me go."

She got up, went and picked up the coffee pot, and brought it to the table.

"Want a refill?"

As she leaned over the table to pour the coffee, I could see her luscious breasts.

"You must have been at Davis at the time of the explosion. What did you see?"

"I was in my truck leaving the parking lot when the explosion happened. I kept driving because I didn't know what happened. Then I saw flames and smoke coming from a building and then a lot of people running around. It took me awhile to get off the campus because there were so many people running around and I didn't want to hit anyone."

While she was drinking her coffee, I quickly asked, "Did you know John was storing dynamite here?"

"Of course not," she snapped.

"Did you have any idea John was blowing up buildings?"

Her face tightened and the tone of her voice deepened.

"Am I John's accomplice? Is that what you are asking?" "You've been living here with him for quite a while. Did you have any idea what he was doing?"

"I don't like where this is going. Did the FBI tell you to ask me these questions?"

"No. They didn't ask me to do anything. I just want to know."

"No you don't," she replied.

"What do you mean, I don't? If I didn't, I wouldn't ask."

"Bob, you'd be much better off going back to Wisconsin and forgetting about this situation," she said in a mellow voice.

"Did the FBI question you?" I asked.

"No."

"Why not? You live here too,"

"The FBI knows even if I did know, which I didn't, I would never tell them anything," she replied calmly.

"And how does the FBI know that?"

"The FBI has been harassing me, following me, trying to discredit me for years. They have a dossier on me that would fill a filing cabinet. As a member of the American Communist Party, I am considered an enemy of the United States," she replied.

"Wow, that's far out. Of all the houses in San Francisco, I pick the one with an avowed Communist and a bomber," I said with a mock laugh.

"Like I said, you'd be better off going back to Wisconsin and getting on with your life."

"It sounds like you want me to leave."

"I like you and I don't want to see you get in over your head," she replied.

"Over my head?"

"There are a lot of things going on here that don't meet the eye. There is a social revolution and a massive class struggle in America. We can't go on the way we have been. A new order is rising and those who keep the poor, working class people under their thumb will have to pay the price."

I sat there taking in her words and wondered if she really thought that a Communist revolution would topple the United States.

"Why don't we change the subject. Where have you been the last few days?" she asked.

"I went to see my friend from high school who is in a hospital near Chicago."

"What happened?"

"He was shot in the leg in Vietnam. It's a pretty serious wound and he had surgery and is beginning rehabilitation."

"Sorry to hear that. It's another example of America's failed policies. Rich kids can avoid the draft and avoid going to Vietnam simply by going to college, even if the college is not an accredited school. They are draft-dodge colleges for wealthy kids," she stated. "It's a poor man's war."

"I think one of my high school buddies did that," I replied.

She reached across the table and picked up the coffee cups and took them to the sink.

She turned around, and with a smile on her face said, "I missed you."

"You missed me?" I asked in a surprised voice.

"Yeah. I enjoyed the last time we made love."

"You mean the only time we made love."

"We have a big empty house to ourselves. Do you want to make love?" she asked.

She untied the sash on her robe and the robe parted, giving me a full frontal view of her stunning body. I could feel the blood rushing to my loins, but I was worried about what she was up to.

"You just finished making love to Patrick and now you want to make love to me!" I protested.

"He doesn't do it as well as you do," she replied in a sexy voice.

I sat there staring at her for a moment, not sure what I should do or say.

She dropped the robe to the floor and she said, "I know you can't resist me."

"You may be surprised, but I can resist you," I said defiantly.

I got up and walked out of the kitchen and kept walking toward the front door.

"Bob, what are you doing?" she called to me.

"No, why are you doing this to me?" I shouted without looking back or breaking stride.

"You're acting like a teenager!" she shouted as I closed the front door.

I walked across the street to Autumn's house. I knocked on the front door and her roommate Oscar answered the door. He informed me that Autumn went with friends to Golden Gate Park, but he didn't know exactly where in the park. I asked him to tell Autumn to meet me at my favorite Market Street bar and that I needed to talk to her.

Haight Street ends at the east end of Golden Gate Park so I went for a walk in the park in hopes of finding Autumn. I needed to talk to her and tell her about my predicament. While I was walking toward the park, I was tempted mightily to go back to the house and make love to Maryanne.

It was Sunday and the park was crowded. Marijuana smoke wafted through the air and there were dozens of groups of people playing various musical instruments. One group consisted of thirty drummers playing different types of drums from bongos to tom-toms to snare drums. They kept a continuous beat for twenty minutes before stopping. Boys, girls, mothers, fathers, and even grandparents were all dancing to the infectious drumbeat.

I stood there watching, listening, and wondering how I was going to deal with Maryanne. My foot was tapping on the ground, keeping time with the drummers, when a girl with white roses woven into her hair grabbed my arm and pulled me into a giant conga line that was snaking its way through the park. For the next thirty minutes, I gyrated from side to side in the two-hundred-person conga line. We danced our way through picnickers, bicyclists, joggers, Frisbee players, and people smoking pot on picnic blankets.

In the conga line I had no identity. I was just one of many and I thoroughly enjoyed it. When people saw us coming they cheered, clapped, gave the peace sign, and smiled. I had never seen so many smiling faces in San Francisco before.

When the conga line finally disbanded, someone handed me a joint and I took a big hit and held it as long as I could. When I tried to hand the joint back to the redheaded guy who gave it to me, he just smiled, gave me the peace sign, and walked away. I could feel the joint burning my fingertip and thumb, so I took another quick hit before dropping it to the ground.

It didn't take long before I began feeling the effects of the marijuana. I wandered through the park for two hours enjoying all the sights, sounds, and scenery. It looked like one massive party with every resident of San Francisco in the park. I was mesmerized by a group of elderly Chinese-Americans practicing Tai Chi.

I came upon twelve-year-old twin girls who were singing in perfect harmony. They were being accompanied by two guitar players, and their voices were absolutely captivating.

Everywhere I looked, I saw people singing, dancing, meditating, smoking pot, playing music, sitting on blankets, flying kites, playing Frisbee, and shouting anti-war slogans.

When the effects of the marijuana wore off, and I tired of walking, I headed off toward Market Street to my favorite bar. I decided to catch a cable car that would take me toward the bar. I walked several blocks to the nearest cable car line and watched tourists pile into the cable car. They all looked so wholesome. Families with kids, couples, and elderly people sure didn't look like the people I was hanging around with in San Francisco in the Summer of Love.

I reached up and grabbed the outside post of the cable car and hoisted myself up onto the exterior running board. I saw my reflection in the cable car window. My hair was getting longer and scraggly, and I had large dark circles under my eyes from lack of sleep. I didn't look at all like the Bob Ralston who left Milwaukee about a month and a half ago.

The Market Street Bar was crowded but I found an open stool and sat down. The bartenders there never asked to see my ID anymore as I was a regular at the bar.

"What'll you have?" the tall blond bartender asked.

"I don't know. What do you suggest?"

"We make some of the best vodka martinis in San Francisco."

"I don't normally drink vodka," I said.

"It's made with peach extract. I think you'll enjoy it," he said.

"What the hell. I'll give it a try."

The bartender was right. I did enjoy it. The martini was very smooth, sweet, and strong. In a matter of minutes, I consumed it and ordered another one. I struck up a conversation with a balding man sitting on the bar stool next to me. He had a long beard and his black hair was pulled back into a long ponytail.

"What's happening?" I asked.

"Just going with the flow," he answered.

"Maybe that's what I need to do, go with the flow. Stop worrying about things."

"Stress is the devil. Live a righteous life and you will find inner peace," he replied.

"I don't think I could find inner peace if it smacked me in the face," I replied, feeling the effects of the first martini.

"It's not hard, if you just look inside yourself."

"Have you found inner peace?" I asked in a condescending tone, as I began drinking my second martini.

"I served two tours of duty in Vietnam and when I came home I was all fucked up. I hated everyone and I hated myself. I saw so much death and destruction and I killed a bunch of Vietcong. I came home angry because I had lost my youth. My youthful innocence was gone. Two things, youth and innocence, I could never get back."

"I think I'm losing my youthful innocence too," I said, feeling the effects of the second martini.

Suddenly I felt a tap on my shoulder. I turned around and Autumn was standing behind me with a big smile. I clumsily got off the bar stool and gave her a big hug.

"I am so glad to see you," I said.

"I'm glad to see you."

"Can we sit down and talk?" I asked.

"Sure, let's go find a table."

We found a small table near the very back of the bar and sat down. Autumn was wearing a ringlet of flowers around her head and she was the most darling flower power girl I had ever seen. Just as we began talking, a waitress interrupted and asked if we wanted a drink. I ordered another vodka martini and Autumn ordered a beer.

"Last time I saw you, you were being hauled off by the police. Then you disappeared for a couple of days," she said.

"I was interrogated by the FBI," I replied, starting to slur my words ever so slightly.

"The FBI?"

"Yeah. They wanted to know if I was helping John Robinson. I told them I had nothing to do with him and nothing to do with any dynamite or bombings."

"Where have you been for the last couple of days?" she asked.

The waitress arrived with our drinks and I threw ten dollars on her serving tray and told her to keep the change. I grabbed my drink and gulped down half its contents. I was really feeling the effects of three vodkas.

"I went to see my friend Hoss in a hospital in Chicago," I said, slurring more of my words.

Autumn looked at me with a blank stare.

"My friend got shot in Vietnam and he lost his innocence. I think I'm losing my youthful innocence," I rambled. "Autumn, they want me to testify against John Robinson. He's the guy who has been blowing up buildings in California, including the one at Davis."

"Testify against him?" she asked, reaching across the table and grabbing my hands.

"Yeah. I am their fucking star witness. If I say I saw him at Davis the night of the explosion, he's going to the electric chair or jail for life."

"Did you see him there?" she asked, tightening her grip on my hands.

"Yeah, I saw him there," I replied while drinking the last of the third martini.

"What are you going to do?"

"I don't know. I haven't had one damn person tell me I should testify."

"If he has killed people, then you have to testify. You have to do the right thing."

I slammed my fist down on the table and raised my voice. "What's the right thing? People are dying in Vietnam, people are dying in America, people are dying all over the world! What difference does it make whether I testify or not?"

"You need to stop drinking. You're drunk."

"Now you're going to be my mother?"

"I am trying to be your friend!"

"Autumn, you're such a Pollyanna. You think we're all on some good karma, astro-physical trip. Humanity is not good. Get that through your head! The world sucks! People are the meanest animals on the planet. They kill each other and always have!"

"You're acting like a real jerk."

She got up and walked out of the bar, leaving me sitting by myself. I put my head down on the table and mumbled, "Shit! What am I doing?"

I tried to get up and chase her so I could tell her I was sorry, but I was too drunk. I fell back into the chair. The next thing I knew, the bartender unceremoniously announced that it was two o'clock and closing time. He said I had to go home and rousted me.

Chapter 41

I don't remember walking home from the bar and I don't remember walking into my bedroom. I woke up with a splitting headache and almost threw up. I dragged myself into the shower and stood there for fifteen minutes trying to get myself straightened out.

My head throbbed from the worst hangover of my life. I went back to my bed and cursed myself for drinking hard alcohol and for making a fool of myself in front of Autumn. My frustration only made my headache worse.

I went back to the bathroom and threw up three times. That was followed by five minutes of gut-wrenching dry heaves. I took two aspirin and tried to eat something to settle my stomach. Then it dawned on me that I hadn't eaten anything the day before. I drank coffee and too much vodka, and I smoked pot. No wonder I felt like crap. When I checked the mirror, I looked like shit. My hair was messy and my eyes were red and puffy. All I wanted to do was apologize to Autumn.

With Maryanne at work and John in jail, I had the house to myself, unless the FBI had planted listening devices. I walked into the kitchen and found a note on the kitchen table from Maryanne. The note said "Bob, I'll be home tonight. Want to get together? I'll cook dinner." I wondered if she made the dinner offer to figure out what was going on with me.

I drank a glass of orange juice, ate a packet of instant oatmeal, and noticed the *Chronicle* folded up on the breakfast table. I picked it up and scanned the front page and saw a photo taken in Golden Gate Park showing a large gathering of bare-chested men, and women with flowers in their hair, listening to a musical performance and dancing. The caption under the photo said, "Good day, sunshine in the park."

A sidebar headline read, "Bombing suspect hires famous local attorney." I read the article intently and learned that radical attorney William Rogers had agreed to act as John Robinson's defense counsel. At the bottom of the article was a picture of John's mug shot.

I started feeling better and walked across the street to see if Autumn was home so I could apologize. Just as I stood up, there was a knock on the front door.

I opened the front door and to my astonishment Jim Gaston was standing there. His hair had grown much longer and he had a full beard that made him look much older than he was.

"What the hell are you doing here?" I asked in disbelief.

"The commune didn't work out," he said with disappointment written all over his face.

"How did you find me?"

"I called your mom and she gave me your address."

"What are you doing now?"

"I'm heading up to an ashram in Oregon," he replied.

"Hold on," I said. "I gotta go talk to someone across the street. Just hang out here for a couple of minutes. I'll be right back."

"That's cool," he said, setting his backpack down on the wooden porch.

I ran across the street to Autumn's house. The front porch was crowded as usual with a dozen people smoking pot, talking, and some sleeping. I knocked on the front door and hoped that I would see Autumn's face through the yellowing lace curtains covering the glass window in the door. I turned to look back across the street at Gaston and then the door opened. It was Autumn's roommate Oscar.

"Is Autumn around?" I asked.

"No, man, she split a couple of hours ago," he answered.

"When she comes home, would you please tell her I want to apologize."

"What happened, man? She came home last night all upset and crying."

"I got drunk and made a fool of myself."

"She told me that you're not the man she thought you were. She's in love with you, dude."

"I really blew it. When is she coming back?"

"She's not coming back."

"What do you mean?" I asked as my face grimaced.

"She packed up her things and moved out early this morning. "I have no idea where she's gone, but she doesn't live here anymore. You broke her heart, man."

A fiery pain shot through my stomach when I heard his words. Autumn was the only real friend I had in San Francisco. I had ignored her feelings because I was so obsessed with Maryanne. My shoulders slouched and my head felt as if it were going to explode. I shuffled back across the street with my head down. Then I remembered that Gaston was waiting for me on my porch.

"I'm hungry. Can we get something to eat?" he asked upon my return.

"Yeah, sure," I said in a barely audible voice.

When he saw the pained expression on my face he asked, "What's going on, man?"

"I'll tell you all about it over breakfast." I said. "Come on, we'll go in my truck."

We walked around to the alley and for the first time there was no sign of the Hell's Angels. No roaring motorcycles to dodge. No mean guys to avoid. No motorcycle mamas dressed in tight black leather outfits glaring at me and flipping me off.

Before we got into the truck, I told Gaston to wait a minute. I crouched down on my hands and knees and began looking at the truck's undercarriage. I was about halfway under the truck when Gaston asked, "What the hell are you doing, man?"

"Just making sure there isn't anything that could go boom." I crawled out and brushed off my hands.

"Are you talking about a bomb?"

"Relax, man, everything is cool."

"You're freaking me out, man!"

"Get in the truck and I'll tell you all about it," I said.

As usual, the truck started up instantly. The interior and the bed in the back were still disheveled from the FBI's ransacking. I put the truck in reverse, but suddenly there was a tap on the driver's side window. James Logan was standing next to the truck.

"What do you want?" I snarled.

"Get out so we can talk," he said.

"I told you to stay away from me," I replied.

"What's going on?" Gaston chimed in.

"It's nothing," I said. "I got to talk to this guy for a minute."

I got out of the truck and walked a few steps away with Logan.

"What do you want?" I asked with a frown.

"John Robinson's preliminary hearing is in two weeks. Have you made up your mind about testifying?"

"I'll let you know," I said.

"This is no game. You should let us put you into protective custody before the Weathermen Underground kill you."

"Don't try to scare me. How could the Weathermen know anything about me testifying?"

"You're so fucking naïve. The Weathermen Underground are well-armed and dangerous anarchists. They have as many spies in San Francisco as we do."

"I'll keep that in mind. I gotta go."

"I told you before. You haven't done anything wrong yet. But when we subpoena you, if you lie under oath, you're going to jail."

"Let's cut the shit, man! So your undercover agents are going to testify that they saw me see John Robinson at Davis? How is that possible? Where were they, inside my retinas? How could they tell what I saw and what I didn't see? Go ahead and subpoena me. That way I won't look like I am a willing witness."

"I'm trying to help you, man."

"I don't need your help. I don't need the FBI's help. I don't need anyone's help," I said, turning to walk away. "If I do testify, I am going to do it because I want to. Not because you are trying to force me to do it."

I climbed into the driver's seat and rolled up the window.

"Who is that guy?" Gaston asked.

"He's an undercover FBI agent."

"Oh man! Now you're really freaking me out."

"Be cool. I'll tell you all about it."

I drove Gaston across the Golden Gate Bridge to Sausalito to get something to eat. He pulled a joint out of his backpack, lit it, and handed it to me. At first, I wasn't sure if I was in a good state of mind to be smoking pot, but then I decided that marijuana might be just what I needed to ease my mind. I took a big hit and held the smoke deep in my lungs for as long as I could. I exhaled and began telling Gaston the whole story of renting a room on Haight Street where one roommate was a communist and the other one was a member of the Weathermen Underground and a terrorist bomber. Gaston listened intently as we passed the joint back and forth. While the milk truck rumbled across the Golden Gate Bridge I told him about Autumn and how I got drunk.

We pulled into the Crescent Moon Café's parking lot and sat in the truck until I finished telling him all about John Robinson, the dynamite in the basement, the bombing at Davis, and the FBI interview. Then I told him how much I was obsessed with Maryanne. He sat listening and shaking his head. When I finished, we got out of the truck and went inside the restaurant.

The waitress led us to a small black circular wrought iron table on the outside deck that overlooked the bay. We could see Alcatraz off in the distance. When I saw Angel Island, my heart ached to be with Autumn.

We ordered breakfast, quickly drank two cups of coffee each, and began to relax and enjoy the magnificent view.

"So now you know what a crazy scene I'm involved in," I said.

"Far out, man," he said. "That's some heavy shit."

"So what happened at the commune?" I asked as the waitress brought our food.

"We were all supposed to be working together for the good of the commune. We had to work a two-hundred-acre farm and that's a lot of hard work, but several people were always getting high on pot, or LSD, or mushrooms. They didn't want to do their share of the work. They wanted the food but weren't willing to work for it. And it got kinda crazy with the free love thing, too. There were lots of married couples, but everybody was screwing everybody else's partner. I even got involved in group sex with four different couples. Don't worry,

I'm still straight. It was either me and two wives, or a man and me with somebody's wife."

"Sounds like you were busy," I smiled.

"But couples started getting jealous and marriages started falling apart. Pretty soon all sense of order and responsibility fell apart. Everybody was doing their own thing. That's not to say there weren't some righteous people living there, but they were definitely in the minority. It wasn't what I thought it was going to be. I'm really disappointed and disillusioned."

"An ashram in Oregon?" I asked.

"Yeah. There are no drugs allowed and you spend a lot of time in meditation and self-reflection. I think it's the best way for me to seek spiritual enlightenment."

"Where in Oregon is it?" I asked, while sipping my third black coffee.

"About fifteen miles outside Klamath Falls."

"How far is that from here?"

"I would guess about a six-hour drive."

"I'll drive you up there," I said.

"No, man. You got too much going on."

"I want to. I'll drive you up and turn around and drive right back."

"Groovy. When do you want to go?" he asked.

"Now."

"Okay," he said with a shrug.

We finished breakfast and walked back to the truck. We climbed in and Gaston started rolling some joints as I pulled the truck slowly onto the road headed north.

"We got to smoke up the last of this baggy. I can't take it into the ashram," he said.

I turned on the radio and soon we were passing through vineyard after vineyard. Thousands of acres of grapevines, bathed in brilliant

California sunshine, covered the rolling hills of Marin County. Gaston handed me a joint and after two drags on it, I passed it back to him. Marijuana smoke filled the truck even though we had the windows rolled down. Mile after mile rolled under us as we headed north to Oregon.

I turned off the radio, and we struck up a serious conversation. We had a common bond: we were two young men who elected not to go to college right out of high school.

"My experience seems a lot like yours. I came to San Francisco hoping to find answers to my questions about life," I said.

"Answers are hard to come by."

"I thought I was so cool. I'm in San Francisco with total freedom to do whatever I want, with whomever I want. I'm tripping, grooving, getting exposed to things I never would have back in Milwaukee, making love to a beautiful woman, and then wham! I wake up and find myself caught in the middle of a battle between two opposing forces. It's hard to tell who is more evil."

"Man, the FBI versus the Weathermen. You're in deep shit, man."

"I remember sitting in my bedroom in Milwaukee thinking if I went to San Francisco I could find the meaning of life and something spiritually fulfilling. Since I arrived in San Francisco, I have met some crazy people with some crazy ideas. Sometimes I think I'm an adult, and other times I think I'm a stupid kid who hasn't a clue what's really going on in this world."

"You're only eighteen years old. You haven't had time to figure things out. You need to focus on your spiritual side and recognize what the materialistic world is doing to you. All this material shit means nothing. Discovering who you are and being at peace with that will bring the greatest personal satisfaction possible."

"You sound like a Hare Krishna," I said and turned my head to see his response.

"Nothing wrong with being a Hare Krishna," he said, clasping his hands in front of his face.

We crossed into Oregon and entered a forest of tall alder trees. Before us sprawled a verdant valley. The last of the sun's rays filtered through the trees and the road ahead stretched as far as we could see. Ours was the only vehicle on the road.

"Beautiful place," I said.

"I hear it rains a lot up here. Probably why it's so green."

Gaston lit up another joint and we returned to our introspective conversation.

"Where did Melissa end up?" he asked while exhaling smoke from his nose.

"I dropped her off in Los Angeles. We saw The Doors perform in LA. Jim Morrison is outta sight. A really far out concert."

"Did you screw her?" he asked looking at me.

"At first no. But later yes," I said. "She was quite a lady. I really liked her. I still can't believe you picked her up right out of that restaurant in Iowa. That was so far out, man."

"We had great chemistry."

"You mean you had great sex," I replied with a chuckle.

"You got to spend some time with her. It was more than just sex. She was a deep person with good karma."

I nodded my head and turned to look out the driver's side window. "I didn't think I'd ever see you again when I drove out of Colorado."

"It's a long and winding road. We have no idea where it will take us, other than to our eventual deaths."

"There are times when I think my life isn't going anywhere, but I should have a whole life ahead of me. I have dreams. I have goals. I want to do something with my life, but when I see what other people are doing and thinking, and hear what they are saying, I feel like I'm only along for the ride."

"Stop with the what-ifs," he said.

"What does that mean?" I asked with an annoyed look on my face.

"Spiritual awareness."

"I'm spiritually bankrupt," I replied, letting go of the steering wheel for a moment. "I'm just trying to make it to nineteen years old. My reality sucks."

"You gotta work at it, man. I'm giving up booze and drugs and sex so I can get my head straight and get some insight on my true self. I can't do that in an altered state."

"I'm lost in my spiritual solitude," I moaned.

"Our only certainty is our mortality. If you accept that, then you can start to find answers about who you are and what you are searching for, and I believe in karma. You do some bad shit, bad shit will descend upon you," he said. "It is the universal law."

"Killing people is bad shit."

"Ultimate bad shit."

"Do you think I should testify against this guy? The guy has blown up a bunch of people, not to mention buildings."

"I can't answer that. Only you can," he said. "Whatever your value system is, then you must apply it to the question at hand. Do you really care that he killed people?"

"I don't really care. I mean, I don't get all bummed out about it. But it sure as shit is not right going around killing people, no matter what the cause."

"But you're being asked to do something about it. The question is, do you care enough about what you believe is right or wrong to do something about it? Make no mistake. There are a lot of very evil, bad people and governments in the world. But we learned a valuable lesson from the Nazis. If you don't stand up to evil, evil will sweep you and society into chaos and death," he replied.

"Sounds like you think I should testify."

"I didn't say that. It's soul-searching time for you. That is a decision only you can make."

Suddenly a highway sign appeared in the impending darkness that indicated Klamath Falls was ten miles away. There were a few homes off in the distance with lights on, but the highway and the surrounding area were pitch black. The truck's headlights only dimly lit up the road ahead. Gaston was busy rolling a large joint.

"Where am I taking you?" I asked.

"You're not taking me anywhere. We're going to find a place to park this milk truck and call it a night."

"No, I'm going to turn around and head back to San Francisco," I protested.

"No way, man. You'll fucking fall asleep at the wheel and kill yourself."

"I can't sleep. My world is imploding. I don't sleep anymore anyway."

"We're going to smoke this monster joint, look at the stars, and watch the universe go by," he said. "Do you have any sleeping bags in this refugee from a junk yard?"

"Yeah, I have a couple of bags in the back."

"Look," he said pointing at a sign for a local park. "Turn in here."

I made a sweeping right turn onto a dirt road and drove slowly through an opening in a wooden split rail fence that bordered the entrance to the park. I drove to the far end of a parking area and turned off the engine. We were surrounded by the quiet darkness.

"Let's go smoke my last joint and call it a night," he said.

I grabbed the sleeping bags and a flashlight from the back of the truck. We walked a few yards and spread out the sleeping bags on a soft grassy area. Gaston lit up the joint and we sat on the sleeping bags passing it back and forth until it expired.

As we snuggled inside our sleeping bags, with the grass providing a soft cushion for our heads, the sky glowed with hundreds of stars and the waning moon was barely visible over the tall trees in the distance. We heard neither crickets, nor leaves rustling, nor any sound of man or animal.

"I don't know what's going to happen when I go back to San Francisco," I said. "I have this damn bad feeling I'm not going to see you again,"

"You'll pull through this."

"I'm lonely there. Other than Autumn, I have no friends. Now that she's gone, I feel lost."

"You haven't lost anything other than dispelling expectations. What do you want from San Francisco? It's a city with a lot of people, many just like you and me. People searching for answers and meaning. It's trial and error, man. At least you're trying, seeking, and searching. You can do no more than that. The answers will come," he said rolling over in his sleeping bag.

"I am stumbling and bumbling through the universe. No, I'm tumbling out of control through the universe."

"It doesn't matter what god you pray to, all things in life will pass. You and everyone else on this planet are traveling through the universe. And what you said earlier is partially true: you are along for the ride, but you are not powerless."

"I can't believe I'm saying this, but I miss some things about Milwaukee. I knew where people were coming from. My friends were my friends. There weren't a lot of hidden agendas. Everybody is not high on drugs all the time, and it's so easy to get laid in San Francisco it's taken all of the thrill out the hunt."

"Holy shit! I never thought I would hear Bob Ralston say he is tired of getting laid."

"Yeah. Hard to believe."

"Tell me about Hoss. How's he doing?" he asked, rolling over and facing me.

"He's gonna make it, but it's taken a heavy toll on him. That sparkle in his eyes, his constant smile, his positive attitude, and his joy of living are all gone. He's not the happy-go-lucky guy that we knew. He's damaged goods."

"Your mom said on the phone that he may not walk again without the use of a cane."

"It's going to take the better part of a year to determine that. They are taking bone grafts from his hips to rebuild the femur in his left leg. He told me about the flight from Hawaii to the Naval Station Great Lakes in an Air Force C-141 cargo plane. It was loaded with seriously wounded soldiers and Marines heading home for major surgery and rehab. He said that the plane was full with more than a hundred people on stretchers, stacked three high in the cargo bay, and seven soldiers and one Marine died before they landed in the United States."

"Big fucking mess. We are losing hundreds of soldiers every month–for what? Lyndon Johnson is bombing the shit out of North Vietnam and it hasn't accomplished a thing, and it isn't stopping the Vietcong. We're getting our asses kicked, just like the French did. The US is a colonial power involved in a civil war in Vietnam. And if we don't watch out, China will come to Vietnam's aid, just like they did in Korea. We don't seem to learn anything from history. It is heart-wrenching to watch countless young men cut down in the prime of their youth because of some asshole like Robert McNamara who hoodwinks our country into believing in a misguided foreign policy."

"How many soldiers have died in Vietnam?" I asked while propping up my head with my arm.

"Several thousand killed this year alone. We have about half a million soldiers fighting in Vietnam. Last week, three hundred

American soldiers were killed, along with twenty-five hundred wounded."

"What's it like in an ashram?"

"I'll tell you after I've been there awhile, but it's mostly meditation: a quiet, self-reflective environment. At this ashram, you are not allowed to speak a single word on Wednesdays."

"Far out," I smiled.

"You ought to try meditating. It will clear your head, get rid of the mental clutter, and you'll see and understand things more clearly," he said. "It puts your mind at peace."

"I'm so screwed up right now that my brain probably looks like fifty miles of bad road."

"If you aren't at peace with yourself, you really can't find happiness and self-fulfillment," he said. "Most of all, you can't find the truth.

Wanting to change the subject, I said, "I wonder what Sharman Stromme is doing tonight."

"Probably banging Freddy Billford," he replied.

"I don't think so. They are over."

"Freddy knew all along that you were screwing his girlfriend."

"No way."

"He's just too cool a guy to do anything about it," he said.

"I'm not proud of doing that," I said. "I don't think I really took anybody's feelings into consideration. I was just a selfish, horny guy."

"If you are aware of it, you can do something about it."

"When I look into a mirror, I don't like what I see."

"Maybe that mirror is trying to tell you something."

"I'm going to sleep."

"Good, because we just finished the last joint."

Chapter 42

woke up to a very light sprinkling of rain falling from a heavily overcast sky. It must have just started because my sleeping bag was mostly dry. Oregon was reminding me that I wasn't in California.

I sat up, rubbed my eyes, and noticed that Gaston's sleeping bag was rolled up next to me, but there was no sign of him. I assumed he must be off in the bushes relieving himself or in the truck. I rolled up my sleeping bag, grabbed the other sleeping bag, and headed for the truck. I opened the back door expecting to see Gaston inside, but he wasn't there. I threw the bags in the back, closed the door, and wondered where he went.

"Jim! Where are you?" I yelled.

There was no response. I walked to the cab and opened the door. On the driver's seat was a handwritten note that said, "Peace be with you. We'll meet again somewhere, sometime. I am walking to the ashram. Jim."

If there was one thing I was sure about Jim Gaston, it was that he didn't like to say good-bye in person. I put the note down and stood in the rain pondering my fate and his. I heard cows mooing off in the distance and the rhythmic pattern of the increasing rain bouncing off the truck's hood. I looked skyward and let the drops cascade down my face, hoping the rain would cleanse my soul, wash away all my problems, and tell me what I should do when I returned to San Francisco.

I climbed into the driver's seat and sat motionless for several moments. I thought about how close I was to Canada and whether I should start driving north, instead of south. I decided that running away from problems never solves them. I turned the ignition key and the truck growled to life. I drove out of the park and turned the truck onto the southbound lanes of the highway. I had attached a small compass to the dashboard when I left Milwaukee, and when the needle indicated south, I took a deep breath and in a hushed tone said, "It was meant to be."

The rain fell steadily and the windshield wipers clattered in a monotone rhythm. The sheer absence of humanity, unlike San Francisco's busy streets, soothed my mind. A large semi-truck rumbled past in the opposite direction, throwing a wall of spray across my windshield and jostling my truck as it sped past. I held the steering wheel tightly and when the truck stopped shuddering I reached up and patted the dashboard in appreciation and said, "You're a friend, Bessie."

Two hours later, when I reached the California border–sure enough–the rain stopped. Half an hour later, I drove into the town of Eureka and stopped to get something to eat. I drove slowly into the main business district and couldn't believe my eyes when I saw a sign that said Kate's Kafe.

"I can't believe it," I said. "There are two Kate's Kafe's in this world."

I parked the truck and quickly looked into the rear-view mirror to see what I looked like. My hair was disheveled and I had noticeable bags under my eyes. My eyes were still bloodshot from smoking so much pot the day before. I climbed into the back of the truck and changed my t-shirt and ran a comb through my hair. The comb did little to improve my looks.

I climbed out the back door and walked into the café. Judging by its rustic wood interior and numerous photos hanging on the walls, it catered to the area's many loggers. It was crowded, but I found an open stool at the counter and sat down. When the waitress asked what I wanted, I told her lots of coffee. When she returned with the coffee, I ordered a Kate's Country Breakfast. Cradling my coffee cup, I looked around and saw a lot of young people hanging out in the restaurant. I ventured a guess that there were only two couples over twenty years old in the restaurant. The young man sitting on the stool next to me struck up a conversation.

"Where you from?" he asked.

"I'm headed back to San Francisco," I answered.

"You live there?"

"Yeah, I live in the Haight-Ashbury District."

"Wow. That must be very cool. Living in Haight-Ashbury in the Summer of Love."

"It's a trip, man."

"What's it like? I'm thinking of going down there."

"It's pretty far out. Kinda hard to describe. It's like an oasis of total freedom. Everything and everyone is accepted," I said in between bites of my breakfast.

"I heard that there is going to be a huge anti-war demonstration in San Francisco this afternoon," he said.

"What time?"

"The newspaper said it starts at three o'clock," he answered.

"Just about the time I get back into the city."

He got up from his stool and gave me a peace sign and said, "Peace, have a good trip back, man," and walked out of the café.

I finished my breakfast, used the restroom, and brushed my teeth with my right index finger. I walked out of the café and noticed a barbershop across the street. My last haircut was four months ago, and I decided to get my scraggly hair trimmed.

I walked into the barbershop and I was the only patron. I sat down in the barber chair and a barber, with lots of graying hair and a dark moustache, asked me how I wanted my haircut. I told him just a slight trim.

We got talking and he told me that his son was a Marine captain serving in Vietnam. I waited to hear his opinion of the war, expecting him to be gung-ho in supporting the war effort. To my surprise, he was really cool about the whole war issue and just wanted his son to come home safely.

"Don't understand what we are doing over there," he offered. "I don't think the South Vietnamese government would last two minutes if the U.S were to pull out."

"Sounds like we're in for a long war," I answered.

"Most people don't know it, but the US has been involved in Vietnam since the late fifties. President Kennedy got us more involved and President Johnson has gotten us deeply involved," he said.

"How is your son doing?"

"He's stationed way up north at Khe Sanh. They are constantly under attack," he replied with a furrowed brow. "But he's doing okay."

I was going to tell him that I had a friend who was almost killed in Vietnam, but I thought better of it. The conversation wandered off onto numerous subjects, even how the San Francisco Giants were doing.

"Ever heard of a group called the Weathermen Underground?" I asked.

"Only what I read in the newspapers and *Time* magazine. They are a violent anti-war revolutionary group that's been going around the country killing police officers, blowing up buildings owned by companies that supply the military, and killing innocent people," he answered. "They want to overthrow the government."

"I heard they have infiltrated every big city in the country," I said.

"I don't believe that, but I read they have a lot of operatives in Boston, Chicago, and San Francisco," he said. "They're a bunch of murderous thugs."

When he handed me a mirror and asked how the haircut looked, I was pleased to see that my hair looked better a little shorter. I thanked him, paid the bill with a dollar tip, and wished his son and him well as I walked out the door.

When I walked across the street to my truck, there were eight people standing next to it, admiring the artwork on the side. When I reached for the door handle, a bearded young man with a long ponytail, wearing tattered bell-bottom jeans, called out to me. "This your truck?"

"Yeah, it's an old milk delivery truck from Wisconsin," I said.

"It's far out, man. Out of sight artwork."

"It gets me around."

"Where you headed?" a girl wearing a long billowing yellow dress asked.

"San Francisco."

She grabbed the arm of the young man standing next to her and they walked up to me together.

"We were just about to start hitchhiking to San Francisco. We're going to the anti-war march there today. Any chance you could give us a ride?" she asked, as her boyfriend stood there smiling.

"If you don't mind me asking, how old are you two?"

"We're sixteen," the young man answered.

"You planning to go home after the march?" I asked.

"Maybe. Maybe we'll hang around the city for a few days," the girl replied.

"I'll take you if you promise me that you will go home after the march, and not hang out in the city," I said.

"Why do you want us to go home?" the girl asked with a perplexed look.

"There are a bunch of people in San Francisco who would love to take advantage of sixteen-year-old kids from Oregon. When you turn eighteen then you can hang out in San Francisco," I said.

"That's kinda weird," the boy replied.

"That's my deal. Take it or leave it," I answered.

"How would you know that we kept our promise?" the girl asked.

"I wouldn't. But if you have no intention of doing what you say, then why say it?" I asked.

"Good point," the boy replied.

"Well?" I asked, as I opened the driver side door.

"Okay. We promise to come home after the march. We'll take a Greyhound bus," the girl stated.

"Let's go," I said, as I climbed into the cab.

They scurried into the passenger seat and she sat on his lap.

Chapter 43

We were barely ten miles out of Eureka when the girl opened her purse and pulled out a joint. She asked me if it was okay to smoke in my truck. I nodded, and she lit the joint.

When she passed the joint to me, I declined. "I'll pass. I smoked too much pot yesterday."

The four-hour drive passed quickly and they spent most of the time chatting between themselves in anticipation of arriving in San Francisco. That was fine with me as I wasn't interested in small talk with a couple of sixteen-year-olds. I played several Beatles eight-tracks and cursed my bad luck for choosing to live at 806 Haight Street.

As we approached the Golden Gate Bridge, I could see the tall buildings in downtown San Francisco. I resolved to be strong no matter what happened. I wasn't afraid. I was resigned that I had been dealt a very strange hand.

John Robinson's preliminary hearing was approaching and something had to give. I pictured James Logan pacing in my parking spot, wondering where I was. I chuckled at that silly thought because I knew damn well the FBI was following my every move. They didn't want to lose their star witness. I wondered if members of the Weathermen Underground were following me too.

When I looked over at my passengers, I realized that I never asked what their names were. I took some perverse pleasure in knowing that there were other young people more naïve than I.

The inbound traffic crossing the bridge was heavily backed up, probably due to the anti-war march. I surmised that it would be impossible to get to the Haight-Ashbury District due to street closures and the humanity that had descended upon the city.

"Look, we're never going to get far in this traffic," I said. "Once we get across the bridge, I'm going to look for a side street and find a place to park. Then you can walk to the march a lot faster than any car or truck could take you."

They nodded their approval in unison.

After thirty minutes of slowly creeping along in traffic, we finally reached the San Francisco side of the bridge. I drove into the Marina District, pulled onto a side street and parked the truck.

"The anti-war marches always go in the same direction. Here's what you do," I said. "Walk on Marina Boulevard and when you get to Bay Street turn right and keep walking to Van Ness Avenue. The march will follow Van Ness and then go up Market Street to the Embarcadero to the Ferry Building."

They climbed out of the truck and bounded off toward the march. I sat in my truck watching them and made up my mind that I was going to go to the march too, if only as an observer.

I climbed out of the truck and started walking toward Van Ness Street. I noticed a handbill in the window of a small grocery store announcing that Simon and Garfunkel were putting on a free concert the next day in Golden Gate Park.

The closer I got to Van Ness, the bigger the crowd of anti-war demonstrators grew. The sidewalks overflowed with people of several generations. There were nuns, girls in skimpy tank tops, grandfathers with white beards, mothers with their children in strollers, couples holding hands, Vietnam veterans, a large group of students wearing San Rafael High School T-shirts, and thousands of protestors with hand-made protest signs.

All the side streets leading to Van Ness were closed to traffic and thousands of people filed onto Van Ness. As I approached Van Ness, I heard a huge crowd chanting anti-war slogans, pounding drums, and blowing whistles. Van Ness teemed with marchers, both on the street and sidewalks. I joined the countless marchers from an intersecting side street.

As I stepped onto Van Ness, the forward movement of the crowd swept me up, so that I was going to participate in the march, whether I liked it or not. I had no choice. Marchers filled the entire length of Van Ness from one sidewalk to the opposite sidewalk as far as I could see, and marijuana smoke filled the air.

Many of the protesters carried artistic and humorous signs, including one that depicted President Johnson being dropped from a B-52 bomber.

As I shuffled along with the masses, I wondered how Hoss was doing. I thought about how much the war had changed him. I just couldn't picture myself serving in the Army. Since I knew nothing about killing someone, I was convinced that I would be killed if I went to Vietnam. The more I walked, the clearer it became to me that what America was doing in Vietnam was wrong.

Although I was dubious of anything Maryanne espoused, I did agree with her that it was a poor man's war and all the rich kids were safely tucked away in college. I took pause because I was contemplating going to college to avoid the draft. Avoiding the draft was a more immediate priority for me than getting a college education.

As the march snaked its way onto Market Street, I hoped by some miracle I would bump into Autumn. I wanted to look her in the eye and tell her how sorry I was and that she was a very important friend to me. I also wanted to make love to her. I decided I should limit my drinking. If I hadn't gotten drunk, Autumn and I would still be close friends.

I passed a group of Vietnam veterans in green camouflaged uniforms standing on the sidewalk holding up the two-finger peace sign. It took an hour to get from Van Ness to Market Street, and another hour and a half to go from Market Street to the Embarcadero. There the atmosphere turned festive and the marchers spread out over the entire Embarcadero waterfront. When I arrived at the Ferry Building there was a stage with the musical group Country Joe and the Fish singing anti-war songs.

While listening to the music, it dawned on me that there were very few San Francisco police officers along the demonstration route and there were no National Guard troops visible. There were no unruly demonstrators. No storefronts were damaged. It was truly a peaceful anti-war demonstration on a beautiful sunny summer day in San Francisco.

I spent the next two hours wandering through the throngs of people just taking in the sights and sounds. It was the most colorful and eclectic gathering of people I had ever experienced. People danced, sang, smoked pot, laughed, hugged, smiled, and engaged in countless discussions–all in agreement that the United States had to get out of Vietnam.

I stopped at one of the many stages along the Embarcadero and listened to disabled Vietnam veterans speak about their experiences in the war. I cringed when I noticed that one of the vets, sitting in a wheelchair, looked a lot like me. Both his legs were amputated at the knees. I felt a knot form in my stomach when I thought about my impending draft physical.

A young lady offered me a joint, and without thinking, I instinctively put it to my lips and inhaled deeply. I smiled at her and handed it back. While holding the smoke in my lungs, I wondered what it was like to take your last breath. That led me to think about my mortality. I wondered if I would ever make it to twenty-one years old so I could actually buy a drink legally. I concluded it was probably better to be killed in Vietnam as a decorated soldier than to be murdered in San Francisco by the Weathermen. I was sure that murder victims, even if they were performing a heroic act for America, would not get buried with honors in Arlington National Cemetery.

Just when I started to feel sorry for myself, I watched a Vietnam vet, on crutches, make his way to the microphone. When he started speaking, I felt ashamed of myself. In front of me was a generation of young men whose lives were forever altered for the worse. Behind me were thousands of young men, members of the same generation, who had unfettered freedom to enjoy the Summer of Love 1967. I didn't stay and listen to what the Vietnam vet had to say. It all seemed very unfair.

My stomach churned at the thought of this huge discrepancy within my generation. I began questioning what I believed in and what I stood for. It seemed my value system was built on a house of cards: no real convictions, only expediency. On one hand, I didn't believe that America was a bad nation, and I certainly didn't want to run away to another country to avoid the draft. On the other hand, I didn't agree with our foreign policy and the war in Vietnam. My country was telling me to do my patriotic duty, and I was trying to figure out a way to avoid it. Was I stupid for not going to college immediately, especially with the draft hanging over my head?

As I started the long walk toward the Haight-Ashbury District, I asked myself how a government and its citizens could hold such divergent views on what was right and wrong. I also hoped I would run into Autumn.

Chapter 44

By the time I arrived at Haight Street, the sun setting over Golden Gate Park yielded to a warm evening.

As I walked toward my house, I saw a steady stream of people returning from the anti-war march. I put the key in the front door lock, paused, and then turned it. "Maryanne?" I called as I entered the living room, but there was no answer. I guessed she was still returning from the march.

I went to my room, dropped my clothes on the floor, and headed down the hallway to the bathroom. I turned on the shower and stepped into the old bathtub with its ornate brass legs.

I stood under the showerhead for several minutes, hoping the warm water would soothe my mind, but I worried about what was going to happen when Maryanne came home. I fantasized that I was James Bond, and like him, I was in a dangerous situation with a beautiful woman. No matter how dire James Bond's situation was, it never stopped him from making love to a beautiful enemy. I thought about how sexy Maryanne was. I made up my mind that I was going to make love to her one last time, no matter how dangerous a proposition that might be.

I got dressed and went into the kitchen to get something food. On the kitchen table was a note from Maryanne saying that my mom had called, and that Hoss was doing well, and to please call home.

As I sat in the kitchen, killing time before going to get my truck, I decided to see the scene of the crime. I turned on the light switch at the basement door and the wooden stairs creaked as I descended. Cobwebs brushed against my face in the dim light. Years of dirt and grime covered the ground-level windows above me and the concrete floor bore the scars of dozens of earthquake tremors.

I walked slowly across the floor and opened a small wooden door and fumbled around looking for another light switch. Finding it, I stepped into the room and saw a long wooden workbench that stood empty. I assumed the FBI took everything as evidence, but this was where John Robinson assembled his explosive devices. I stood at ground zero where a murderer had done his fiendish work. It seemed an unlikely place for such death, destruction, and despair to originate. Since there was nothing to see, I turned around and headed back up to the kitchen, turning off lights as I went. The visit to the basement reminded me that John Robinson's preliminary hearing was just a few days away.

As night fell over the city, I put on a light sweater and started walking to the Marina District to retrieve my truck. When I reached the Marina Green, near the St. Francis Yacht Club, an acoustic music concert was taking place. The headliner was anti-war protester and acclaimed singer Joan Baez. As I walked through a large crowd of concertgoers, I heard Baez's melodic voice riding on the gentle breeze blowing in from the sea. The sweet smell of marijuana permeated the air. It was a pleasant evening in the Summer of Love, but there was no love in my heart.

I stood and watched Baez perform, while much of the audience sat intently on the grass. I got an urge to get into my truck and start driving anywhere away from San Francisco. I began walking again and told myself that I wasn't going to run away. For better or worse, I was going to face this situation and hope for the best. I steeled myself to face Maryanne and keep my wits about me.

As I approached my truck, I saw the majestic Golden Gate Bridge lit up in the distance. I climbed into the truck's cab and sat silently for several moments, enjoying the peaceful sanctuary that my ever-faithful milk truck provided.

"We gotta go home, Bessie, for better or worse," I said quietly as I grabbed the steering wheel.

When I approached the alley leading to my parking spot, I discovered the alley was blocked by several police cars with their red lights flashing. I wondered if something had happened in my house. Maybe the Weathermen Underground blew up the house in an attempt to kill me.

I pulled up slowly to the police officer directing traffic and rolled down my window.

"What happened officer?" I asked.

"The alley's closed for a police investigation," he replied, trying to wave me on.

"I live in the second house on the left and my parking spot is right there," I said, pointing at the parking space. "What's going on?"

"There was a double homicide. Two members of the Hell's Angels were shot. It was a drug deal gone bad," he answered. "They've been dealing a lot of shit heroin lately and a lot of junkies are getting real upset with them."

"Can I get into my parking spot?" I asked.

"Okay. There's room to squeeze past the patrol car on the left. But don't go any farther down the alley. One of the bodies is still lying in the alley and we're waiting for the coroner," he said.

I parked the truck and I could see the kitchen lights were on in the house. That meant Maryanne was home. I took a moment before leaving the truck to get my story straight on where I had been and what I had been doing.

I walked in the back door and Maryanne was sitting at the kitchen table grading her students' papers. She was wearing bell-bottom jeans and a San Francisco Mime Troup t-shirt with a large red star on her chest. I assumed it was the red star of the communist party of Russia or China.

"What have you been up to, my absentee roommate?" she asked with a smile.

"I drove up to Oregon to see an old friend of mine," I replied.

"You've been seeing a lot of old friends lately. Do you have any new friends?"

"Not sure I would call them friends–maybe acquaintances."

"I'm going to cook some pasta like my grandmother taught me. Would you like to join me?"

"I would love some pasta, but I gotta get cleaned up. I've been on the road for a couple days."

"I have a fresh baguette and a delicious Italian sauce recipe for the pasta," she said.

I walked down the hallway to my room, took off my clothes, and headed to the bathroom with a towel wrapped around my waist. I wasn't expecting a dinner invitation from Maryanne upon my return, and I completely forgot that I had just taken a shower a couple of hours earlier.

The aged plumbing reduced the shower flow to a soft sprinkle and shampooing my hair relieved my itchy scalp. I picked up the bar of soap and lathered my upper body. I was startled when the shower curtain was suddenly pulled back. Maryanne was standing completely naked next to the tub.

I was going to ask her what she was doing, but I took a moment to relish her stunning body, beautiful face, and streaming long black hair.

"I missed you, Bob Ralston from Wisconsin," she purred.

"You missed my stunning intellect," I smiled back, trying to look at her eyes instead of her breasts.

She burst out laughing and said, "And that's not all."

"If you don't want me to get an erection right here on the spot, you should leave immediately."

"That's exactly what I want."

She stepped into the tub, pulled me close, and began kissing me. Water ran down her long hair and dripped from her breasts. I wrapped my arms around her and began French kissing her. I pulled back slightly so I could look into her gorgeous green eyes.

If she was singing a siren song, I was ready and willing to crash onto a craggy shore. I slid my hands down to her buttocks and squeezed them lightly. I tilted my head down and kissed her left nipple. She moaned softly with delight.

She reached down and felt that I was fully erect.

"Have you ever made love in a shower?" she whispered.

"No, but I want to," I lied.

She lifted her left leg onto the side of the tub and inserted my penis into her vagina.

We began thrusting together. The pace grew faster. I kissed her neck and told myself to hold out as long as I could. I wanted this to last as long as possible. She moaned louder and louder, which heightened my excitement.

Suddenly, she stepped back and we disengaged. She turned her back to me, leaned forward with her outstretched arms against the tile wall, and looked back at me.

"Let's do it doggy style," she said with a nasty smile.

I moved toward her and we reengaged. I grabbed her hips and began thrusting.

"Don't worry about me. I've already come," she said in a barely audible voice. "Now I want you to come."

I lost all control, thrusting as fast as I could without falling down in the tub.

"You have the sexiest ass," I blurted out as I reached my orgasm.

Ten minutes later, I sat at the kitchen table while Maryanne busied herself cooking dinner. The delicious smell of pasta and pesto wafted throughout the house. She poured two glasses of Chianti wine and proposed a toast.

"Here's to Midwestern boys who know how to use their farming implements correctly," she laughed.

I laughed too, appreciating the view of this rare beauty in a t-shirt without a bra. She must have driven all the boys in high school crazy.

"Do you like younger men?" I asked while sipping my wine.

"Not really. But your tight ass and washboard abs just get me all worked up."

Maryanne didn't find it difficult to look and sound sexy with her seductive voice, her enchanting eyes, her rock-hard body and her strong but alluring personality. The combination of these attributes gave her a commanding presence. When she entered a room, people looked. When she spoke, people listened. When she walked away, everyone's eyes followed her.

Although dinner was as delicious as she said it would be, I took care not to drink too much wine out of fear I might say something I would regret. After dinner, we went into the living room and sat on the couch together.

"How long have you been here now?" she asked.

"About two months."

"So what do you think about San Francisco?"

"What do you mean?" I said, shifting slightly away from her.

"You came all the way from Wisconsin for something. Have you found it?"

"If I was looking for the meaning of life, I haven't found it. I had no idea what to expect. I know that only being here two months isn't going to grant me some great enlightenment, but I've learned that expectations are rarely ever met when you idealize something. I also discovered that friendships are as precious and fragile as porcelain dolls. I've listened to numerous points of view on religion, karma, universal order, war, peace, and love that I would have never have heard in Milwaukee. I've seen some great concerts, smoked some awesome pot, and met people from all over the country and the world. In the short time I have been here, I have realized that there is a lot more to the world and that I am not the center of the universe. I have been emboldened and humbled at the same time. I hope these experiences lead me down a path that I can take for the rest of my life."

"You didn't mention the Vietnam War. What do you think about that?" she asked, while putting her wine glass down on the coffee table.

"I think it's a big mistake."

"So you're against the war?" she asked.

"I don't think we should be there."

"Why?"

"Because a lot people are getting killed, and for what?"

"Do you think John was responsible for the UC-Davis explosion?" she asked.

"Wow, where did that come from?" I asked, feigning surprise.

"He's against the war," she answered, looking at me intently.

"I don't know if he did or didn't do it."

"What did the FBI say when they interviewed you?" she asked, looking directly into my eyes.

"They said they had witnesses that saw him come out of the building, and they had enough physical evidence to charge him," I replied.

"Did you see John at Davis that night?"

"I don't think so."

"I visited John last week. He is being held in the county jail," she stated. "He said you saw him at Davis."

"When I was trying to get in the truck, I got knocked to the ground twice by people fleeing in a panic. If he was there, I sure didn't recognize him," I said, trying to cover my tracks.

"He says that you two literally ran into each other and you even called him by his name."

"I don't recall that."

"John's attorney says the FBI will not release the names of the witnesses who are going to testify against John at the preliminary hearing," she said, still staring at me.

"When is the preliminary hearing?" I asked, feigning ignorance.

"In three days."

There was a knock on the front door.

"I'm expecting some friends," she said as she walked toward the front door.

"I gotta go to the bathroom," I said while walking the other way.

I went in the bathroom and locked the door. I knew the jig was up and I was in trouble. Playing dumb wasn't going to work any longer. The unexpected visitors were probably members of the Weathermen Underground.

Quickly, I opened the bathroom window, climbed out, and dropped five feet to the ground. I ran to the wooden fence that surrounded the back of the house and climbed over it into the neighbor's yard.

I scurried across the neighbor's backyard, climbed over the opposite fence, and ran down the side street that intersected with Haight Street. Then I ran into Golden Gate Park where I would be hard to find in the dark.

Chapter 45

As the right wing tip of the United flight from Milwaukee to San Francisco gently dipped starboard, I craned my neck to get my first glimpse of San Francisco in forty-six years. I could see the Bay Bridge below me, chockablock full of traffic. When the flight attendant's pre-landing announcement blared over the speakers, I was completely oblivious to it. Instead, I was thinking about the Appreciation Award my company was about to bestow on me, at the company's headquarters in San Francisco, for forty years of loyal service.

I would turn sixty-five years old in a few weeks and I pondered what retirement would be like. I also contemplated how much longer I would live, as my mortality was becoming a subject of greater interest to me. I looked down at the many liver spots on the back of my hand and remembered that they were just like the ones my great Uncle Walter had.

Flying into San Francisco gave me a unique perspective of the city. I immediately recognized Coit Tower and Candlestick Park, and recalled the San Francisco Giants baseball game I watched with Jim Logan in the miserable cold and fog.

The landing gear touched down and snapped me out of my reminiscing. With the retirement ceremony taking place that evening and my return flight to Milwaukee the following evening, I planned to spend a full day sightseeing and to take a walk down Haight Street and see what the house at 806 looked like.

My retirement dinner took place in the elegant Top of the Mark Restaurant at the Mark Hopkins Hotel. My fifteenth floor room provided a stunning view of the Golden Gate Bridge. I stood looking out the window remembering when I had first laid eyes on the bridge and recalled the time I drove Jim Gaston to Oregon in my milk truck, forty-six years prior.

I received a wooden plaque of appreciation with my name and a large number 40 engraved on a shiny brass plate. Several company executives, many of whom I had never met before, attended and thanked me and wished me well. Two hours and one large dessert later, I was no longer employed. I shook everyone's hand and then left the dining room. I got into an elevator and went down to my room.

I placed the plaque on the bed, took off my coat and tie, unbuttoned my shirt collar, and slipped off my shoes. I sat down in a large blue armchair and stared out the window at the brightly lit city. I called room service and ordered a scotch and soda.

I leaned over, turned on the clock radio and dialed in an Oldies station. By sheer coincidence, the station was playing a lot of music from 1967, the Summer of Love. As each song played over the inferior speakers, I attached some importance or event to it.

"Light My Fire" by The Doors rekindled how enamored I was with my communist roommate Maryanne Cetio. Forty-six years later she still stirred lustful thoughts in my mind. The Buckingham's "Kind of a Drag" reminded me of my other roommate, the mad bomber John Robinson with his deranged views of a revolution.

A knock on the door broke the musical trance and reminded me that I had ordered room service. I shuffled to the door with a five-dollar tip in hand. When I handed the young man the tip, I asked if he had ever heard of The Doors. He shrugged and said he thought so, but he was in a hurry to get to the next room. He gladly accepted the tip and scurried down the hallway. I watched him go and guessed that I had been about his age the last time I was in San Francisco.

I walked over to the window and looked down at the cable cars, crowded with tourists, laboring up and down Powell Street. Then the song "I Think We're Alone Now" began playing and it reminded me of the wonderful day I spent with Autumn on Angel Island. I was never able to find her after she moved from the house across the street.

The twenty-year-old scotch was very smooth and the radio kept cranking out songs from the 1960s. I sat back down in the armchair just as The Beatles' "All You Need is Love" filled the room. I put the glass down and felt pangs of loss because I never experienced love in the Summer of Love in San Francisco. For forty-six years, I regretted never speaking to Autumn again. I wondered where she went and where she was living now.

As midnight approached, I finally finished the scotch and got undressed for bed. While brushing my teeth, I heard Scott McKenzie's song "San Francisco" ("Be Sure to Wear Flowers in Your Hair"), which was the anthem for the Summer of Love 1967. I looked into the mirror, shook my head, and thought how naïve I had been in San Francisco in July 1967.

I put on my pajamas and sat on the edge of the bed just as Tom Jones's big hit "Green Green Grass of Home" began playing. I thought about the circuitous path that life takes and how ultimately we must face the consequences of our choices. There are no re-dos, no second chances, and no escape clauses.

I switched off the radio and climbed under the covers. I just stared at the ceiling and finally had to accept that coming to San Francisco in the summer of 1967 wasn't what I had hoped it would be, yet there were many valuable lessons of life I learned here. I drifted off to sleep with verses of "San Francisco-Be Sure to Wear Flowers in Your Hair" reverberating in my head.

Chapter 46

I was in a deep sleep when a knock on the door jarred me awake. I heard a woman's voice calling out, "Room service."

I struggled to my feet, still half asleep, and opened the door to a tall African-American woman with a breakfast cart and a coffee pot.

"I didn't order this," I said.

"Is your name Robert Ralston?"

"Yup, that's me."

"This is courtesy of Northwest Casualty Life Insurance."

"Wow. Well okay, bring it in."

I looked at the clock radio and it was nine, probably the latest I had slept in a decade. After the scrumptious breakfast, I showered and got dressed in blue jeans and a sweatshirt and headed out on my sightseeing excursion.

I walked to the Hyde-Powell cable car line and climbed aboard a passing cable car. When a tourist with four children asked me for directions to the curvy Lombard Street, I answered that I was a tourist too and I didn't know how to get there, even though I really did. The cable car surged forward and I decided to stand on the outside step to get a better view. The conductor rang the car's bell aggressively, much to the delight of the tourists aboard. I recalled riding this cable car numerous times with Autumn.

"Oh, Autumn," I said to myself.

I walked to the Marina District to the edge of the bay. It was a weekday and the Marina Green was virtually empty. I stood in the very spot where Joan Baez had performed after the 1967 anti-war march. Then I walked to Golden Gate Park where I still had vivid memories of the Summer of Love. Long gone were the throngs of young people who had danced, sung, marched, smoked pot, and loved here that summer. A new mother went jogging by with her baby in a high tech three-wheel stroller.

The marine layer receded. The sun broke through and shone brightly. As I walked toward Haight Street, I felt anxious to see my summer of 1967 home. When I turned the corner onto Haight Street, I felt my emotions swelling. I didn't know what to expect. So much had happened to me on this street, so long ago.

The Victorian houses were magnificently restored. Their intricate paint jobs highlighted every piece of colorful trim and relief, in distinct contrast to how shabby they had looked in 1967 when the owners let them fall into disrepair. The bright and extensive palette of colors made Victorian after Victorian regal looking. I noticed that many Victorian owners had converted their basements into garages. The street level garage doors were an unappealing addition to the architecture. One Victorian had a "For Sale" sign, and I grabbed the realtor's flyer from a plastic holder attached to the front porch railing. The asking price was an eye-popping $1.8 million dollars. I mused that it was a far cry from 1967, when you could have purchased it for about $250,000.

I approached 806 Haight Street with reservation and strong emotions. I remembered cursing my bad luck for renting that room.

I wondered how in the world I ended up there. I turned slowly to look across the street and I stared at the house where Autumn had lived. She was the closest thing to finding real love that summer in San Francisco. But like her name, she disappeared in an early fall breeze.

I didn't realize that I had been standing in front of 806 for five minutes when a young, handsome Asian-American man opened the front door and walked out onto the porch.

"Can I help you with anything?" he asked.

"I, um, I–I lived here a long time ago," I stammered.

"In this house?" he asked while walking down to the sidewalk where I was standing.

"Yeah, I was one of those crazy kids who came here in the summer of 1967. I rented a room here for a few months."

"Where are you from?" he asked.

"Wisconsin."

"You haven't been back here since 1967?"

"Nope. This is the first time in forty-six years."

"Wow. Forty-six years. Would you like to come in and see it again?" he asked.

"That's a very kind offer, but I wouldn't want to impose," I replied.

"It's fine. While you are looking around maybe you could tell me a little history about the house. My wife and I bought it two years ago, and we've been remodeling the interior ever since."

"I can only tell you about the few months I lived here," I replied.

"My name is Justin Liu," he said, extending his hand.

"I'm Bob Ralston," I said, shaking his hand.

We walked into the living room, beautifully decorated with freshly painted walls. It was a far cry from the dingy, faded living room I recalled.

"I rented the bedroom down the hall from the bathroom on the right," I said.

We walked down the hall to the bedroom and I walked in.

"This is my son Jeremy's room," he said. "He's twelve years old."

The walls were covered with sports memorabilia and pictures of Jeremy's favorite athletes. The old sash window had been replaced with a modern double-pane sliding window. I barely recognized the room.

We walked down to the master bedroom, which was Maryanne's. Then he offered to show me the third bedroom, which was John Robinson's, and I graciously declined.

"Could I see the kitchen and the basement?" I asked.

"You can see the kitchen, but the basement has been converted to our garage. Nothing to see there."

"I guess parking is as difficult now in San Francisco as it was forty-six years ago," I smiled.

"No, it's much worse now."

We walked into the kitchen, which had been completely remodeled. The only thing I recognized was the window over the kitchen sink. From there I used to look out and see my milk truck parked in the alley. When I looked out the window I could see the parking spot had been turned into part of their small fenced-in backyard.

"Would you care for a cup of tea?"

"That would be great, but am I imposing on your time?" I asked.

"No. I'm waiting for my wife. We're going to a parent-teacher meeting."

We sat down at the kitchen table and I appreciated how much time changes things. He handed me a cup of tea and he sat down across from me.

"What do you do for a living?" I asked.

"I'm an attorney, and my wife is an attorney too," he said. "What do you do?"

"As of today, I am officially retired. I was an insurance broker selling life and casualty insurance in Milwaukee."

"What brought you to San Francisco in the summer of 1967?" he asked.

"I guess I was like so many other young people back then, searching for answers, the meaning of life, and looking for love and understanding."

"Was it as wild as movies and books make it out to be?" he asked.

"It was a pretty wild time. You could do about anything you wanted to do. Drugs were plentiful and readily available. Most people smoked pot and a lot of people experimented with LSD. There was increasing use of heroin, which attracted a very unsavory group. What you don't hear much about was how bad the Hells Angels were and there were a lot of rip-off artists stealing anything they could get their hands on. This was especially true of junkies who needed to support their drug habits. Almost every house on this street, except this one, had about twenty people living in it or sleeping on the front porches. It was non-stop, all day and all night in Haight-Ashbury. But all in all, most everyone got along and everyone opposed the Vietnam War."

"How long did you live here?"

"I arrived in early July and left in early September," I replied.

"Why didn't this house have twenty people living in it like all the other houses on the block?"

"Because of the two renters," I answered.

"Who were they? They were your roommates, right?"

"That's a long story," I replied.

"Well, I have time until my wife gets here," he said with a chuckle.

"One of my roommates was a famous professor at the University of San Francisco."

"That's where I got my law degree," he said.

"Her name was, I mean is, Maryanne Cetio."

"No way! Maryanne Cetio, the famous communist professor at USF?" he asked in disbelief.

"Yup, that's her. Her room was the master bedroom."

"No kidding. She's pretty well known. You can see her pictures in the library and in the political science building at USF. They tried to fire her a few times, but the ACLU always stepped in and saved her professorship," he said. "She was a pretty good-looking woman by the looks of her pictures."

"What ever happened to her?"

"I heard she retired a few years ago and moved to Europe," he replied.

"When I lived here, the FBI was keeping a close eye on her," I said. "We got to know each other rather intimately." I smiled.

"Who was the other renter?" he asked.

"The other roommate was a guy named John Robinson. He was a deranged dude."

"What did he do?"

"John Robinson went around California blowing up buildings belonging to companies and universities that were in some way involved in supporting the Vietnam War. They either did research or manufactured war materials. It was his way of protesting the war. He was a member of the Weathermen Underground."

"Oh, man, this is unbelievable. Are you making this up?" he asked, wide-eyed and leaning into the table.

"It's the absolute truth. And all three of us lived in this house in the summer of 1967."

"What did John Robinson use to blow up buildings?" he asked.

"Dynamite."

I took a drink from my teacup.

"In fact, he was making the bombs right here in the basement, unbeknownst to Maryanne or me. Or at least I don't think she knew."

"Holy shit! He was making bombs in the basement of this house?" he asked in an astonished voice.

I nodded my head.

"Did he kill anyone?" he asked.

I nodded again. "He killed twenty-eight people. I think that was the final number."

"Whatever happened to him? Did he get caught?"

"That's another long story," I replied.

"Man, your long stories are fricking unbelievable!" he said. "Tell me more."

"John Robinson was indicted for murder, mayhem, and the destruction of property." I decided to stop at that point.

"Did he get convicted and go to jail?" he asked.

"The FBI's case hinged on being able to identify him at the scene of a crime. When Robinson blew up a building and killed a couple of people at the University California, Davis, the FBI thought they had finally caught him in the act. The problem was their eyewitnesses were all paid informants. Robinson presented fifteen people in court who testified that he was fifty miles away at a party and couldn't possibly have been the perpetrator."

"Then what happened?"

"Well, there was one eye witness who was not a paid FBI informant," I said.

"Who was it?" he asked with growing interest.

I paused and put the teacup on the table. "Me."

"Oh, come on, man! You are pulling my leg. This is the greatest story I have ever heard. Are you for real?" he asked, raising his voice.

"I'm sorry if I offended you. I was telling you what happened and who lived here. Maybe I should leave."

"No fricking way! I gotta hear the end of this. My wife isn't going to believe this," he exclaimed.

"The FBI wanted me to testify that I saw John Robinson at UC, Davis on the night of the explosion. They had collected substantial physical evidence against him. In fact, they carried dozens of dynamite sticks out of the basement in this house with his fingerprints all over them. The FBI needed me to testify that I saw him at UC, Davis the night of the bombing."

"You said he was a member of the Weathermen Underground. Weren't you afraid to testify? That was a pretty radical and vicious group of anarchists," he said.

"I was scared shitless, but I never admitted to seeing Robinson at UC, Davis. So no one really knew if I was going to be an eyewitness. I never said yes or no to the FBI."

"Did you see him?" he asked, staring at me intently.

"Yes. I accidentally ran into him in a parking lot as he was running away from the scene of the crime."

"Well, did you testify?"

"I decided I wasn't going to do it. But the more I thought about it, the more the idea of killing innocent people really bothered me. I asked a couple of my closest friends, one who was wounded in Vietnam, and they both told me not to testify. Their rationale was that the United States was killing innocent people in Vietnam and all John Robinson was doing was trying to stop people and companies that supported the war from killing civilians for a corrupt South Vietnamese government."

"And?"

"I have come to learn that war is a very dirty business."

"Did you serve in the military during Vietnam?" he asked.

"No. When I left San Francisco in September 1967, I went back to Wisconsin and enrolled at the University of Wisconsin-Madison and started school right before I would have been drafted into the army. I eventually got my insurance broker's license and worked in that industry for forty years."

"So whatever happened to John Robinson?" he asked.

"He was sentenced to ten consecutive life sentences without parole," I said. "He's going to die in a federal prison."

"Who testified against him?"

"I did."

He sat back in his chair in disbelief. "I thought you said you weren't going to testify against him," he asked while shaking his head.

"I wasn't, but I came to the conclusion that wantonly killing someone for a cause is a lot different than killing someone in the heat of battle. Killing an unarmed combatant is inexcusable. It's a crime. It's cold-blooded murder," I stated.

"Weren't you afraid the Weathermen Underground would kill you?" he asked.

"Absolutely. I couldn't do anything to tip my hand before the trial because my other roommate, Professor Maryanne, had close ties to the Weathermen. She seduced me trying to learn whether I had seen Robinson at UC, Davis. She was a very attractive woman with an incredible body. I must confess she was the most beautiful woman I ever made love to. Just don't tell my wife that," I said with a chuckle. "Three days before the trial started, I was afraid the Weathermen Underground were going to kill me, just in case I was a witness. After all these years, I can't recall all the details, but I was able to set up a clandestine meeting with an FBI agent in Golden Gate Park. I asked him to take me into protective custody and the FBI did. Two days later, I was escorted into a heavily guarded federal courthouse where I testified, without any doubt or reservation, that I had clearly seen John Robinson in a parking lot about three hundred yards from the building that exploded at the University of California-Davis. His famous defense attorney tried to tear me apart on the witness stand, but I didn't cave in one bit."

He sat silently for a moment with an incredulous look on his face and then finally spoke, "Weren't you afraid that the Weathermen would kill you for testifying?"

"Sure. But I wasn't going to give up my convictions based on fear. The FBI hid me for three months in Colorado, helped me get enrolled in the University of Wisconsin, and then on January 15, 1968, I walked onto the UW, Madison campus and joined twenty-eight thousand other students in the pursuit of a higher education.

"At first, I was always looking over my shoulder and afraid to make friends. But then I decided that I wasn't going to live my life in fear. I believe that if God intended me to be killed by the Weathermen, then so be it. God always gets his way. As you can see, I'm still here. I got a business degree, got married, have three kids, and have had a good life," I said.

"Wow. What a story. But I thought it was the Summer of Love," he said. "Doesn't sound like you had a lovely time in San Francisco."

"To this day, I can't get anyone to tell me what a hippie was. It's too difficult to define. I think our generation did a lot to change society for the better, but being a hippie and the Free Love thing didn't exactly turn out the way it was portrayed. For sure, it was sex, drugs, and rock and roll. But a lot of people had their lives altered forever, and many of them were Vietnam veterans. What bothers me the most is we don't seem to learn from our mistakes. Our country is involved in two wars and I wonder what good will come from them," I said and got a little choked up, "Thank you so much for letting me come in. You have a wonderful house."

I stood up and shook his hand, turned around, and let myself out the front door. I walked briskly down the sidewalk and stopped momentarily to take one last look at the house at 806 Haight Street. And then I took one last look at the house across the street where Autumn had lived.

As I walked under the iconic street signs at the intersection of Haight and Ashbury, I knew I would never return to San Francisco. It was a city that harbored too many painful memories.

THE END

About the Author:

Robert Rice, Jr. was born in Milwaukee, Wisconsin, the only boy in a family of five children. He attended Riverside High School and served in the US Air Force from 1966–1970. He drove from Milwaukee to San Francisco in a VW Bug in the summer of 1967, where he experienced the Summer of Love on his way to a new duty assignment. He began writing as a college student in Hawaii and captained a forty-four foot sailboat that sailed halfway around the globe. In addition to *My Summer on Haight Street*, he has authored two screenplays, a dozen short stories, and several published magazine articles. He also wrote and produced two television sports documentaries. He has been a public affairs/public relations and political campaign consultant for more than twenty-seven years. He lives in Santa Barbara, California, with his wife and twin daughters. His son lives in northern California.